THE BORROW A BOYFRIEND CLUB

"Charmingly chaotic and keenly observant, with real emotional depth. Page Powars's debut is an absolute joyride." —**Becky Albertalli,** *New York Times* bestselling author of *Imogen, Obviously*

"Humor, hijinks, and a whole lotta heart abound in this romantic and affirming debut. An utterly charming and delightful read." —**Dahlia Adler,** author of *Cool for the Summer* and *Home Field Advantage*

"With a chaotic found family, a dynamic hate-to-love romance, and all kinds of silly shenanigans along the way, this book is one you won't be able to put down." —**Tashie Bhuiyan,** author of *Counting Down with You* and *A Show for Two*

"Equal parts sharp, comedic wit and heartening romance, Page Powars's *The Borrow a Boyfriend Club* is a powerhouse of a debut." —**Amelia Diane Coombs,** author of *Exactly Where You Need to Be*

"With an endearing protagonist, heartwarming romance, and a powerful message about being enough, this book is sure to charm readers, no matter their type!" —**Isaac Fitzsimons,** author of *The Passing Playbook*

"A complete delight. Noah and Asher's hate-to-love romance is matched only by Powars's shimmering and honest trans coming-of-age tale." —**Carlyn Greenwald,** author of *Sizzle Reel* and coauthor of *Time Out*

"Powars has written the swooniest romance that'll leave you breathlessly wondering will they or won't they." —**Naz Kutub,** author of *The Loophole*

Text copyright © 2023 by Page Powars
Jacket art copyright © 2023 by Steffi Walthall

GetUnderlined.com

Educators and librarians, for a variety of teaching tools, visit us at RHTeachersLibrarians.com

Library of Congress Cataloging-in-Publication Data is available upon request.
ISBN 978-0-593-56858-3 (trade) — ISBN 978-0-593-56860-6 (ebook)

The text of this book is set in 11-point Iowan Old Style.
Interior design by Ken Crossland

Printed in the United States of America
10 9 8 7 6 5 4 3 2 1
First Edition

Random House Children's Books supports the First Amendment and celebrates the right to read.

For timestamp 17:20 of the *SK8 the Infinity*
episode 8 English dub

CHAPTER 1

The last thing I expected to see on my first day at Heron River High was *FA LA LA LA FUCK THIS SCHOOL* spelled atop the snow in festive holiday lights.

Crowds of my new classmates gathered around the flickering green and red profanity. Three teachers gesticulated at the students to keep walking, but no one paid attention. Instead, the kids lingered, taking pictures with their phones.

When Mom and Dad asked during our weekly burger night what my new school was like, this would not be mentioned.

As I passed by, I pulled the hood of my puffer jacket down lower over my forehead, just in case someone felt like the new kid was more interesting than a flashing *f*-word. Once inside the building, I quickly found the main office.

My heart rate picked up. *Game time.*

I gripped my backpack straps tighter and kept up my turtle impersonation until the office doors shut behind me. The administrative assistant, who somehow didn't appear a day over twenty, was bundled in a festive argyle cardigan. He pressed a phone between his ear and shoulder as he typed on a laptop, sweat beading above his brow. On the countertop, a nameplate had *Sonny* written in cursive.

"Fa la la la what, now?" he murmured. Sonny was in a bad mood.

My shoulders shrank into my narrow frame. I tried to snap them back into a loud and proud position. A masculine, broad, very much *boy* position.

Everything would go fine today. I'd been transitioning for years. I passed.

Sonny, the admin assistant, muttered something along the lines of *I'll get back to this later* and hung up the phone. He gave me a fake smile. "Welcome back from winter break."

As I stepped up to the counter, students passed by the fancy domed window framing the downtown streets of Ann Arbor, Michigan. I'd heard rumors that Heron River High was disgustingly nicer than Pinewood High, and the admin office alone proved that. Its sparkly white walls and chrome furniture were ten times better than Pinewood's brick hallways lined with rusty lockers. Whoever wrote the twinkling profanity by the front doors seemed misguided.

"I'm actually a new junior here," I said. "I transferred from Pinewood. My name's Noah. Noah Byrd."

"Anything I can help you with? Class schedule good to go?"

"Yeah. The vice principal emailed it to me last week. But I was wondering if I could get more information on how to join the boys' sports teams?"

"Which team?" Sonny asked.

It didn't matter which one. All that mattered was joining

something ASAP. By the end of the semester, I had to show everyone who I was. I wasn't about to let my classmates draw their own conclusions about me again, and a boys' sports team emblem pinned to my chest would establish who I was from the start. The less time they had to develop their own ideas, the better.

I considered which sport would destroy my scrawny body the least. A non-contact sport. "Tennis?"

He gave me a once-over. "I can email you a list of our sports, if you'd like. That would include more information on the tennis team. Unfortunately, there aren't any tryouts during the winter semester, but you could try to join in August."

My heart sank. It was only January. I couldn't wait that long. "There's really no boys' team that will let me join now? Don't some seasons start in the winter?"

"They do, but we require our students to sign up and pay any necessary registration fees for their sport during the first week of the school year." Sonny typed a bit more, then turned the screen to show me a spreadsheet labeled *Heron River High School After-School Student Clubs*. "Most of our clubs accept new recruits during both semesters, though. If you're hoping for an extracurricular to hold you over, how about you check these out?"

I pulled his laptop toward me and scrolled through the club names, keeping an eye out for any words that sounded overtly masculine. They had French and Spanish. No and no. Anime. Nope. Classic literature. Not quite. Math. God, no. Dance.

I paused.

Definitely, definitely not dance.

I kept scrolling. Something called the Football and

Lamborghini After-School Club eventually showed up on row eleven.

My insides recoiled. I had no clue what this club was, but being *that* enthusiastic about football and cars was maybe too manly. The goal wasn't to stand out here. I wanted to blend in like a normal teenage guy.

There had to be another choice.

Four more rows passed by, offering debate, sculpture, film, and, finally, chess. Then I skimmed back up to the top again in case I'd missed something.

I had not.

I faced Sonny again. If no sports teams would let me try out this semester, then there were no other options. I swiveled the laptop back around. "How do I join this football and cars thing?"

Sonny scrolled on his laptop. "Hm. I can't sign you up. You need approval from the club president."

"How come?"

"There's an interview process," a voice said from behind me.

Startled, I spun around. A boy my age with light tan skin sat in a chair against the wall. His legs were so long that they stretched across nearly half the office, his chunky red Prada sneakers only a foot away from my worn Converse. I hadn't noticed him when I first came in.

"For just a football and car club?" I asked.

"Yep. You need to go to one of their weekly meetings first."

"Quiet," Sonny called his way. "You're in the main office for defacing school property. Not to chat with your classmates."

The boy defensively tossed up his hands, and I saw that

4

his fingers were dripping with silver rings. His smirk was as chaotic as his mess of brown hair, which was half tied into a lopsided bun, the rest falling loosely above his shoulders.

This must've been Mr. *Fa La La La Fuck This School.*

"So, I might not be allowed to join?" I asked Sonny.

He shrugged. "That's what their club rules say."

What kind of person would make people interview for a basic school club? "Their president sounds like a prick," I mumbled.

"He's actually pretty great," Mr. Fa La La said behind me. Clearly, my voice hadn't been low enough.

A door swung open, and a woman in a fancy maroon suit stepped forward. A plaque on the door read *Principal's Office.* "Mr. Price. A word—"

"Yeah, yeah, yeah." He rose to his feet using the chair armrests, slung a canvas tote bag covered in environmental patches over his shoulder, and disappeared into the principal's lair.

Even if there was a chance I wouldn't be accepted into this bro-of-all-bro clubs after going through the president's ridiculous interview process, I had to try. This was the clearest, and currently only, way to make sure these students knew exactly who I was.

I was a boy just like Mr. Fa La La. I had always been a boy. This time, no one at school would question that.

I faced Sonny again. "One last question. Do you know where this football and Lamborghini club meets?"

CHAPTER 2

As the bell rang at the end of my sixth-period chemistry class, I kept my head tucked into my hoodie and followed the hallway signs toward the theater, where the Football and Lamborghini After-School Club met on Mondays and Wednesdays until four o'clock.

How did such a cringe club even exist?

I entered through the main audience doors. The theater was an expanse of red velvet seats and fancy carpeting that reached up to a balcony. Heron River High was certainly living up to the "fanciest public school in Ann Arbor" rumors.

In the lower bowl, there were clumps of students with bound scripts and snacks on their laps. To my left, a girl spoke very dramatically to a wall about how aliens were taking over the world. I didn't recognize the scene she was rehearsing. At least, I hoped she was rehearsing.

I cleared my throat to snag her attention. "Do you know where the Football—?"

The girl thrust a finger at the stage. "Follow the signs for the basement. There's a door backstage right."

"Oh. Uh. Thanks."

As I headed backstage, some people stopped munching on their veggies and chips to watch me. Nerves flooded up into my face and down into my toes. So far, I'd survived my first day at Heron River High without being noticed much. Before each class began, all the teachers had asked if I wanted to be introduced in front of the room, and each time, it was a very hard pass. And in most classes, my assigned seat was some leftover desk in the back. Walking across a literal stage now was going from zero to ten real quick.

I had no clue what these drama kids were thinking when they saw me. For all I knew, they were just like the students at Pinewood High School. Never subtle with their stares. Never correcting their so-called *slipups* because they didn't care enough to remember my name.

My time front and center lasted six seconds, which felt like six years, and then I was backstage.

Three students faced a solid metal door in the corner. One of them, a fit boy who wore a varsity football jacket with the last name Ngo on the back, paired with ugly orange joggers, shoved a hand inside a party-sized bag of spicy cheese puffs.

This had to be the place.

Two other students stood in front of the boys, guarding the door. One was a pretty Black girl in a pink blouse and tulle skirt, which hung off her slender frame like a ballet tutu. Her brown coily afro had a smattering of blond highlights.

The second girl, a whole head taller than the first, had a light-olive complexion and a slicked-back black ponytail. She sported a bold red pantsuit and cat's-eye-glasses combination, and a notebook with a *Trust me, I'm in charge* sticker was pressed against her chest.

Was I in the right place?

The girl in charge smiled so brightly that her whole face crinkled. "Good afternoon, boys! You almost didn't make it on time."

Spicy Cheese Puffs rolled his eyes as he wiped a dusty hand on his jeans before plugging numbers into the insulin pump on his hip. "Who cares?"

"Asher," she responded, still smiling.

"Figures. He really needs to chill on the micromanaging."

Asher.

That must've been the president. The one I had to impress.

I stepped closer and waved. "Is this where—"

They were already disappearing behind the mysterious metal door.

"—the interviews are," I muttered to myself as it closed shut.

I followed. The door creaked open to reveal a steep, dark, wooden staircase. A cool draft blew past me, raising the hairs on the back of my neck.

I swallowed hard and headed down the stairs, which moaned with each step. Either I was lowering myself into an after-school cult or the pits of Hell. Some source of light from below the staircase started stretching along the walls.

This was the basement. A normal, cluttered theater basement that smelled like mothballs and wet dirt. The room was split into several narrow lines of costume racks, leaving hardly any space between them, like in a warehouse.

This place appeared abandoned. What happened to the others?

Mumbling sounds came from somewhere past the sea of costumes.

I headed toward them, shoving my body through the mess. Puffy dresses scratched against my cheeks. Belts and ties drooped to the dusty floor like snakes, threatening to trip me at any moment. Finally, the path led into a room.

I blinked.

The dusty concrete floor led to maroon carpeting as fuzzy as dandelion fluff. The cement walls were draped in matching curtains with rhinestone embellishments that glistened in the fluorescent lights. Playing cards in the hearts suit were stuck to and scattered across the ceiling. Way-too-thick cologne replaced the scent of mothballs.

At the very back, multiple mini fridges, an electronic keyboard, and seven or so boys surrounded a billiards table. A few hovered around the table while others slung themselves across bright-red pleather love seats. Above them hung a red flag with a logo at the center: two *B*s faced back to back, forming the shape of a heart.

Two guys held cue sticks. The one on the left was Asian American and had cotton-candy-blue hair with slightly grown-out roots. Combined with his rainbow-patterned jacket, he could've been a movie star. He was aligning the tip of his stick with the cue ball, about to make his next move. The other had a light-brown complexion and wore a knit sweater and collared undershirt. A laptop labeled with *Camilo Torres* rested nearby him as he sat on the edge of the table, bored.

Bored. In a bizarre underground club like this.

Had I tripped down the basement stairs and slammed my head too hard?

I stepped deeper into the basement. "Hello?"

My voice rang out right as the one with blue hair pulled back his cue stick. He yelped.

The boy looked familiar, but I couldn't place from where. With hair as loud as his, I'd probably spotted him walking around downtown. "Sorry!" he said. "You caught me off guard."

"Who left the door unlocked?" that Camilo guy asked. "A customer broke in."

The two girls who guarded the door earlier stared at me, stunned. The one holding the notebook reached into her pantsuit blazer pocket to pull out a key ring. "I locked it, Camilo."

He pointed my way without breaking eye contact with her. "Using what? The imaginary knob?"

Pastel Blue Hair Boy waved his hand dismissively through the air as he walked over to me. "No worries! We're technically only open to customers on Wednesdays, but that's okay. What type of boyfriend are you looking for?"

A bleating sound propelled out of my mouth. "What am I *what*?"

Camilo hopped off the table. Now that he was no longer seated, I could see he was nearly as short as me, and notes written in black pen ink were scribbled all over his hands. *Politics club send newsletter* and *#88-101 chapter 3.2* were the only decipherable ones.

The human to-do list moved closer, glaring my way.

"Lenny, I can't place a name to this person. They don't go to our school."

Pastel Blue Hair Boy, aka Lenny, held up his cue stick as a sword. "STAY BACK, NARC!"

Others in the room made various startled noises and leaped off the love seats as backup. Meanwhile, Camilo pushed up his turquoise glasses and muttered, "Do you even know what that means?"

I threw my hands up. "Whoa, whoa, whoa! No! I'm here because I want to interview for your club!"

"You can't interview for a club at a school you don't go to!" Lenny said.

"He transferred here today from Pinewood," a voice called out.

In a faraway corner, a door marked with a fake *Do Not Enter* road sign opened. Someone stepped forward.

A mess of brown hair, half down, and half tied in a bun. Chunky red overpriced sneakers that made each step sound like an earthquake. A full set of silver band rings.

Mr. Fa La La La.

My chest instinctively deflated, but I forced myself to puff it out again. *Look like a* boy, *Noah.* "So that's why you knew so much about this club this morning. You're a member?" I asked him.

"That I am." He passed the billiards table, where everyone had gone back to focusing on the game instead of us. Crisis averted, I guessed. Fa La La stopped at a glowing retro jukebox to select a song, and an odd electronic, jazzy song started to play.

A *jukebox.*

"How are you even here right now?" I asked. "I thought you'd get suspended."

"I did. For two days, including today."

"So, you snuck back into school?"

"It's not like I can miss our club meetings."

Part of me was impressed at this guy's dedication, but another part couldn't get past the fact that he wasn't supposed to be on school grounds. Of course this club attracted degenerate bad boys who frothed at the mouth at getting suspended in the name of screwing the system.

Still, I had no other prospects. So I summoned my most passionate dude aura. Tall stance, broad shoulders, hands in pockets. "I love cars. And sports. I want to join."

Instead of the club members swarming me for high fives and bro handshakes, Spicy Cheese Puffs burst out laughing so hard on a sofa, he started choking on his spit.

"This guy started here today," Camilo murmured, picking at the tip of his cue stick. "I doubt he'd know what we really are yet."

I just stood there, confused.

Fa La La finally stopped fiddling with the flashing jukebox buttons long enough to lock eyes with me. "This is the Borrow a Boyfriend Club."

I scanned the bright-red furniture again, the hearts playing cards all over the ceiling and walls, the flag with two Bs forming the shape of a heart. I remembered what Lenny had asked me when I first arrived. About what type of *boyfriend* I wanted.

No. Way. "Students don't actually come here to borrow boys for dating purposes, right?"

"Sure they do," Fa La La said. "For social events. Dances. Weddings. Awkward family dinners . . ."

Duh, yeah, of course. "The school allows something like that?"

"Nope. Which is why we're down here. And operate under a different club name." He tapped his temple twice with a pointer finger.

"And every student here knows about this?" I asked. "They really use your . . . services? For this Borrow a Date thing?"

"Borrow a Boyfriend. And it's a club, not just a *thing*."

"People borrow temporary dates, though? Not permanent boyfriends?"

"Yes, but—" Fa La La huffed. "Borrow a Boyfriend has a better ring to it, okay?"

Lenny knocked another ball. "You would've heard whispers about us soon enough. That's how the freshies find out. With so many boys wanting to join, and so many other students wanting to borrow us, learning about the club was bound to happen."

"And it's not"—I hesitated—"weird?"

"Only weird if you make it weird," Fa La La said. He was now resting against the jukebox with his arms crossed. "There's no kissing or off-limits touching allowed."

A few boys pointedly shared looks.

If this bizarre roundup of Disney princes was really telling the truth, then the possibility of joining a football and Lamborghini club was dead-dead. But nearly every boy did want to join this instead, or so they claimed.

And the word *boy* itself *was* in their name.

Maybe joining this strange basement crew could be worthwhile. Proving myself was worthwhile. "Okay, then. Can you tell me who the club president is? Asher? I've been wanting to talk to him."

"Oh?" Fa La La gave me a good up and down, arms still crossed like the pretentious criminal he was. "But earlier this morning, didn't you say he sounded like a 'prick'?"

I shoved the feeling of irritation down as best I could. "No. Well, yes, but no. It was a joke. I want to have an interview with him."

"Come back in two days. Our winter membership process starts this Wednesday."

I couldn't wait two more days. If I didn't move fast, the *slipups* and *little mistakes* would be right around the corner. "We can't do an interview right now while I'm already here?"

"No. It's my club rules."

My eyebrows shot into my hairline. "*Your* rules?"

He closed the distance between us with an outstretched hand, showing me the same infuriating smirk he had given Sonny this morning. "I'm Asher Price. The Borrow a Boyfriend Club president."

My blood ran cold.

This guy was the president. And I had called him a prick.

Asher gave up on waiting for me to shake his hand, which must've docked another fifty points against me, and pointed toward the basement stairs as a cue for me to leave. "I look forward to our interview on Wednesday. Don't be late."

CHAPTER 3

Two knocks sounded on my bedroom door.

"Knock-knock," Mom called from the hallway. Seemed redundant.

I locked my phone, which had been flooded with searches for Asher Price's social media presence over the last half hour, and slipped it beneath my blanket. Although he had accounts, they were inactive. I assumed he was trying to capitalize on the whole "boys who don't have social media are hot and mysterious" thing. "Yeah, Mom?"

The door cracked open farther. Mom's head peeked through the crack. She was wearing her Avocadia sales-floor outfit of the day, her body drowning in owl-shaped jewelry. Her downtown boutique was mostly popular for its painfully older millennial white-woman jewelry selection, since that was exactly what Mom was. The shop was located right next door to a breakfast bar where oat-milk lattes cost ten dollars and pesto aioli toast went for twenty.

Once Mom assessed that the coast was clear to enter my bedroom, she opened the door fully. Dad's shadowed figure stood behind her. "Burgers are ready. Can't wait to hear all about your first day, N!"

My heart shriveled.

Like always, it was N. No other nicknames. And Mom and Dad had never once called me Noah.

When I'd told them my name was Noah three years ago, it took every single cell of confidence I had inside me. But they continued to call me N. The same first letter of the name they'd given me when I was born.

A few months later, I told them again over dinner. *Call me Noah.*

We know.

Still N. Like they couldn't push themselves to say the new name instead.

At first, I told myself this couldn't be true. Mom and Dad were supportive. When I'd asked for help with health insurance, they answered questions. When I'd worked early weekend shifts at Bitterlake Coffee for a year to raise money for new clothes and top surgery in addition to my college tuition, they took care of me during summer vacation. But a voice inside me whispered they still didn't see me as *enough*. That deep down, they thought the wrong name first.

So that meant I had to work harder to make them see who I was.

My lack of response kicked Mom into first worry gear. "Was your first day okay?"

"Fine," I said. "First day was fine."

"No probs?" Dad asked from the hall. I could make out his stubby facial hair and bare, muscular arms in the dim light. Must've been wearing one of his workout tank tops.

The only reason there weren't any *probs* was because I'd hidden in a hoodie all day, but I gave them a thumbs-up anyway. "So far."

Mom walked over to my dresser. She absentmindedly picked up one of my silver ballet trophies from middle school, only to set it down five seconds later. A shopping bag was tucked behind her back, but I couldn't tell what could be inside. "Hopefully it'll stay that way, honey. But if anything does happen, don't hesitate to tell Dad and me. We can talk to the school if anyone starts giving you a hard time."

They didn't understand. If talking to the school had worked, I wouldn't have needed to transfer. My time at Pinewood High wasn't some movie where everyone ganged up on me by shouting insults and shoving me into lockers. Everyone would nod when I'd say I was a boy, then keep addressing me by the incorrect name.

And slipping out the wrong name or the wrong pronoun doesn't count as bullying. Not on paper. They were little mistakes. Accidents. At least, according to the principal.

But these *little mistakes* hit differently than being ganged up on and bullied. A small part of me would've preferred they'd shoved me into lockers as long as they got my name right. That way I could've written off their behavior as them being horrible, hormonal monsters. But all I could think was that their *little mistakes* were my fault. That I didn't look or act enough like a boy for them either.

If I did, I wouldn't have distanced myself from everyone—even Jas and Everly and Rosen, my best friends for years—and started eating lunch alone.

I transferred schools because I was tired.

Worry oozed from Mom's and Dad's pores. I'd bet ten bucks that this would cause me more *probs* if I didn't assuage their fears now.

"I've decided to join a club at school," I mentioned.

Their faces lit up.

"Yeah?" Dad said.

"I think that's a great idea, honey." Mom lifted another gold tap trophy off my dresser, which was beside the photo of Jas and me dancing during our sophomore year *Les Misérables* dress rehearsal. "Is it a dance club?"

I tensed up. "No."

Never.

The room entered another stretch of silence, only interrupted by a dog barking outside.

"I'm kinda tired," I said to officially kill the conversation.

"Of course," Dad said.

Mom finally pulled out the Avocadia paper shopping bag from behind her back. "Oh, we got a new line of spring clothes at the shop today," she said, as if she'd forgotten the one thing she was hiding. "I spotted some new button-up shirts that I thought you might like. Don't worry, I can return them." She hung the bag on my closet doorknob.

The gesture was nice, but we'd been through this routine before. Button-up shirts didn't hide enough of my face or arms or chest or shoulders or neck. I'd just shove this into the back of my closet with the other pieces she had bought.

"Thanks," I said instead of burning the shirts on the spot.

"Of course, N."

The name whirled into my heart like an arrow, flooding my whole body with a sudden burst of rage. "I want to change my name. Legally."

Bringing this up probably made Mom and Dad doubt everything was fine at school, but I didn't care. I'd add more grueling shifts at Bitterlake Coffee to my weekend plans so I could afford it, and then, maybe, if Noah were government-official, they'd get me.

"Remember what you researched back in April?" Mom's voice instantly sounded more *Oh God, I don't know how to deal with this.* "How the process can be pretty tedious and long?"

"Yes."

"And pricey?"

With the Bitterlake gig, that wouldn't be a problem, but the way her voice squeaked as if she'd need to spend money on this herself made my irritation churn. "Yes."

"You'll have to go to court. You sure you want to go through that while adjusting to your new school?"

"Yes."

"It just seems so sudden—"

I sighed. "If I request a court date literally right now, they won't be able to schedule me for several weeks. Maybe even months." The words came out sharp. But if Mom and Dad would've looked this up themselves or had offered to help me, they'd know, too.

They shared a few parental blinks and nods.

"Okay, kid," Dad finally said. "We're cheering you on."

Mom smiled before joining Dad in the hall and shutting my door.

The moment they were gone, I fell back onto my bed and stared at the ceiling. Mom and Dad *were* cheering me on. And I appreciated that. But I still had to breathe deeply to try to calm myself, to stop my guilt over getting angry with them, and to prevent the mental bullet-pointed list of reasons why I wasn't enough from unraveling out of control like a medieval scroll.

No matter how hard I tried, my fears kept winning. Soon, my imagination wouldn't stop painting Asher Price's name across my dull beige walls in bright-red letters. That condescending president stood in my way of joining the Borrow a Boyfriend Club.

He was the one hurdle I was less and less confident I could clear.

CHAPTER 4

Wednesday was achingly slow to arrive and even slower as I moved through the school day. I'd become a pro at being invisible, dashing in and out of class, not talking to anyone.

At least, invisibility was the plan until I established myself among a solid group of guys at Heron River High. Popularity would likely bring some level of safety and ease the fear of others making mistakes. If or when I passed the Borrow a Boyfriend Club interview today, then I could stop being a ghost.

When the time finally came, I dashed out of my sixth-period chemistry class to head toward the theater basement. A clacking noise came from behind me.

"You dropped something!"

A girl was reaching down toward a mess of pencils and erasers on the classroom floor. Her hair was bleached blond and pin straight, and her clothes were labeled with a mishmash of brands I could never afford.

Reaching for my bag, I checked the front pocket. Unzipped.

So much for my invisibility cloak. I rushed over to help her clean up, pulled my hood lower onto my forehead, and prepared for the first inevitable slipup of the week. "Thanks."

"No prob."

"Sorry if anything, like, flung at you."

"Nah. Here you go." She handed me back three of my pencils with a smile, and then she was standing and walking out the door with some friends.

No *little mistakes*. I wasn't even referred to in the third person. At least, not yet. With my bag closed, I restarted my course toward the basement as fast as I could. One minute later, I was gripping the sparkly red curtains that hid the ugly concrete walls and nearly heaving out both my lungs.

Once I caught enough breath to glance up from the carpet, I met Asher Price's gaze a few feet away. He was at the back of the room, surrounded by four girls. All of them were holding origami swans.

At the sound of my huffing and puffing, they turned away from Asher to face me.

"I—" I coughed and pounded my chest. "I'm not late."

"You're not breathing either," Asher said.

"You told me to be on time. And I wanted to be first."

One of the girls, who was clearly uninterested in my sweaty body, faced Asher again. She shoved her origami swan into his chest. "There's a secret letter hidden inside of mine, Asher! I wrote it just for you."

"There's one inside of mine too!" Another swan shove attack.

"And mine!" Another.

His face remained serious as he collected his swan army. "Thank you."

The pack of enlarged pupils and leaking hormones erupted into giggles like he'd told the funniest knock-knock joke in the world. As they passed me and disappeared through the costume racks, I heard whispers like "so mysterious" and "a literal rebel."

Weird. More like *so rude* and *a literal clout demon.*

Even weirder, Asher seemed unfazed by the whole encounter. After the girls were long gone, he walked over to a wastebasket in a corner of the basement and tossed the swans inside.

Was being swarmed by fans *that* much of a common ordeal for him?

Asher gestured at me, then toward the bright-red love seats. "The other members aren't here yet. Sit while you wait."

I followed orders. Showing up early to my interview must've gained me back the points I had lost for calling Asher a prick. And since I was first in line, I'd have to interview first.

I *needed* to. My odds of being accepted into this club already felt low since Asher was the president. But gaining entry would prove I was a boy, and fast. I had to get accepted.

I had to win over Asher Price no matter what.

Minutes ticked by. I kept myself busy by inspecting the hearts playing cards scattered across the ceiling and walls, then the assortment of energy crystals stacked on the mini fridges. A few footballs and basketballs were shoved into a nearby corner as well. Above the ball pile was a poster advertising something called the Anita Kömraag Dedicatory Club Talent Show, happening in March.

More unfamiliar faces emerged from the cluttered costume racks. A few offered me acknowledging nods as they claimed their own seats. Most ignored my presence entirely.

This didn't feel like a simple interview. This felt like a competition.

Eventually that human to-do list, Camilo, appeared too. There were even more illegible homework reminders penned all over his hands than last time. Other members I vaguely recognized followed, like Spicy Cheese Puffs and Notebook Manager. Then Lenny, who instantly spotted me and grinned.

The nerves in my chest dissipated slightly.

Asher finally stood before us prospective members. As if on command, the official members formed a single-file line behind him.

Everyone went silent, all except for the jukebox, which played that same upbeat electronic song, an odd mess of drums and trumpets and synthesizers.

I glanced around and counted heads. Eighteen other rivals.

Fine. This was fine. I'd remain on my best behavior from now until my interview was long over. And I'd go first. That meant there would be no risk of following up someone ten times more impressive and manlier than I was.

"Welcome to the start of the Borrow a Boyfriend Club's semesterly membership process," Asher's voice boomed across the basement. "I'm the club president, or CEO. Behind me are our CFO, Constance Adams, and product manager, Isabella Vanentini"—he nudged his head toward the two girls I'd seen guarding the door that first day—"as well as my seven club members."

Lenny, who stood at the end of the row, stepped forward.

Asher gestured at him. "This is Lenny Kawai: Influencer Type."

Type?

Camilo stepped forward while Lenny stepped back.

"Camilo Torres: Smart Type," Asher said.

He stepped back. Another boy came.

Asher kept going through names and Types like a grocery list. "Pascha Coombs: Musical Type. Aiden Ngo: Sporty Type. Everett Miner: Psychic Type. Max Booker: Artsy Type. Liam Robinette: Gaming Type." He paused. "And I'm Asher Price: Popular Type."

I couldn't hold back a snicker any longer.

My competition shot glares at me. Some also came from members, including Spicy Cheese Puffs, better known as Sporty Type. He lightly punched the shoulder of a scrawnier member beside him, whose body was drowning in a scrappy beige cardigan and flowery scarf. "Look who it is."

"Pardon?" Scarf Boy asked.

"New kid. He's in our pottery class."

"Ah, so that is why I sensed an oddly familiar aura surrounding him."

My shoulders tensed. Had Sporty Type been monitoring my several failed attempts at making pinch pots and already marked me a loser?

I shifted awkwardly. "Sorry. But do you all really categorize yourselves like this? Publicly?"

"Unfortunately." Camilo was busy texting.

Asher snatched Camilo's phone out of his hand and slapped it down on the table. "Different people need their boyfriends to possess different qualities depending on the circumstance. A boy who will impress a strict family is completely different from one who will impress friends from other schools. Or a borrower may simply request us because they want to spend time with someone. We have Types so borrowers know who to best select on our request forms."

Camilo rolled his eyes.

Asher pulled a red pamphlet out of his tote bag, which nearly blended in with the curtains behind him. No other color was allowed down here. "Before we begin, I'll make one thing very clear. All members receive the *How to Be a Good Boyfriend Training Handbook*. If accepted, you must memorize and master all twenty rules listed in this pamphlet."

I furrowed my brow, expecting the other prospective members to do the same. Instead, they all nodded and hung on to Asher's every word like he was Christ reincarnated.

No, not like Christ. Something more powerful. Like he was the most popular boy in school.

"If you can't commit to following all the rules, leave now." Asher stared us all down. "Including rule number one: you must stay single."

"*What?*"

A boy with a buzz cut leapt to his feet beside me. Both his backpack brimming with textbooks and smaller frame instantly signaled him as a freshman. "You're telling me I have to break up with my girlfriend just to make extra cash off your borrowers?"

"Yes." Asher's voice was flat. Indifferent. "No single status, no membership, and no tips. That's the rule."

So that's why so many also drooled over getting into this club. Cash. Students paid real tips for this so-called service.

Just how much money were we talking?

"But these dates aren't real," Buzz Cut Freshie went on. "Why would we need to stay single for that?"

"The rule is a club tradition, and for good reason. It stops drama. Conflicts of interest. Nothing can harm the club's integrity if members come with no strings attached." Asher's voice morphed into a more robotic tone the longer he spoke, like he'd heard this complaint a million times. "We are here to be marketable and bring in borrowers. Not to have fun. Our borrowers want what they know they can't have. Being unattainable keeps them coming back."

"But—"

"No dating. No real girlfriends. Someone's been kicked out for this reason, and I'll happily make that happen again. Any more questions?"

A few club members behind Asher shifted their weight. Lenny pressed his lips tightly together.

Everyone fell silent again.

Eventually, Buzz Cut Freshie squinted. He scoffed and flounced away, disappearing into the costume racks. Two other boys slowly got up and trailed behind him.

Fifteen boys remained, myself included.

Asher seemed unaffected by the outrage. "Rule number two is also vital: never admit to being in the Borrow a Boyfriend Club. If accepted, you agree to register as a member of the Football and Lamborghini Club and continue regular study of Italian culture and language. You are more than welcome to discuss being a part of this club publicly at any time."

Everything finally clicked into place.

Football and Lamborghinis, two things the boot country was known for in America aside from pasta and pizza. So, in other words, they were fronting as an Italian club.

"Does everyone understand?" Isabella, the product manager, asked from behind Asher. Her sharp cat-eye glasses caught in the light as she tilted her head only at me. The honorary new kid. "We operate under a real, registered club with the school. Especially with Ms. Vora. She's our sponsor, so if she leaves her art classroom to check on us, you throw out a *ciao* and start cheek kissing. M'kay?"

How this scheme stayed undercover was eons beyond my understanding. If every student understood the facade, then didn't it only take one person to screw up in front of all the prowling teachers? Could the student body be that loyal?

"We'll now begin," Asher said.

There was no time for doubts or concerns now. *Time to shine.* I got to my feet.

Asher's silver rings glistened obnoxiously in the fluorescent basement lights as he thrust a finger at the boy sitting farthest from me. "You. Follow me."

I raised my hand. "But I got here first."

Asher glanced my way for only the briefest of seconds, then walked away and ignored me. The lucky interviewee trailed him like a giddy golden retriever, as did Asher's seven club members. They all vanished through the mysterious door at the far end of the room.

Seriously?

That self-centered, lowlife jerk.

Five minutes passed before Asher stepped through the door again. The once-lucky interviewee beside him now looked like a dejected basset hound. He wandered toward the staircase, failure seeping from his pores.

Asher pointed at another interviewee who, of course, was not me. Five minutes later, another miserable face stepped out of the room. And another. Another. Worst of all, that electronic song must have been on loop because it was *still* playing.

"What song even is this?" I asked my rivals sitting around me.

One stared at me like I was the universe's ultimate doofus. "You mean 'The Borrow a Boyfriend Club Theme Song'?"

I nodded a couple of times. Of course they had a theme song.

After an hour of the same synths and trumpets and drums repeating from the jukebox, I was the only body left. Asher stepped out for the fourteenth time and finally pointed at me.

I followed him into a space no bigger than my bedroom. The scent of wet dirt overpowered the cologne that had engulfed me over the last hour. The place was as empty as an interrogation room, with only a single light bulb hanging above us, a few shelves on the wall stacked with paperwork, and a folding table sandwiched between two chairs.

All seven members stood along the wall, their eyes on me.

Camilo and Lenny, the only two I recognized enough to remember by name, were at the end of the lineup. Just like Asher, they both had freakishly symmetrical faces. And perfectly styled hair. And arms that, although on the skinnier side, showed off visibly toned muscles through their sweaters. I fought the temptation to pull my sweatshirt hood over my whole face.

Asher gestured toward an empty chair. "Sit."

I did, then Asher took the other seat. The slimmest laptop I'd ever seen was open in front of him.

Asher typed away, his silver rings clinking loudly against the keyboard. "If you pass a question, we continue on. If you fail a question, we stop. No retakes are allowed."

I nodded a few times.

"Who are you?"

"Um. Noah Byrd."

"Thank you, Noah Byrd. You failed."

Camilo let out a sharp cackle. Lenny elbowed him.

I nearly choked on my own spit. "All I said was my name."

"Your name isn't the problem." Asher tapped his screen like a barbarian. "Question one is the problem. Your image. Your brand."

I scoffed. "My *brand?*"

"What are you trying to sell me? Your popularity and attractiveness? You transferred here two days ago. It's impossible for you to provide us with a steady track record that proves you have a strong enough image at this school to pull borrowers."

"Can't freshmen apply days into starting here? They wouldn't have an image, either."

"Nearly every student from the three middle schools in our district funnel here. Their peers carry over. No one from Pinewood goes here except for you."

He had a point. This school was far from home, but worth the commute for me.

Asher rose from his chair.

"Wait!" I stood up so quickly that my sweatshirt hood flung off my head.

Every imperfection that my hoodie kept hidden was revealed underneath the flickering light bulb. The messy clumps of blond curls on top of my head. The full shape of my small, angular face. The peach fuzz around my cheeks. To top it all off, my sweatshirts smelled like coffee beans from my early morning shifts at Bitterlake instead of expensive cologne.

Now there was utterly, truly, no point in continuing this interview.

Asher tilted his head. "You're not half bad."

I blinked at him. "What?"

He sat back down in his chair, then propped his chin on a fist. "Nice curls. Heart-shaped faces are getting popular again."

A part of me felt borderline uncomfortable, and I couldn't believe this was all he had to say. But Asher spoke in a way that made me feel like I should be thanking him for even glancing my way, and I hated that I did.

He set his phone on the table, then opened a timer. "I'll accept your first answer for now, Byrd."

"It's Noah."

"Question two," Asher said. "Recite every member's name and Type. You have sixty seconds." He tapped the start button on his screen.

The numbers started counting down from sixty.

A strange squawking sound shot out of my mouth as I

searched the faces behind Asher. When I landed on Lenny Kawai at the end of the line, he showed his dimples.

"Can I ask what this has to do with being a good boyfriend?" I asked.

"Memory retention. Matching faces with names. Borrowers expect us to remember everything about them from previous dates. Forty seconds."

I swallowed hard. "Lenny. Influencer Type." Whatever that meant.

Lenny beamed even brighter.

"Camilo," I went on, finding his face beside Lenny. "Smart Type."

Camilo imitated the sound of a buzzer, and my anxiety shot through the ceiling. "Wrong. I'm Candice Type."

"What's a Candice Type—?"

"Can this dic—"

Lenny elbowed him again. "Ignore him, please."

That was much easier said than done considering I felt as vulnerable as if I were naked. I racked the deepest corners of my brain to remember more names and Types from Asher's welcome speech, but hardly any more came.

"Well." I pointed at the varsity jacket on Sporty Type. *Ngo* had been written on the back, but what was his first name? "There's Sporty. And a psychic?"

The timer sounded at zero.

Asher pressed stop. He didn't type anything on his laptop, didn't say whether I answered correctly. But he didn't tell me to leave either. I hoped my obvious effort was enough. "Next question. Members must have a passion for romance. Explain why you care about love and dating. Sixty seconds."

My stomach flooded with dread. I had never been in a relationship. I had never asked someone to a school dance. I had never kissed someone before.

I wasn't sure if I *wanted* to. A romantic fairy tale seemed too impossible for me. I hadn't even trusted Jas and Everly and Rosen to see myself for the real me. My best friends.

How could I trust someone to see all of me in that way? How could anyone? Because I'd never experienced "romance," I wondered if it was even real.

But that didn't matter, here, now.

"I'm an expert in dating!" The lie shot out of me.

Asher hitched his brow.

Sweat beaded along my hairline. "Yeah, yeah. I've dated someone. Lots of someones. At my old school." I made a face. "Not like I dated a lot because I kept getting dumped. Or because I dumped them either. Because that would mean I don't care about romance. And I do. So much. Actually, I didn't date many someones at all. Just a couple. We'd walk around downtown, and get lattes at Bitterlake—"

"Has anyone ever been in love with you?" His stare drilled right into me.

"Sure."

"Do you have proof?"

My mouth opened. Nothing left it.

The timer on Asher's phone beeped. My sixty seconds were up.

He shut his million-dollar laptop once more, slipped it into his tote bag, and then walked over to open the door. A stream of basement light filtered into the dimly lit room.

I royally screwed up the third question, and I hadn't been

able to continue my lie, but hope danced inside me, nonetheless. "Did I pass?"

"Nope, you've failed," Asher said in the doorway.

The hope dropped dead.

Camilo whistled from his viewing position against the wall. "I wasn't even drilled this much when I first interviewed."

"But didn't you goof it and say you only wanted to prove you were cool enough to get in?" Lenny asked.

"That's my point," Camilo said. "This guy's bad, but not *that* bad. What gives?"

"He has no experience being a boyfriend," Asher said. "How could he care about the club? A recruit like him would break all the rules in our handbook. He'd get a girlfriend the moment we turned our backs—"

"I have enough to worry about, so I'm not going to randomly start trying to figure out who I'm into now," I interrupted to help my case, only to instantly realize the error.

Great. I admitted to lying. I was no love expert.

At least this dragged Asher's attention back to me. "Or a boyfriend. Or *anyone*. What I'm trying to say is, you'd break the rules."

The desperation simmering inside me heated to a boil. I rapidly flickered my gaze between him and Lenny and Camilo. "Can I redo my last question? I can clarify—"

Asher turned around slowly, steadily, regarding me with so much disdain that I was stunned into silence.

His voice was bold. Cold. Clear.

"No retakes allowed."

CHAPTER 5

I leaned against the brick wall beside the school entrance after the most embarrassing interview of all time, watching the traffic grow denser as Ann Arbor rush hour approached.

An icy wind blew by and sent a chill down my spine, and the smell of road salt blasted my nostrils. I stuffed my hands deeper into my parka pockets instead of starting my journey home. I felt too drained to move.

Asher had rejected me. How was I supposed to prove I was enough now?

I let out a long sigh and forced myself to head toward the downtown streets lined with orderly parked cars. Before the end of the semester, I had to solidify who I was some other way. Trying to stay invisible would only work for so long. Eventually, my classmates would notice and draw their own conclusions about me.

Just as I was about to turn the street corner wrapping around the school, a loud groan came from behind.

"Then I'm gonna quit!"

Then shushing. Lots of it.

I froze in my tracks, then slowly crept closer to the noise. Only a few feet away, most members of the club, including their product manager and CFO, stood beneath the awning of a school side door. Sporty Type's mouth was covered by Lenny, whose pastel-blue hair was mostly hidden by a fuzzy, hot-pink hat that matched his full-body pink parka.

Sporty Type ripped Lenny's gloved hand off his mouth. "I'm not doing that cringe talent show."

Talent show. I'd seen flyers hanging up in the basement about this earlier.

"I've already discussed the idea with Asher," Constance, the CFO said, wincing. Her fuzzy coat was a burst of lacy frills and pom-poms, like the rest of her wardrobe, cute cat paw prints sewn onto the front pockets. "We need to stay a lucrative business, and ever since we had to cut our base rates after this year's Homecoming, not enough is coming in anymore."

"Not our fault we had to do damage control," Sporty said with a tsk. "It's *his*."

"Would you rather have all your tips start going toward our funds instead?" Isabella interrupted, pressing a finger to his chest. "Or do a cute little talent show?"

That shut up Sporty Type.

Constance sighed. "Asher agrees winning the cash prize is our only option. Otherwise, according to my spreadsheets, between wardrobe, transportation costs for dates, and website fees, we'll . . . go broke and close by the end of this semester."

The other members shared tense stares.

"Without my cut from the old base rate, I'm gonna have to

quit regardless and get some part-time job downtown," Sporty said, kicking at a dirty snow pile beside the sidewalk.

Camilo was too busy messaging someone again to look up at the conversation happening around him. "Yeah? You won't miss people writing essays for you for free? How are you gonna cope in first period without your morning groupie latte? Ready to start buying your own?"

Sporty towered over Camilo's tiny frame. "I will, bro!"

Camilo didn't even flinch.

Isabella bent down so quickly to tug on Sporty's ugly orange athletic shorts that her high ponytail slapped him across the face. "No one will buy you anything when you wear these. What did I tell you about them?"

Sporty winced in shame. "Not allowed."

"Who dresses you?" Isabella flailed around her pointer finger. "Who dresses all of you?"

"You do, Isabella," a few boys muttered.

"You won't quit, my friend," interrupted Psychic Type as he pressed his fingertips together. His voice was calm. "None of us will. We're gonna wow 'em onstage for that sweet cash."

Sporty nudged Psychic with an elbow. "That a premonition or a bet?"

"Common sense. Our yearly hundred dollars from the school vanished in a week. The savings Sebastian left for us was gone a month later. Our funds are drier than an ant husk. Or would you rather pay for your borrower dates with your own money?"

Sporty groaned again, earning him more shushes.

"Okay, hi!" Lenny's loose hot-pink parka bopped around his lanky frame as he rushed over to Constance and slung an arm over her shoulder. "Please, *please*, keep it down. If Asher hears any of this, he won't be happy."

I couldn't tell the specifics of what was going on, but they clearly needed help winning prize money from the talent show to keep its members happy and the club alive. Desperately.

So desperately that they might be willing to make a deal.

"I could speed-draw people in the audience," someone suggested, holding up a sketchbook. Must've been Artsy Type.

"Way too quiet." Sporty Type held up a single finger. "We should spin basketballs on our fingertips."

"I can predict how soon you'll drop them, friend," Psychic Type said.

Lenny waved his hand high in the air. "I'll do our makeup using only kids' paint."

"I'd rather chew cement," Camilo replied.

"Hey," I shouted, stepping farther around the corner, startling all the boys. "What about a dance routine?"

Everyone else shared several nervous glances.

Lenny rushed toward me and slapped a gloved hand over my mouth. With his other hand, he gestured wildly at Psychic Type. "Hypnotize him! Make him forget what he heard!"

Psychic shook his head. "Outside of my moral range."

I ripped Lenny's hand off my lips. "But I can help you. With the school talent show."

The fear on everyone's faces flipped to intrigue.

A familiar voice piped up from behind us. "Help us how?"

Asher stood beneath the awning wearing a gray wool peacoat that fell above his knees. I hadn't even heard the door open.

Asher's thick brow hitched. "Well?"

"With dancing," I said, and the words sizzled on my lips. Under normal conditions, I'd never consider being an instructor. I hadn't danced in four years and swore I never would again. But I'd do anything to be let into their club. "I can teach your members how to do a cool routine."

"It's the Anita Kömraag Dedicatory Club Talent Show." He emphasized each word like there was weight to the statement. Like this wasn't any ordinary high school show.

"And?"

"The prize is five thousand dollars."

My eyes nearly bulged out of my head. "Where's that kind of money coming from?"

"Anita. She's an alum. A Tony Award–winning actress on Broadway who donates to Heron since she loved the theater and Improv Club. The talent show's in its second year, and the prize money has already tripled because Anita keeps getting more famous."

"Which means everyone and their mom wants to sign up," Sporty Type muttered.

This biography was starting to sound familiar. If she really was a hometown hero, then she must've been mentioned at my old musical rehearsals. Maybe Jas and Everly were fans.

"Anita alone decides who wins the money," Asher went on. "A lot's on the line."

I shrugged. "Well, I'm good. Really good. I can send you a picture of my dresser. It's covered with dance trophies." I conveniently left out the "haven't danced in four years aside from in my bedroom" part.

Lenny approached Asher, apologetically. "I'm really sorry, Asher. He snuck up on all of us. I'm sure he won't tell anyone what's happening to the club—"

Asher lifted a hand to shut him up, his focus still on me. "You want something in return."

"I failed your interview," I said. "But if you let me pass, I'll save your club."

Deep down, I doubted my past middle school knowledge of ballet, tap, jazz, or any of the other various dances I dabbled in were worthy of five thousand dollars. But that was a future-me problem.

Asher crossed his arms and studied me. "Passing yesterday's interview was just round one of the process. You get that, right?"

"What?"

"There is a total of three rounds an applicant must pass to be accepted, the first of which is an easy interview."

Easy. "Really?"

"Really."

"But why?"

"Club rules. A well-known one. Have you not cared enough to ask around the school and do a sliver of research on who we are the last few days?" Asher started walking away.

"Let me pass the first round, then," I shouted at his back. "I'll pass the other two rounds on my own and become a member by demonstrating my excellent boyfriend skills."

Asher turned. The surprise on his face lasted a moment before morphing into amusement and intrigue. "Oh?"

"Yeah. Whatever it is, I'll prove that I'm a great boyfriend. The perfect boyfriend."

"If I agree, you won't *help* us with the show. You promise to secure us a win."

I swallowed hard. "Okay, I promise."

His classic smirk came rushing back, the same left corner of his lip tilting upward in a way that made me want to punch him in the jaw. He fished the club's training handbook pamphlet from his tote bag and handed it to me. "Then you should get started on that research."

I took the book. "So, this means . . . ?"

"You're our new dance instructor. We'll start your lessons next month; the show is March twenty-first, so starting from the end of February should leave us with enough time to practice. And you have one week to convince me to go on a date with you."

My heart nearly stopped. "Sorry. What?"

"Round Two: Romance the President. Best of luck."

CHAPTER 6

HOW TO BE A GOOD BOYFRIEND HANDBOOK

PART I—MEMBERSHIP PROCESS

To be accepted into the illustrious Borrow a Boyfriend Club, all prospective members must pass three rounds to prove his potential as a good boyfriend:

Round One: Impress the Club President
Round Two: Romance the Club President
Round Three: Entertain a Borrower

Assessment for passing each round is at the discretion of the club's president and its members. No second chances are permitted. Please see back of handbook for details and list of exceptions.

My eye twitched as I stared at the club handbook open on my bed.

What *was* this?

I skipped down to the second portion.

PART II—RULES

1. Members must stay single.
2. Never admit to being in the Borrow a Boyfriend Club.
3. Early is on time. On time is late. Late is inexcusable. (More than three tardies to meetings and/or dates will result in dismissal from the club.)
4. Off-limits touching is not allowed between members and borrowers.
5. Members must always look good.
6. Style is at the discretion of the product manager. Wardrobes must be followed both while on the school premises and during dates.
7. Weekly meetings must be attended. One excused absence is allowed per semester.
8. Discrimination of any kind will not be tolerated or allowed.
9. Members must not discuss other borrowers while on dates so all clients feel special.
10. Dating hours must fall between 7 a.m. and 11 p.m.
11. Borrowers must be walked or driven home to ensure safety.
12. Members must not be under the influence of any mind-altering substances on dates.
13. A maximum tip payment of $20.00 per date from a borrower is allowed.

14. Tips earnings must be reported to the CFO by the first of each month via the website.
15. Reimbursement requests must be submitted in the form of a receipt by the first of each month. (See back of the handbook for what can be reimbursed by club funds.)
16. ~~Borrowers must pay their base-rate payments of $29.99 through the website and never through members (20% commission split between product manager, CFO, and club funds).~~
17. Dates with non–Heron River High School students must be approved by the president.
18. Scheduling conflicts must be reported to the president within 24 hours of a date.
19. All borrowers and fellow members must be treated with respect.
20. Any borrower behavior deemed inappropriate or unsafe toward members must be reported to the president immediately.

Failure to adhere to these regulations can result in dismissal from the club. All rules are at the discretion of the president and can be amended at any time.

I tossed the pamphlet across my bedroom. Rotting garbage. That's what this was. At least with rule number sixteen randomly crossed out, there was one less to memorize.

This process could take longer than I'd expected. If I wanted to stop with the invisibility act at school anytime soon, I had to figure out how to *Romance the President* fast.

How was I supposed to do that when I barely believed in romance myself?

Snatching my laptop off my bedside table, I opened my internet browser and began to Google.

BEST PICKUP LINES TO ASK SOMEONE ON A DATE!

1. Are you a bonfire? Cause you're so hot,
   I want s'more.
2. I'm in the mood for a pizza. A pizza you!
3. Did you eat a magnet? Because you're attractive.

I pulled my focus away from the article shining across my face to find the mirror that hung on the far wall, ran a nervous hand through my hair, and then held it out awkwardly. "Did you eat a magnet? Because you're attract—" I stopped myself before I dropped dead from embarrassment.

What had I said? *I'll prove that I'm a great boyfriend?* I'd seriously told that to Asher Price?

I'd charged into that theater basement expecting to pass a few simple questions. Now I needed to seduce one of the most popular guys in school in under a week to get a step closer to being accepted. *And* help them win a club talent show that was two months away. The odds of me pulling this off were . . . lower than Asher's expectations of me.

Lifting one of my noodle arms, I flexed my bicep. The tiniest bump in the universe rose.

I sighed and dropped my arm. The odds of me becoming a high school athlete instead of a pseudo boyfriend were just as miserably low. And could I pull off staying invisible until then?

More research.

I clicked on another article from an official magazine website. If whoever was writing this guck was being paid real money, then they had to be pros.

TOP FOUR WAYS TO ASK OUT A BOY YOU LIKE!

1. Give him a flower.
2. Leave a love note on his car—extra points if using a romantic language like French or Italian!
3. Take blueberries or sweets like cupcakes and spell out your lovey-dovey confession!
4. When he least expects it, just give him a great big kiss, even if it's in public!

I slammed my laptop lid shut and fought the urge to press a pillow to my face and suffocate myself. Asher Price was a boy who had enough audacity to spell swear words in front of the school, and he was running something as ridiculous as a Borrow a Boyfriend Club. And he was the club's Popular Type. Putting all of this together, there was no doubt everything he did was to score popularity points. To get with girls.

I hadn't even had my first kiss.

Meanwhile, Asher probably had more experience than I would ever collect in my lifetime. How was I supposed to impress him?

I hesitantly opened my laptop again and reread the article.

Use blueberries or sweets like cupcakes to spell out your lovey-dovey confession!

Had to start somewhere.

* * *

Baking eighteen cupcakes was only a thirty-minute process, but spelling out each letter of *ASHER, IM YOURS, BE MINE* on the tops with frosting cost me two whole hours.

The sentence took forever to think up since I needed precisely eighteen letters to fill Mom's heart-shaped cupcake baking tray. But the time spent was worth it. This was the perfect way to deliver a romantic message to Asher.

A half hour before the first-period bell rang, I made a beeline for the theater with the tray of cupcakes and rushed down the basement staircase, taking the steps two at a time, then blasted through the overflowing costume racks until I reached the very back. No Asher. No Lenny. No Camilo. No anyone. The coast was clear.

Exactly as planned. No one would dare come to school this early.

I walked toward the billiards table, nearly tripping over a football and stepping on a paintbrush along the way, then set the tray down. I pulled out the sticky note that I'd written *From, Noah* on with a pink highlighter.

This had to work. The cupcakes were homemade. That showed time and effort were put into this. And everyone loved food.

As I stuck the note beside the cupcakes, a side table pushed into the corner of the basement caught my eye. A vintage gold picture frame sat on top of an embroidered doily. Above it hung a banner on the wall with the phrase SERVE LOVE.

I grimaced. This sounded like a club slogan. "Serving love" as if they were serving spaghetti on a platter.

And here I thought I couldn't believe in romance any less.

I approached the photo for a better inspection. The framed image was of a boy signing papers at a fancy mahogany desk, a fountain pen in one hand and a Rolex watch on his wrist. Along the bottom of the photo, the same phrase was printed in a gold font.

Whoever this was, he had perfectly styled short brown hair and sophisticated dark glasses, and if it weren't for the slight blur likely caused by a shaky photographer, I would've assumed this was a *Business Insider* cover. Nickels and dimes and packages of gummy bears were scattered around the photo in a way that mimicked offerings. The table was like an altar.

Had someone died?

My gaze drifted toward an index card taped to the doily on the tabletop.

The Sebastian Shrine
A living legend! Please offer your respects
before serving love to others.

Before I could figure out what respects to pay, let alone who this Sebastian guy was, creaking footsteps came from the staircase.

Panic surged through me. Why was someone coming here before school had started? I searched for a place to hide, landing on the room behind the *Do Not Enter* door, which was left ajar. I jogged over and slipped inside, peeking through the crack.

Camilo. Hands stuffed in his pleated slacks pockets, he sauntered over to the billiards area and came to a sudden halt.

I couldn't see well from this angle. Only the back of his beige knit sweater and collared shirt tail sticking out around the waist. But it was obvious what he was doing. He was reading the cupcakes.

My insides withered. Embarrassing. *So* embarrassing.

Camilo's back blocked my cupcake display from view, but he was clearly moving something. Was he eating all eighteen?

Another set of footsteps came closer, more rapid and louder than Camilo's.

Lenny jogged across the room in a whirlwind of pastel blues and purples. He tackled Camilo with his lanky limbs, making the two of them stagger and the rhinestone curtains flutter. "Ready for our incredible, amazing morning-announcements club feature?"

"No," Camilo said, shoving him off. From a distance, I could make out to-do lists scribbled on both his hands *and* arms. More than usual. That meant he had better things to do than poke his nose in my business. And yet.

"Come on, Camilo."

"There's no *point* in announcing that no one got accepted this semester to the whole student body."

I couldn't see Lenny's face, but his weary sigh made it clear Camilo was successfully smothering the sunshine radiating off him. "Any club that's accepting new members during the winter semester has to participate even if they have nothing to say." He patted Camilo on the head twice. "Let's get prepped before Asher shows up."

Of course. The club had to meet before school to prepare for some special morning announcements, today of all days. And Asher would be here any moment.

"Wait." Camilo tugged on Lenny's jacket sleeve to keep him within the vicinity of my cupcakes. "Check this out."

Lenny's blue hair tilted. "What's this?"

Another bold voice came from the staircase. The one I dreaded hearing the most.

"Stop fooling around. It's almost time for the announcements."

"Someone left you a gift, Asher," Camilo said.

"A gift?" Asher passed by the crack in the closet door as he approached, his sneakers shattering the dusty basement floor with each step.

Silence.

"What the hell?"

A pit dropped into the depths of my stomach, never to be found again. Was the *Be Mine* phrase too commanding? Was the cupcake idea that much of a turnoff?

"*Byrd!*"

My palms sweat as I kept them pressed against the metal door, one no one was supposed to be near except for Asher. Definitely not me.

I was screwed.

I slowly, gradually, painfully stepped out of the forbidden room.

The three stared at me. I stared back. The many kings and queens of hearts on the walls grimaced and shook their heads.

Asher pointed at the table, his jaw tense and brow wrinkled. My heart tray wasn't there anymore. Instead, the cupcakes had been taken out of the tray and reordered. Half of the cupcakes had even gone missing. They didn't spell *ASHER, IM YOURS, BE MINE* anymore.

They spelled SMASH ME.

"No," I muttered. Was this a fever dream? Where had the other cupcakes gone? Had they walked off the tray and jumped into the billiards table's pockets? What had Camilo done? "No, this wasn't me—"

Asher waved the sticky note with my name on it in the air.

"Little Byrdie is more forward than I thought," Lenny whispered. Camilo let out a short laugh, then pressed a hand to his mouth. Between *#12-45 pg 107 bio* and *meeting 2pm NHS* written on his palm, there was a smear of bright-pink frosting.

"That's not what I wrote, though! I wrote—"

Asher thrust a finger toward the exit. "Leave."

CHAPTER 7

The Borrow a Boyfriend Club wasn't worth the trouble.

The thought repeated in my mind as my first-period pottery class passed by. After this morning's mortifying cupcake escapade, the mushy clay spinning on the wheel was a replica of my brain. There was no way I could keep acting like a clown to romance Asher Price. I had some dignity left.

I'd prove who I was to the student body some other way.

"*Goooooooood* morning, Heron River High!"

I startled on my stool and lifted my hands right off my wheel. The morning-news announcer boomed from the television at the front of the room.

A student with sweepy black bangs and a lip ring flashed the camera a painfully forced smile. "Today is Monday, January sixteenth. My name is Michael Whitten, and here is our famous quote of the day, from Osamu Dazai's *No Longer Human*: 'Human beings work to earn their bread, for if they don't eat, they die.'"

The room fell quiet.

Another anchor showed up on-screen. She cleared her throat. "And my name is Sarah Janay. First on the docket today: now that the winter semester is here, some clubs would like to take the opportunity to celebrate their newly inducted members."

The camera angle switched to a wider shot of three girls, all wearing argyle sweaters, in front of a green screen. "I'm Savannah, president of Chess Club," the one in the center said, "and I'd like to welcome sophomore Tina Kulkarni and freshman Alex Wu!"

More clubs came and went with their announcements, but the classroom chatter drowned out most of the names. Mr. Alberich tried and failed to shush us. Three familiar faces soon appeared on camera. Asher Price, sandwiched between Camilo Torres's bright turquoise glasses and Lenny Kawai's even brighter blue hair.

Someone shushed ten times louder than Mr. Alberich ever could, slashing through the noise. All mouths zipped shut, and all eyes were glued to the television.

None of the Borrow a Boyfriend Club—or, rather, Football and Lamborghini Club—members spoke at first. Lenny and Camilo eyed Asher awkwardly.

Finally, Asher locked his stern gray eyes with all of ours. "No one has been accepted."

The classroom chitchat returned in a crashing wave.

"That Italian Club is so exclusive," Mr. Alberich commented through a grin, a curious sort of tone coating his voice. Maybe he didn't know the true reason why all the students cared, but he could at least tell the obvious: everyone thought the members were hot.

A familiar groan came from a few pottery wheels to my left.

My gaze traveled toward Sporty Type in his usual varsity jacket with football patches decorating the arm. "Sebastian would be so pissed. Asher couldn't even take this seriously enough to introduce himself or the club."

"He cares," Psychic Type said beside him, a floral, droopy cardigan hanging off the back of his pottery stool. "His aura was pink. Caring. Kind."

As Lenny recited a polite statement about the competitiveness of the club to assuage their overflowing rejection pool, two girls and a boy swiveled around in their stools.

"Asher seriously still isn't letting anyone new in?" one asked, leaning very far over Psychic Type's wheel.

Both members hesitated. Eventually, Psychic Type showed a slender finger covered in gemstone rings. He was so pale that his skin practically glowed in the lights. "Our president keeps his standards immensely high to ensure our"—he paused and lowered his voice, probably to stop Mr. Alberich from paying attention—"*club visitors'* souls are satisfied." Then he lifted his scarf to his face, as if he were suddenly too shy to directly make eye contact with his fans. "Especially you three."

I stared at an invisible camera. These boys were *not* real.

Even if their personas were exaggerated, or entirely fabricated, everyone else treated them like the elite regardless. Getting accepted was that big of a deal.

This was exactly the stamp of approval I needed. But I'd already made up my mind. I refused to keep embarrassing myself to become a member.

"*But,*" Asher's voice boomed. He was still on-screen, and speaking louder now, like he knew there were crowds to silence. "One candidate has made it to round two of the membership process. That is all."

The camera stayed on the members a beat too long before switching to the next club.

"Seriously?" one girl near Sporty Type asked, tugging his jacket sleeve. "Who, Aiden?"

Now most of my classmates tuned in, watching the conversation from every part of the room. They all had the same question.

"That new kid. He's actually in this class." Sporty—I guess he had a real name, Aiden—scanned the room until he landed on me. He waved his arms high. "Congrats on making it to the second round, mio amico."

All eyes lasered in on me.

I blanched. A brief hint of joy trilled through me, knowing I was the candidate in question, but now that everyone in the room knew that too, my fears rose fast.

If I didn't become a member, the whole student body would find out I failed. Word traveled quickly. They'd assume I wasn't enough in the end.

I waved back at Aiden, my insides recoiling. There was a slim chance I could ever be a perfect boy for this club, but now I couldn't give up.

To romance Asher Price, I'd just need to trick him into thinking I was.

CHAPTER 8

The worst life mistake I'd ever made was accidentally calling my eighth-grade teacher Mr. Lobb *daddy* while turning in a geology test. The second worst mistake I'd ever made was waiting for Asher Price to pull into the juniors' parking lot in the freezing Michigan winter.

I kicked my left Converse sneaker out of a deep pile of snow, then went back to scanning the lot from behind the pine tree I'd claimed as my hideout post. *Leave a love note on his car* was the remaining suggestion I'd read on that *TOP FOUR WAYS TO ASK OUT A BOY YOU LIKE!* article that seemed dramatic enough to catch Asher's attention. But there were only ten minutes left until the first-period bell rang, and he hadn't shown up to school.

Where was he? Two weeks had already passed since I transferred. I had no time to lose.

Almost everyone my age walked in Ann Arbor. But Asher Price wore Gucci sweaters and Prada shoes and had a face that looked just as Photoshopped as it was punchable. He must've gotten some bougie million-dollar sports car for his sixteenth birthday.

Minutes later, an obnoxious rumble came from the main road.

A bright-white Mustang swung into the parking lot. The car took a sharp turn into the farthest possible spot away from the school. Asher Price stepped out of the driver's side in his fitted peacoat and trusty tote bag.

Predictable.

As he headed toward the school doors, I held my knit scarf higher on my face and stealthily ducked my way through the pine trees lining the lot until I reached his car. Up close, it was much more beat up, like something out of the late nineties. There were scrapes on the doors and dents along the rear bumper, like he'd slammed into ten mailboxes. Probably had. Good. He needed a flaw.

I pulled out the piece of construction paper I'd cut into a heart the night before and read over my love letter one last time. I'd used an online translator to write the confession in Italian, mostly because that was one of the most stereotypically romantic languages in the world, but also because I wanted to prove my knowledge to President Prick. The Borrow a Boyfriend Club operated under the guise of the Football and Lamborghini Club, and my Italian skills had to score me some points.

Still. This was very mortifying.

My heart raced as I struggled to lift the left windshield wiper and slip my letter underneath.

The wiper wouldn't budge, so I tried the right one instead.

Nope. Both were frozen to the window. I glanced around the rest of the car, searching for somewhere else to easily stick this love letter without it flying away in the wind.

If someone else found this piece of paper fluttering around the parking lot later, the embarrassment would kill me, revive me, and kill me again.

The driver's side of his Mustang suddenly caught my attention. Through the window, the door lock was visibly left unlocked. Before the odds grew of someone spotting me lurking like a creep, I whipped open the driver's-side door, dove into the front seat, and leaned over the steering wheel to place my note on the dashboard.

A car horn blared through the parking lot.

I looked at my chest, which was pressed against the wheel. Of course. Then toward the school entrance, where Asher had stopped. He was digging through his tote bag and pulling out his keys.

He turned around to return to his Mustang.

I tossed the letter on the dashboard before jumping out and slamming the door shut. Adrenaline coursed through me as I sprinted for the nearest pine tree.

As Asher approached his car with a furrowed brow, he inspected the sides like he was searching for clues. After one full circle around his car, he noticed the heart love-letter cutout.

My legs turned to jelly. I gripped the tree as hard as I could to keep standing, hoping its thick trunk and snowy branches hid me completely.

Asher tilted his head, then dipped in and out of the front seat to grab the letter.

"Will you go out with me?" Asher enunciated clearly. "Check yes or no. Love, Noah."

My face flared with heat. Asher Price actually spoke Italian? Of course he did.

He glanced around the parking lot. "Where you hiding, Byrd?"

I stepped into his view. "I—"

"You broke into my car."

"I mean, technically yes, but—"

"Congrats. I've gotten a few of these on my car before, but never inside. And never in Italian." He handed over the piece of paper. "Come on. Read the letter to your crush."

I snorted. "You are *not* my crush."

Asher's thick brow shot up. "Really killing your chances here."

"I mean—that's not what I—"

"You gonna read the note or not?"

Blood was pumping loud in my ears. My heart raced as I approached him. I cleared my throat. "View usk ear cone—"

"Vuoi uscire con me."

"Vuh—"

"*Vuoi.*"

"Voo?"

"Jesus Christ, man," Asher said.

I frowned. "I see you speak Italian. Fluently?"

He shrugged. "My dad's from Florence. Lives there full-time. That's why we operate under the Italian culture and language disguise. Easy to pass off." Asher gestured to the note. "Why didn't you go with English?"

Calling Mr. Lobb *daddy* in the eighth grade was no longer the worst mistake of my life. I couldn't meet his eyes. "The internet said Italian was a romantic language."

He sighed dramatically, then started walking back toward the school.

"Is that a yes?" I shouted. "Do you check yes?"

"Try again, Byrd. You're gonna have to get more creative if you want to impress me. Any idea is fair game."

Crackling came from the branches above, and before I could look up, a clump of snow fell on my head.

CHAPTER 9

I'd been working on my name-change petition paperwork in the library since lunch started twenty minutes ago, yet I had several more pages to go to prove that I wasn't running from the law or fleeing to a foreign country. The paperwork was standard for anyone wanting to change their name, and the only way the Ann Arbor City Clerk would schedule my court date. But you'd think I was an FBI-wanted criminal instead of a sixteen-year-old with a clean record.

I sighed and opened my laptop to take a break. The tabs on my browser were packed with influencer videos from the night before, all explaining how to ask someone out.

God. I had two days left to get Asher to agree to a date. If I was going to pull off getting him to see that I was worthy of the school's most esteemed club, then I needed to do a *lot* more research.

"Heya, Little Byrdie!"

Before I got the chance to glance up from my grilled cheese

and laptop, my sweatshirt hood was yanked down, exposing my head. I scrambled to pull it back up as Lenny slid into the seat across from me.

What had he called me? *Little Byrdie?*

At least it wasn't N.

My stomach dropped once I realized my name-change forms were out for him to see. I rapidly slid the papers underneath my laptop. "S-sup?"

"Wow." Lenny tried to speak quietly since the librarian's front desk was close by, but his voice cut through the silence anyway. "You're doing homework during lunch?"

Three girls greeted Lenny in singsong voices as they passed. One set a sugary drink topped with an obscene amount of whipped cream beside him. The cup had heart stickers all over it.

Lenny thanked them in such an endearing way, they literally sighed. The painted portraits of Edgar Allen Poe, Fyodor Dostoevsky, and Agatha Christie on the nearest wall watched in horror as the library became a hormone-filled zone.

I studied Lenny's pastel-blue hair that showed a hint of black roots, his diamond-stud earrings, and the fluorescent spray-paint-patterned jacket he wore over a high-neck sweater that was straight out of a street fashion magazine. This kid looked *so* familiar.

I shut my laptop. I obviously hadn't been doing homework, but it was better Lenny didn't know the truth. People sat in the library during lunch to study or avoid feeling like an outcast. If he knew my situation was the latter, my growing image could be destroyed.

"Camilo mentioned how he sort of screwed up your cupcake confession last week." Lenny's eyes were full of pity. "On paper, he's Smart Type, but I think he should really be Academically Gifted but Gets Bored Too Easily Type."

"I've noticed," I droned.

"But he did feel bad! And he told Asher the truth."

Relief flooded through me. "So, Asher knows? That I'm not some weirdo?"

"Well, he knows you didn't mean to spell *Smash Me*. But he's also seen that same cupcake trick a good thirty times now."

That *was* the first search result I'd seen online.

I banged my head on the table. "How long did it take for you? You know, to make it into the club?"

"A day."

Cool. "I see."

Lenny lifted a finger, the baggy sleeve of his jacket sliding down his arm. "But the process was so much easier then! I joined when Asher's brother created the club his senior year, back when he was president. See, Sebastian didn't implement the three rounds until he graduated last year and passed the club to Asher."

Sebastian. The one with the altar of gummy bears and nickels in the basement that had *Serve Love* engraved on the bottom of the photo of him. That was Asher's *brother*?

"Wait," I said. "That Sebastian guy created the club? Not Asher?"

"Yeppers. Asher just used to be another member. We both joined as sophomores. They also already knew me because I'm neighbors with the Price family, so."

So, nepotism.

The fact that Asher hadn't created this ridiculous popularity-based dating club surprised me, considering he was the exact self-obsessed asshole who would. Like brother like brother. Also meant Sebastian hadn't died, despite the altar—he was just that much of a legend to them. "Did his brother explain why he added these extra steps?"

Lenny shrugged. "Asher thinks it's because Sebastian doesn't trust him to choose the right members now that he's gone. Added rounds, fewer errors."

Ouch. "Oh."

"See, Sebastian's a business wiz. With Constance helping with the numbers, the two were unstoppable. Every member made over a thousand bucks last year."

"Whoa." If Asher's older brother graduated last year, then Asher had been in charge since September. Even though his ego was bigger than Mars, the fact that he was struggling to fund the club like his business-savvy brother must've stung. "What about Camilo? When did he join?"

"Last year. First freshman to ever be accepted! But he failed miserably the first time he tried to pass round one. He knew nothing about romance either. So have faith, Byrdie."

"Doesn't that club's handbook, or whatever, not allow re-takes?"

"Usually. Camilo's secretive about what went down, but Asher mentioned once that he had to do some convincing with Sebastian. To get another shot, I assume? Asher must've seen something special in Camilo. And if he's letting you seduce him instead of flat-out ignoring you, then he must feel the same way about you." Lenny patted my hand.

There had to be gaps in this story. The Asher I'd come to

know didn't have kind feelings. "He's only giving me a second chance so the club can get a free dance instructor."

Lenny's mouth twisted, but his whole face remained magically symmetrical, his nose perfectly pointed and straight brows perfectly shaped over his deep brown eyes. "No, no, no. He's failed at least seventy other applicants before you. You witnessed some. Everyone sees how the school treats members—free homework answers, food, attention, tips— Asher's seen every bribe in the book. But he's only accepted yours."

"Seriously?"

"Yep. Handing out free passes isn't normal for him. At all. Don't take it lightly."

My chest fluttered with hope.

Wait. Rewind. "*Seventy* others have failed the first round since he became president last semester?"

"Seventy-seven, according to our database."

That hope inside of me dimmed quickly. Between the clout, tips, and report-card boosts, this unofficial club was more sought-after than a perfectly crafted college application. Even with these perks, I couldn't believe so many people wanted to join a club all about dating, which required being vulnerable · and open and confident. Maybe the problem wasn't them. It was me. Romance was for boys who were enough. Who were worthy of it.

I still had a long way to go before I saw love as anything more than another hurdle.

With only two days left to convince Asher to let me through to round three, I needed help figuring out my next strategy.

"Can you give me any advice?" I asked.

He leaned so far forward in his chair that his chin nearly touched the tabletop. I leaned back an equal amount. "You mean, with *Romancing the Asher?*"

"Um. Yeah."

"Listen." His voice became severe, and for a split second I worried I'd blacked out and asked who the school's weed dealer was instead. "I'm not technically supposed to help you. Or anyone else who's trying to get in. So, don't snitch, got it?"

The librarian at the front desk shushed us.

Lenny lowered his voice. "You'll need to shock him! Show him you're bolder than he is."

"Bolder than him?"

"Yep."

"He spelled *Fa la la la fuck this school* with holiday lights in front of the school. You're saying I need to do something stronger than that?"

"Yep. Ash will love a big romantic gesture." He bit his bottom lip like he'd said something he shouldn't have. "But don't call him Ash. At least, not to his face. He hates that. And don't give him any Band-Aids. The latex gives him hives."

"Okay . . . ," I said, even though I wasn't sure how we'd gotten on the topic of Band-Aids. "Why did he do that, by the way? With the lights?"

A hint of a grimace showed on Lenny's face. "Asher and the admin don't exactly see eye to eye." He played with his baggy sleeves instead of elaborating. "I don't think you'd have to be bold in public, or at Heron. Think outside the box. Outside of school hours, even. Use Ann Arbor to your disposal. If you get stuck on ideas, my mom has a video that's all about crushes."

"Your mom?"

Lenny grabbed my laptop without asking and opened it. "Oh, good. You're already watching *How to Woo Men* videos."

My humiliation skyrocketed to the very highest of heights. I took a bite of my buttery grilled cheese to dull the pain. "Who's your mom?"

"Reina Kawai."

I choked on my sandwich before spitting pieces out. "Like, the beauty guru? Reina Cosmetics?"

Lenny stared at my chewed-up bread chunk between us on the table, grimacing. "Yep."

"Doesn't your mom live in Los Angeles?"

"She has this thing about wanting me and my younger sisters to have a *normal high school experience*. My dad grew up in Ann Arbor, so we live here with him while Mom does her own thing in L.A., going to influencer events, collaborating with sponsors, and such. She stops by whenever she can. Lots to unpack."

This was why I'd always thought Lenny looked so familiar. I'd never watched Reina Kawai, but several of her videos were viral hits. I vaguely recalled seeing Lenny's face in thumbnails, showing off intricate eye shadow looks and glittery cheekbones.

It was clear why Sebastian had accepted Lenny into the club. He was the son of a beauty guru who racked up millions of views on every makeup tutorial she posted. Reina had her own freaking makeup line.

This was the type of boy I had to compare myself to. Famous, handsome, perfect. Influential.

Lenny pulled his phone out of his pocket. A few seconds later, my own phone vibrated on the table. He Airdropped an address. "In case you want to stop by for more of my wonderful advice. Fun fact: I live one house to the left of Asher."

Then he clapped me on the back and started heading out of the library.

"Wait," I whispered, just soft enough that the librarian wouldn't laser me with her swirling black irises. "How come you're willing to help me? You said you weren't supposed to."

Lenny grinned. "In all my years of knowing Asher, I've never once witnessed someone stand up to him the way you do. I could really get used to that."

CHAPTER 10

The Art of Romancing: Notes & Research

As I sat on my bed and wrote those words down in my spiral notebook, a chill raced up my spine. The ghosts living in my century-old apartment must've been looming over my shoulder and laughing their translucent asses off.

Thankfully, I had scored a key advantage from Lenny Kawai: Asher Price's home address. Even with this premium knowledge, romancing Asher successfully would take research. Effort. Skill. I couldn't waste this key advantage on a bad idea.

I first conducted research by watching a playlist of Lenny's mom's videos that focused on love and crushes. One was even in collaboration with a well-known dating coach. Reina Kawai always talked quickly and high-pitched like Lenny did, but while applying a full face of makeup. I struggled to keep up as she rambled about how important it was to give your partner flowers on days that weren't just anniversaries or times when you wanted to apologize.

By the time I was done with the playlist, the sun had gone down, leaving the glow of my laptop screen lighting up my bedroom. After sixteen pages of collected research and one page of doodles, which were mostly sketches of stick-figure versions of me kicking stick-figure versions of Asher in the shin, I felt a little more confident.

Next was romance movies.

Couples in movies made big moves. *Bold* moves. And I was in desperate need of a bold idea. I searched for a list of the top fifty most famous rom-coms of all time. If I stayed up all night to watch the first ten, assuming the constant variable of two hours per film, I would be ready to pull off my next attempt by tomorrow night.

I made a bag of buttered popcorn, crawled underneath my bed covers, and hit the space bar on my laptop to begin the movie marathon. The first protagonist sprinted to the airport right before her crush's flight, carrying a stuffed elephant doll and fancy chocolate, which seemed super cliché. The next main character proposed to his love interest in the snow despite family disapproval, which seemed like a cold and miserable experience. Neither was applicable to me.

I didn't realize I was drifting off during the third movie until someone shouted on my screen. I shot awake and gripped my bed for dear life. A man stood outside of someone's window. He held massive note cards with words written on them in permanent marker.

Interesting.

I paused the movie on my laptop, then reached for my

phone to pull up Lenny's note that included his and Asher's home addresses.

Their neighborhood *was* only a thirty-minute walk away.

* * *

I should've known Asher Price lived on Rich Bitch Street.

Really, the road was called Ridgebirch Street, a long windy road on the outskirts of downtown that ran through the most expensive real estate in the city. The houses weren't taller than two stories, but the square footage was huge compared to the apartment buildings near me. Each house was custom designed with fancy fences and front gardens. Some even had fountains.

Lenny Kawai's mom supplying her son with a normal high school experience by living on Rich Bitch Street was a . . . choice. The fact that Asher lived in the same area made me wonder what his family did to live next door to the Kawais.

Three steps onto Rich Bitch Street, and I already felt hundreds of invisible eyes staring at me, the basic apartment dweller who dared to step into their territory.

But I had the perfect plan. The romance movies had taught me well.

My backpack slipped lower on my shoulder, and I hiked it back up. It was a struggle, since it was zipped halfway to fit the stacks of poster board I'd bought from Ann Arbor Family Pharmacy. I kept my head low as I passed Lenny's house, which was mostly shrouded by rows of pine trees. The next house was blocked off by hedges a head taller than me.

I came to an abrupt stop in front of Asher's place. His white Mustang was visible in the driveway through the shrubbery.

Was I really attempting this uncharacteristically Romeo move and tracking down Asher Price at his home? What if he called the police?

Asher *had* said any idea was fair game.

No blockades would stop me from romancing Asher Price. I heaved my backpack over the hedges. As it made a parabola and hooked over the hedges, the poster boards slipped out of the bag, and everything landed in a messy pile on the other side.

Good enough.

Using the branches in the hedges, I climbed up, twisted myself over the top, and jumped onto the ground. The soles of my Converse slipped along a sheet of black ice, and I fell backward and landed on my ass. Getting up as quickly as I fell, I shoved the poster board back into my backpack. The universe was fighting to keep me down, and that only fired me up more.

Until I saw the house in front of me.

The house's half-white, half-black exterior could've easily been some modern-art exhibit piece. And the front lawn was just as artsy with its perfectly trimmed diamond- and sphere-shaped topiaries decorated with holiday lights.

Asher's mansion definitely had invisible laser sensors crisscrossing the lawn. And security cameras. And stun guns set to fire and paralyze an invader's nervous system.

I winced as each of my steps crunched in the snow. No wild guard dogs were attacking me yet. So far so good.

Once I reached a sidewalk that wrapped around his house like a moat, I knocked the snow off my Converse. One room on the second floor was lit while the rest of the house was dark. His curtains were open. I could make out wooden bed-posts and perfect white walls, not a single picture frame or poster in sight.

Asher Price crossed the window.

I couldn't hide down here forever. I had to be confident. Bold.

I needed to get his attention. As I searched his lawn for pebbles or sticks, I was quickly reminded that this was Rich Bitch Street, and these families cherished their lawns. There were no rocks. No sticks. Only a perfectly even sheet of snow covering the yards. I pulled out my house keys, which weighed as much as a small toaster with my Pinewood High School key chain. I threw the keys.

The window cracked.

Too bold. Too bold!

Asher rushed over to lift the window and peered into the dark abyss. "What the hell?"

"Uh. Good evening!" *Why?* "It's me."

"*Who?*"

I forced myself to pull back my knit hat off my forehead so he could make out my face. Ducking beneath hoods and hats wasn't bold behavior, but my brain yelled at me to stay hidden. "Noah."

"Byrd? What did you throw up here?"

"My keys. If you happen to see them, can you toss them back down?"

Asher stared incredulously at me, then up at the spiderweb of cracks in his window. At least his broad shoulders were slightly less intimidating because of his loose black undershirt, and the top half of his dark hair tied at the peak of his head was more like a frizzy badminton birdie. He must've been getting ready for bed before I barged onto his premises. "You do realize that damaging private property *isn't* a turn-on?"

"I know. Sorry. Did your mom hear that?"

"My mom isn't home. Care to tell me what you're doing here?"

"Right. Yeah." I scrambled to pick up the poster board sticking out of my backpack, then held out the first one that read *HI, ASHER* his way.

Asher just rubbed his eyes and stretched.

I cleared my throat and flipped to the next board.

HOW IS YOUR NIGHT GOING?

"Just talk," Asher called. "I can hear you fine. You cracked my window, not my head, remember?"

"But I made this whole— Please. Bear with me."

I could practically hear Asher's eyes roll. I showed the next poster board.

I THINK YOU'RE CUTE

Asher didn't react. Didn't even flinch.

I kept going, dying inside.

AND IF WE WEREN'T SEPARATED
BY YOUR WINDOW

I'D ASK FOR YOU TO FEEL MY JACKET

BECAUSE IT'S MADE OUT OF

REALLY NICE BOYFRIEND MATERIAL

Still nothing. Asher's face remained flat.

The silence between us clung to my body like dripping sweat, and the awkward tension in the air became too painful to endure. I wished I had prepared some sort of music to fill the background. I would even have taken "The Borrow a Boyfriend Club Theme Song" over this.

Actually. That worked. I started humming.

Asher made an odd face. "Are you humming our theme song right now?"

"Mhm." I kept on.

HOW ABOUT WE GO TO THE
ANN ARBOR WINTER FESTIVAL

TOGETHER THIS WEEKEND

SO YOU CAN FEEL IT

THERE?

I set the poster boards on the brick sidewalk as I wrapped up the chorus.

Asher studied me. The outdoor lights shone upon his face, casting a warm, regal glow around him.

Undoubtedly, I'd failed again.

But then Asher laughed. He laughed so hard that he had to

grip the side of his window frame to stay upright. It was a high and twinkly sound, one that hardly matched his usual deeper voice. How could someone so icy have such a warm laugh?

Once I recovered my senses, I took a few wild glances around the courtyard, preparing myself for some massive beast dog to maul me.

"Let me get this straight." Asher continued laughing. "You found out where I lived. You snuck into my gated home at night. You broke my window. And now you're asking me to the winter festival?"

This grand gesture wasn't supposed to be illegal or damaging, but Asher Price wouldn't care about my intentions. All that mattered was execution. Asher Price was perfect, and selective, and probably expected the same from everyone who surrounded him. Although he made me want to rip my hair out on the daily, I wanted to be someone like him too.

Channeling all the confidence I had left inside of me, I straightened and stood my ground. "You bet I did."

Asher stayed silent. My dread shot up to the moon.

"Then, sure," he finally said.

"Sure, what?"

"I'll go on this date with you. Meet me at the winter festival this Saturday. Noon. Be on time." With that, Asher smirked before closing the curtains in front of his freshly cracked window.

CHAPTER 11

When I showed up to the festival after an early morning shift at Bitterlake Coffee, the crowds were thick and the sky was gray. The downtown roads had been obstructed with road signs for a span of six blocks, which Dad loved to complain about this time of year. Now the sidewalks were full of sketchily built amusement rides and carts selling high-calorie snacks.

Three kids shrieked and giggled as they sprinted past me, their bulky coats and boots clunking as they chased each other. One kid slammed into a towering Christmas tree beside the entrance, which was still lit up despite it being January, and knocked down several ornaments.

Asher stood leaning against a road blockade nearby, his hands stuffed in his peacoat. Crumpled hot-chocolate paper cups surrounded his Prada sneakers as if he were the sacrifice of a séance, and wireless earbuds jutted out of his dark hair.

He looked good.

I shook my head to clear the thought. This wasn't a real

date. I had to remain focused. This was a test. The only thing that mattered was succeeding.

I checked my phone. One minute until noon. I was right on time, but at a cost. I'd sprinted out of work with my hands sticky with syrup and shoes splattered with an oat milk latte gone wrong.

A follow notification suddenly popped up on-screen. Someone named Jennifer Chang. I'd heard her name often in class.

A message showed up next.

> hey noah!! i heard you made it to second rounds and just wanted to wish you good luck! i think you'd make a great boyfriend ☺

A burst of courage surged through me. This must've been because of the morning announcements from last week. People were already associating me with the club, even when I wasn't a member yet.

Someone tugged on my puffer-jacket sleeve. I jolted, glancing up from my phone.

Asher stood beside me. "You lied."

What happened to hello? How are you? "Huh? When did I lie?"

"Your poster-board nonsense claimed your jacket was made of boyfriend material. If that were true, then you would've been on time."

I readjusted my sleeves. I hadn't seen Asher much since assaulting his bedroom window over a week ago. Just when passing him by in the halls. He'd always been swarmed by people, so he could never glance my way. Now he was waiting for me and only me, and that had a grin tugging at my lips.

"I was one minute early," I corrected him with confidence.

Asher crossed his arms. "Rule number three of the Borrow a Boyfriend's *How to Be a Good Boyfriend Training Handbook*: Early is on time. On time is late. Late is inexcusable."

"But I was *still*—wait, rule number three? I thought that was that I had to entertain a borrower." Speaking those words aloud made my face flare with heat, but I had a point to prove.

"That's the name of the third *round*. Of our acceptance process." His expression was laced with judgment. "Did you even read the handbook I lent you?"

My heartbeat quickened. "Well, a bit. But—" Not long before I deemed the content all garbage.

Asher sighed. "After becoming a member, there are twenty additional *rules* to being the perfect boyfriend, which my brother notated in the training handbook while he was president. All rules must be memorized."

My insides shriveled up. I'd do better memorizing the quadratic formula.

"Anyway, don't get ahead of yourself, Byrd. I doubt the other rules will end up concerning you much," Asher said. He headed off deeper into the festival.

My stomach boiled as I watched him walk away. The shrub to my left had a lump of snow on top, tempting me to make a snowball and chuck it at Asher's head. *Byrd*, this. *Byrd*, that. Could he not even care enough to remember my first name?

If only sports tryouts were happening this semester. If *only*.

I bit my tongue. *Ace the test.*

"Wait!" I chased after him, stepping on several crinkled hot-chocolate paper cups that crunched under my feet, and pulled a white rose out of my miniature travel backpack. Thankfully, the festival was free, so I could invest in a gift. "This is for you."

Asher took the rose. He twisted the stem between two fingers like he was evaluating how many points this gesture earned me. "Not bad."

The dating advice I'd picked up from that one article and Lenny's mom's videos worked. Now all I had to do was remember what Reina said. *Be kind. Have a smile. Show patience.*

But then there was also Lenny's advice. *Be bold.* Lenny had known Asher for years, so his advice held weight, but his mom had millions of views. I still wasn't sure what type of boy I wanted to be for the next few hours. I needed to act in a way that fit Asher's ideal date, and who knew what that was? His lackluster social media presence didn't provide any answers.

Giving Asher a white rose at the start of our date was a bolder move. But it was also a kind one. Two Byrds with one stone.

As Asher and I walked side by side through the crowds, a jazz ensemble from Detroit played on a pop-up stage nearby. The aroma of cinnamon sugar elephant ears and hot chocolate flooded my nose. I glanced over at Asher. At six-foot-one, he was a whole head taller than me, and the added bun on top of his head made him appear even taller. I suddenly wished I'd slipped inserts into my Converse to bump me up an inch or two.

Silence grew more powerful by the second.

My nerves consumed me. Money. We could talk about

money. His family had a lot of it. I tried to show a very kind, very patient smile. "How about that Bitcoin stock market crash?"

"What?"

Never mind. "Nothing." I rubbed my gloved hands together, then readjusted the thick knit hat Mom made me for my sixteenth birthday. January in Michigan was a tropical retreat compared to February and March, but the temperature was still just under freezing. I had no clue how Asher wasn't suffering from hypothermia in that thin wool peacoat.

Loud whispers and shushes came from a kettle-corn food stall beside us. Four girls drenched in fitted parkas and Ugg boots were staring obviously at Asher. The group pushed one toward us, who was armed and ready with her phone to take a photo or get his number, but then she swatted at their arms to stop them.

"Is there a reason why you transferred schools?" Asher suddenly asked me. Either he hadn't noticed the commotion or was so used to fangirls that he didn't care.

His question made my heart sink into my toes. "No."

"Everyone has a motivation behind every choice they make."

Okay, Sherlock. I played with my hat a bit more to buy myself some more time. "My family moved deeper into Ann Arbor. I was out of district."

"Where'd you live before?"

Mayday. SOS. "Around Pinewood Park?"

"That's still in the Ann Arbor district. Camilo lives in the Pinewood neighborhood."

"I was on the dividing line."

From his narrowing gaze, Asher didn't buy my story, but he stopped with the questions. A hot-chocolate stand caught his attention.

Drinks could occupy our mouths instead of conversation.

I drifted over to the stand. A sign on the counter said two for sixteen dollars.

Sixteen?

Rest in peace, name-change funds. I made a mental note to request an additional shift at Bitterlake next week, then begrudgingly grabbed some bills out of my wallet and bought two hot chocolates, which were decked out with snowmen marshmallows and rainbow snowflake sprinkles. I came back holding two cups and offered him one, trying to ignore the hole burned into my wallet.

Asher's eyes softened a bit. "Thanks, Byrd."

My stomach flipped. The only expressions I'd ever seen on Asher were various forms of condescension. But this face was kinder, like he'd genuinely appreciated what I'd done. For a fleeting moment, it gave off the illusion of a real date.

Stop. This *wasn't* a real date.

We turned left onto the Freedom Street Plaza, where a few game tents were set up around the main clock tower. We passed a balloon dart throwing challenge, a ring toss, and a strength-testing station. Stuffed animals hung from awnings by the necks and limbs. Playing games together seemed like date material.

I stopped and pointed toward the tents as an offer to meander that way.

Asher scoffed. "You want to get scammed? Cork is added

to the throwing balls. The darts are twisted in ways that affect the physics—"

"Hey, hey, hey!" a high, upbeat voice called from a booth. An older festival worker wearing jingling reindeer antlers had zoned in on us. Behind her was a table stacked with glass bottles in the shape of a pyramid, which must've been why she was tossing a softball in her gloved hand. "Bet you two can't knock these down."

A flicker of competitiveness flashed over Asher's face. Without a single word, he straightened his back and headed toward her.

I couldn't help the small laugh that escaped me as I followed. Asher's never-ending scornfulness, when directed at others, was, unfortunately, entertaining. Once he paid the reindeer four dollars to play a round and slapped both of our hot chocolates down on the counter, she handed me a softball. Definitely filled with cork.

Before getting into place, I surveyed the stuffed animals dangling from the awning. A good boyfriend would win his date a prize. The biggest and the best.

"Which one do you like?" I asked him. The teddy bear was a classic, but the dolphin was the biggest.

Asher studied our options. Eventually, he landed on one stuffed animal that had his typically hardened gray eyes practically glowing. "The dino."

I followed his gaze toward a green *Tyrannosaurus rex* with an oversized head and tiny noodle arms. "You mean the dinosaur?"

Maybe it was the icy breeze nipping at our bodies, but the

pink tinging his cheeks was much deeper now. "That's what I said."

"You said *dino*."

"Yeah, well. Sure." Asher patted the back of my puffer jacket. "Go get 'em."

Nerves rushed through me at the sudden and first-ever contact between us. Asher wasn't supposed to touch people. He wasn't supposed to *like* people.

Positioning myself as best as I could in front of the milk bottles, I collected my focus. Then I wound back my arm and chucked the ball as hard as I could.

The softball hit the pyramid with a clink. One bottle tipped onto the table.

A burst of adrenaline shot up into my head. The game was rigged with hot glue and lead and only Satan knew what else, and I still got one down. I was strong. An absolute *warrior*.

I beamed at Asher, tossing up a fist. "Did you see that?"

He smirked back. "Congrats."

The reindeer handed me another softball. This, of course, felt even lighter than the last. "One done and nine to go! You have two more very merry tries left."

All right. Two more chances to win this dinosaur for Asher, or else all the boyfriend points I'd gained would plummet. With another windup, I set my aim for the bottles and fired.

The softball zoomed right past the pyramid and slapped the tent wall.

My shoulders deflated.

There went the dino.

"Darn, guess you weren't strong enough!" the reindeer

whined through flat orange lipstick, but she was smiling. She offered me a third and final softball.

Before I could lift a hand, Asher stepped in the way to snatch the ball instead. Within seconds, he was backing himself up to take a running start at the glass-bottle pyramid and whirled the softball through the air with the force of a rocket launcher.

The pyramid exploded.

Glass bottles flew. Clangs and clanks rang through the air. I stumbled back and instinctively lifted a protective hand, then peeked back at the tent with wide eyes. Nothing remained on the table. The reindeer's mouth hung open.

Asher pointed at the hanging stuffed *Tyrannosaurus rex*. "We'll take that one."

The reindeer nodded three times in quick succession, then jingled her way over to the prized stuffed animal.

I blinked up at Asher, whose eyes held a glint of fire I didn't recognize. "How'd you do that?"

He locked his gaze with mine. "I never lose."

We were handed the dinosaur, and that was the end of that.

As the trial date went on, we passed by a scrambler ride whipping people around in dizzying circles, entered a fun house, and evaded a rusty carousel playing unnerving church-organ music. More vendor stalls were selling flashing reindeer headbands and glow-stick necklaces, and all shone as brightly as they would've during the night, thanks to the overcast sky.

In the distance, a cluster of people I recognized caught my eye. They were mid-laughter as they placed headbands on each other's heads over by the carousel.

Everly Walsh. Rosen Mallet. Jas Ohja.

The people I sat with during every lunch since middle school. Who I matched all my classes with at Pinewood High, and did every musical with in the spring and fall.

Who I ditched once the *little mistakes* ate away my trust in everyone, so much so that I never even gave them a chance to see if they'd do the same.

"Um—" I blurted. "Could we turn around? I want to—" I scanned the road in a panic, then the stage farther down. "Pick up a flyer! For that jazz band! Over there."

Asher made a circular motion with his pointer finger, the stuffed dinosaur tucked underneath his other arm. "We'll pass it again on the way out. The festival goes around in a square. You know, like blocks?"

Have a smile. Be kind. Show patience. "Right. Yeah. I just don't want to forget—"

Everly looked my way.

My heart pounded so hard I thought it would punch through my skin and plop right onto the sidewalk. Lowering my head, I grabbed Asher's peacoat sleeve and dragged him in front of me as a shield, only to instantly regret it. Bold boyfriends didn't act like terrified dogs in a snowstorm. But my old friends couldn't spot me. They couldn't ruin this test.

They couldn't *out me.*

Asher subtly glanced over his shoulder to catch a peek at the three. "You know them?"

I gripped his sleeve harder. "Can we go somewhere else for a second? Please?"

Asher didn't ask why I was panicking or where we should

go. He simply took my gloved hand into his bare one and led me behind the carousel, which was surrounded by a tall iron fence. He shook off his wool peacoat and spread it on the snowy pavement before we sat down.

Laughing kids riding fiberglass animals punctured through the church-organ music swirling around our heads. There were dumpsters a few feet away. Each one smelled slightly like sugary snacks but mostly god-awful.

Asher let his hot chocolate hover near his lips, holding the sides with both hands, his dino leaning against his thigh. He was only wearing two layers: a navy sweatshirt with some thin, white undershirt, and blue jeans. His shoulders twitched like he was staving off a shiver.

"Aren't you cold?" I finally asked.

"No."

"You are."

"Not."

Screw patience. Screw being kind. Screw being the nice boyfriend who smiles and hands out white roses. I slapped my empty *eight-dollar* lukewarm hot chocolate cup on the ground, pulled my knit hat off, revealing my full face, and shoved it on top of Asher's head.

Asher let out a choked sound. "Hey, no, I don't need this."

"You do." I considered reaching into my coat to put on my sweatshirt hood, but there was no one around to see us.

He reached for the thick brim of the hat to take it off.

I swatted his hand away and readjusted my pretzel position to face him. "What is *wrong* with you? It's below freezing outside. All you have on is a sweatshirt thinner than paper.

Where are your gloves? Your scarf and your hat? If I left the house wearing only a coat in January, my parents would punt me into the sun."

Asher looked too stunned to form words. I swore his face was turning too rosy to just be from the crisp winter air. Had I embarrassed him somehow?

"Well." His voice was softer now. "My parents aren't around much."

I paused. "What? Where are they?"

"I told you how my dad's in Florence, doing whatever single, middle-aged architects do. Has been since he divorced my mom back when I was in middle school. According to my mom's work calendar, she's in Thailand at a marketing conference. Then she's off to South Korea for two days, then Japan for another four. Can't remember the rest. But I do remember she won't be back for three more weeks. That a good enough answer for you?"

I paused.

"Is she always gone that long?"

"More or less." Asher leaned back and stretched out his long legs. "Not that I'm complaining. I get to do whatever I want whenever I want. Sucks that your parents sound like people who wouldn't let you stay out all night. Otherwise, we could make this date last a little longer." He winked.

I rolled my eyes. "I'm sure your mom would be thrilled about all the girlfriends you've brought over to your house while she's gone."

"Rule number one: members must stay single."

"But you're the club president. And one of the most popular guys in school. You've honestly never broken that rule?"

"No."

"You're not even a little tempted to? I bet ninety percent of the girls at school are in the Asher Price fan club."

He sniffed. "I have fanboys too, you know."

"Sure," I said through a weak laugh that wisped in the air, "but we're talking about people you'd be tempted to date."

"I know." Asher smirked at me. For a long time.

My heart rate rose.

Asher was also interested in fanboys. Boys who were fans. Boys.

Was this a real date?

No. Asher was the same self-absorbed president of a boyfriend-borrowing club. He still radiated fuckboy vibes, and who he was attracted to didn't change that.

"People can't find out about what I told you," Asher went on when I stayed silent. "About my mom always being gone. Everyone would probably take advantage of that and show up unannounced, ready to party or whatever. Or, hell, try to rob us. You saw how easy my place is to sneak into. So now that I've told you way too much about me, it's your turn to tell me why we're hiding behind dumpsters."

If I told the truth about why I transferred schools, Asher could tell the whole school. The *little mistakes* might come back. The *accidental slipups*.

"C'mon. You keep my secret, and I'll keep yours," Asher said. His stare was calm, patient, like he'd actually wait as long as it took for me to answer. Like he cared.

I inhaled. Exhaled.

"Those people go to Pinewood High," I finally said. "They know who I used to be before I switched to Heron. Before I changed my first name. Before I started hormones. Before I got surgery last summer."

The music from the carousel ride came to a stop, leaving behind distant chatters and hollers from the main road.

"Gotcha." Asher rose to his feet and offered a hand. "How about I walk you home?"

My heart dropped. That was it, then.

I'd failed the test.

CHAPTER 12

As Asher walked me home, I tried my hardest not to drop to my knees and beg for another chance. Since I lived in one of the many century-old townhouses bordering downtown that had been converted into cramped apartment complexes, the trip took a short ten minutes.

At first, I assumed I failed because of what I'd revealed, but I'd also acted the exact opposite of a bold boyfriend and ran away from my former friends. Regardless, there was no way Asher viewed me as boyfriend material, and I wanted to be mad.

But I wasn't. Not even a little.

I was too scared about what would happen next.

Once my bright-blue apartment complex came into view, my brain searched for any last-minute ideas that could save our sinking pretend date from falling further into the depths of ultimate catastrophe. I implemented nearly all the advice I'd picked up from the internet, and now I had nothing left in my arsenal. I'd written Asher a love letter. I'd given him a white rose.

We reached the bottom of my driveway. No sphere topiary or fountains to be seen. Just a cracked sidewalk leading toward my porch with a wooden swing.

"This is me," I muttered.

Asher pulled my knit hat off his own head. His top bun was deflated and sad now—did he ever wear his hair down? Maybe he was always grumpy because these buns gave him headaches? His lips were chapped from being out in the cold with me for so long. He offered the hat back, his damp peacoat dangling over the rest of his arm. "Thanks."

I shook my head, gently pushing it toward his chest. "You should keep this."

Now was the time for him to tell me I didn't make the cut. That I'd failed like the other seventy prospective applicants. That securing my label as a top boy at Heron River High School was officially out of reach.

No. This *couldn't* be over.

Asher's mouth opened. "As far as the date—"

Adrenaline surged through me. I mentally riffled through the paragraphs of the article I'd read.

There was one last option I hadn't tried yet. Something I'd never done.

Something I never thought would first be with Asher Price.

I let my instincts take over as my left hand snatched his peacoat cuff. The other grabbed his shoulder. I tugged him down to my height and aimed his lips for mine.

Asher let out a half cry, half bleating sheep noise. He shoved a hand against my chest. "You don't need to do that!"

The air between us deadened. Mortification rang through every fiber of my being.

I had no brain cells. Not a *single* one.

Asher's mouth moved like a gasping fish as a car passed by us on the street. We stood so close that I could smell chocolate and cinnamon on his breath.

The move was too sudden. Too reckless. Too desperate. Of course he was uncomfortable.

I squeezed my eyes shut. Could this nightmare end already? "I'm so sorry. I thought maybe this would score me some points before you told me I'd failed. I should've asked—"

Asher coughed. "I was going to say that you passed."

I peeked an eye open.

And there was his usual smirk again. But it looked a little different than all the other times. The edges softened, like some iciness had melted off. "That kiss was about to have a lot of passion, Byrd. Have you already fallen for me?"

I stuttered over my words, unable to form a coherent sentence.

A twinkly laugh wisped from his lips as he started down the sidewalk. "Come to our meeting tomorrow. Theater basement. Two o'clock."

"Wait, really?"

"Don't be late."

"But isn't there one more round for me to pass?"

"We'll discuss things then."

My chest burst with so much exhilaration that I felt like I'd blow up into a million meat chunks and become one with the snowflakes drifting from the clouds.

I'd passed.

I'd *passed* the second round.

"Does this mean I don't have to pay for your broken window anymore?" I shouted.

"Don't be late," he repeated.

"Okay! I'll be on time! And not, like, *on time* on time. Early! Super-duper early!"

Asher tossed a lazy wave goodbye before disappearing around the corner.

CHAPTER 13

The jumping-up-and-down exhilaration I'd felt after passing the second round of this ridiculous membership process didn't last long.

Asher claimed we'd go over my third and final round at the meeting. But this could've been some sick prank. For all I knew, I'd misheard Asher after nearly kissing him, and he'd actually told me to *never* show up to the Borrow a Boyfriend Club after the last bell rang.

The training handbook claimed the final test was to "Entertain a Borrower." From the title, I assumed I'd become a magician for a full audience of borrowers, spinning plates and pulling bunnies out of hats. Still, that all seemed much less challenging than romancing the club president, so I could do this. Maybe?

"What do you mean, not enough funding? You spent fifteen thousand dollars on a statue of Henry Ford for the main entrance two months ago."

I stopped in my tracks. The main office door was cracked open.

Through the tinted window, I could vaguely make out Asher's broad figure in front of the counter, gesticulating wildly. Two other figures stood behind Sonny's desk. One of them must've responded to Asher in a way that thoroughly pissed him off because he slammed his palm on the counter.

"Want me to keep lighting up the entrance myself? I got more Christmas lights in my garage. I'll happily get this story on the news, and that'll cost you more than a few sidewalk lights."

More murmuring came from the counter.

Then Asher stormed out of the main office.

My heart rate spiked as I rushed away. Asher was clearly giving more *FUCK THIS SCHOOL* energy in there, and I wanted no part in that.

Once I was a safe enough distance across the cafeteria, I peeked over my shoulder. Asher still stood by the office, now distracted by classmates who'd swarmed him with what appeared to be deformed homemade chocolates from some cooking class. Bless you, Asher Price fan club.

I continued toward the theater without looking back.

Two steps into the basement, my wrists were snatched.

A flurry of hands twirled my body like I was about to smack a piñata. A set of fingers covered my eyes, and I yelped as I was dragged and shoved into what felt like a metal chair.

The pressure against my eyes finally lifted.

Everything was still dark.

There was a snap, and then light shined right into my eyes.

Lenny's mop of pastel-blue hair was the first thing I saw

when my focus returned. He hovered over me, gripping the light bulb pull chain above us. Behind him was a concrete wall with a shelf packed with cardboard boxes. Asher's office, or the *Do Not Enter* side room.

To my left, Camilo guarded the door. Between his tightly crossed arms and the pen scribbles on his skin giving off the illusion of tattoos, he was like a bouncer. His "day at the golf course" outfit toned down the implied threat, though.

"What did you do?" Lenny's voice broke into a low baritone instead of his usual tenor.

I felt the impulse to ask for a lawyer first. "Why did you pull me in here? You could have just asked—"

Lenny reached for my face and smushed my cheeks together. "Answer the question!"

"*Whut?! Whut dih I duh aboot wut?*"

"You know what, bro," Camilo said. He sounded exponentially calmer than Lenny. "Asher updated our prospective applicant list in our database last night and inputted that you passed the second round. No one's ever gotten this far."

I peered at him. "What do you mean? What about you all?"

"*Asher's* never let anyone pass. We've all been here since Sebastian graduated last year. No one else has been accepted since."

Lenny snapped my face back toward himself. "Tell us how you did it."

I slapped his fingers off my cheeks. He cried out and gripped his left hand.

"What do you mean, how did I do it?" I asked. "You were literally the one who gave me advice. You told me that if anyone could pull this off, it was me!"

"Yes. But. You did it so fast! Like it was no big deal!"

"Asher gave me a *one*-week deadline—"

He put his fingers to my temples. "Did you use mind control? You did something ginormous, didn't you?"

Nothing *ginormous* came to mind. Attempting to kiss him right on the mouth was probably pretty ginormous, but Asher claimed he was already planning to let me pass the second round before that. Aside from that, all I did was act like a wimp by hiding from my past and reprimanded him for not wearing enough warm layers.

Three knocks came from outside. Lenny's eyes widened.

Camilo answered the door. Asher Price stood in the doorway wearing a sweatshirt with a fancy vine logo embroidered on the chest.

The sight of him made my stomach flip. The scene of me nearly kissing him played on a loop in my mind, and I couldn't find the freaking "I need a minute to process" pause button.

Asher narrowed his eyes. "What's going on in here?"

"Nothing!" Lenny practically shouted. "Just chillin'!"

"We have a lot to discuss about Byrd. It's two o'clock. All of you are late."

I frowned. Was the extra syllable in "Noah" *that* hard to say?

"But we're in the basement," Lenny whined.

"Meetings start around the *billiards table*. You're late. Three tardies, and you're out."

Lenny sighed as if he's heard this many times. We followed Asher to where most of the other club members sat with their laptops open. Everett the Psychic Type, however, was finishing paying his respects to the Sebastian Price altar in the corner. He dug into his backpack and relinquished a brand-new bottle of ginger kombucha as an offering. A hippie's ultimate sacrifice.

A few heads popped up to watch my trip across the room, interrupting their discussion about a soccer banquet they were attending with borrowers that week. Isabella was too busy scolding Aiden—again—about *rule number five: members must always look good* to notice my presence, tossing a pair of jeans at his mesh basketball shorts and fluffing his shorter black hair.

Constance sat nearby, typing on a laptop I assumed was full of reported tip calculations and club income reports or reimbursement requests. Camilo gave her a poke on the forehead as he shuffled by, then claimed the last vacant love seat.

Instead of taking the other side for himself, Lenny offered the spot to me. I muttered a quiet thanks and sat down while he claimed the fuzzy carpet in front of my legs.

As I set down my backpack, my sweatshirt hood slipped off my head. I reached back to lift it back up, then hesitated.

It was only Asher. And Lenny and Camilo and the others.

I kept the hood down, but I still readjusted my sweatshirt a few times to make sure the fabric wasn't sticking anywhere I didn't want it to.

"We'll now start today's meeting," Asher declared.

In the distance, a door shut.

Rustling came from the costume racks soon after. Everyone fell silent as we peered at one another. I mentally counted heads. Ten, including me. We were all here.

"Oop, oh goodness."

A higher voice. Whoever this was, it didn't sound like a student.

"Factions, go," Lenny hissed.

All of the boys popped up from their seats, assembled into groups of three, and split up.

Group one—Aiden, Everett, and Musical Type—went into the interrogation room and came out seconds later with hands full of green-and-white pillows. Aiden and Musical Type chucked them at the red couches. Meanwhile, Everett pointed a remote at a wall covered in hearts playing cards. A projection screen fell from the ceiling. Another click, and a black-and-white movie with Italian subtitles silently played.

Group two—Gaming Type, Artsy Type, and Lenny—rummaged through a mini fridge to pull out unboxed lasagna, prepackaged tiramisu, and San Pellegrino sparkling water. They set everything on the table.

Group three—Constance, Isabella, and Camilo—stormed to the back, where the Borrow a Boyfriend Club logo was displayed proudly on the red flag hanging on the wall. They ripped the flag down to reveal an alternate version that was striped red, white, and green. The two *B*s facing opposite ways inside the heart had been replaced by the acronym FALAC.

I stared at the new flag. "Uh."

Artsy Type stopped beside me. "What's up?"

"Which syllable do you put the emphasis on?" I asked.

He flicked his gaze at the flag, me, the flag again. "It's the Football and Lamborghini After-School Club's initials."

"Right . . . Never mind," I muttered.

Like a coordinated dance troupe, they all finished the room transformation and twisted and tumbled back to their seats.

Asher headed toward the jukebox. With one click, the theme song changed from synthesizers and electronic drums to mandolin, violin, and harpsichord. I guessed this was "The Borrow a Boyfriend Club Theme Song: Italian Version."

After that, he headed toward the costume racks right as a teacher emerged. She had a rich brown complexion, was model height, and had a *I HATE ADULTING* pin stuck on her cross-body bag. She looked to be in her thirties. Asher's sudden presence startled her, forcing out another "Oop!"

"Well, hello, Mr. Price!"

To my absolute horror, Asher smiled at an adult. "Benvenuta, Ms. Vora."

Ms. Vora. I vaguely recalled Lenny mentioning her as the club's official sponsor last month. This was who they hid their true activities from.

How?

As Ms. Vora faced those of us drowning in the green and white pillows on the couches, her hip knocked against another rack. She tripped forward in her studded cowboy boots, accidentally stepping over her long tie-dye skirt in the process. Other than using Asher's shoulder for balance, she didn't acknowledge the stumble. "How are things going for my favorite football and Lamborghini–loving club?"

Camilo nudged Lenny's shoulder. "Buono. Vero, Lenny?"

Lenny's face flipped to panic, like every word in the Italian dictionary had jumped out of his brain. "Lasagna?"

Ms. Vora gave Lenny a quizzical look before becoming

distracted by the jukebox playing the theme song. She shimmied. "Love this little bop of yours! So sorry I haven't been stopping by as much this year. I'm teaching nearly every art class because of the budget cuts, you know, and my AP Art kiddos are scrambling to finish portfolios. They're obsessed with *making the right choices* in the eyes of the establishment, but there are no right or wrong decisions in art." She stared off like she was daydreaming.

So, they picked the whimsical, overworked art teacher as the sponsor. Clever.

Asher offered a seemingly genuine nod. "We're always thankful for your sponsorship when we aren't technically affiliated with art."

"You too are! You know old Italian sculptures are my bread and butter. And the cuisine? Cooking is its own art form." Ms. Vora kissed her fingertips.

Asher followed suit by kissing his own. I held in a laugh.

"It's a shame we don't offer Italian language classes," Ms. Vora went on, messing with her paisley ascot. "With the influence of all your cute faces, we'd have the whole student body scrambling to sign up. What if I talk to the principal—?"

"*No*," Camilo interrupted. Lenny stomped on his foot.

"What he means is"—Asher's voice was silky and smooth as he spoke—"we wouldn't want to burden the school's small foreign-language budget when Isabella and I are fluent. Thankfully, we're able to teach our members well."

Everyone nodded a little too vigorously.

Ms. Vora smiled at them, then at the black-and-white movie projected on the wall as she retreated toward the stairs. "Well, then. Enjoy your cinematography."

A few members offered a cheery *grazie* in unison.

Once the clacking sound of Ms. Vora's cowboy boots faded into the distance, the reassembled groups put the room back in order, concealing FALAC's existence.

I stayed in my seat, useless and too floored to move. They had acted as if this song and dance was normal. As easy as uno plus uno. I wasn't sure what must've been harder for them to pull off: the group executing this cover-up so often, or Asher forcing such a massively fake smile. Even if this club was ridiculous, I couldn't help but admire their dedication to keeping it secret.

Asher returned to his whiteboard, the politeness he'd shown Ms. Vora long gone. "Back to business."

Most members were typing on their laptops instead of devoting their attention to Asher. They were likely messaging each other. Maybe about Ms. Vora, but some not-so-subtle glances flew my way, too.

My shoulders sunk deeper into my frame as Asher passed everyone a sheet of paper. A flyer packed with tacky clip art and poor font choices to advertise Heron River High's annual Valentine's Day formal happening in two weeks.

Asher walked to a rolling whiteboard beside the billiards table. He erased some old game scores. "The cutoff for all six hundred students here to submit a borrower request form for the Valentine's Day formal ends this week. According to Camilo, the number of request forms we've received so far is reaching the forties."

"Forty?" I repeated. "There are only eight of you. Is it first come, first serve? That's so many requests."

Gaming Type sneered at the video game on his phone.

The strictness seeping off Asher shockingly hadn't deterred him from muting the slashing and grunting sound effects. He shoved his outdated hipster glasses up into his orange curls as he made pointed eye contact with everyone. "Back when Sebastian was pres, we were forced to cap off the form at a hundred."

Artsy Type snorted beside him.

Asher peered at the two seniors calmly. A little too calmly. "Well, my brother isn't here, Liam. Is that a problem?"

Liam, aka Gaming Type, sunk back in his seat with a huff, so Asher scanned the rest of the room for an answer.

Awkward sniffs and throat clears were the response.

"Forty requests are much better than zero," Lenny announced, serving the left-out prepackaged tiramisu onto paper plates and passing around slices. Probably to break the tension. "Especially when we had to spend so much of the fall focusing on damage control, yeah? Cutting our base rate brought some borrowers back!"

"True," said Aiden, who sat to my left and was tossing a football in his hand.

This wasn't the first time I'd heard of alleged damage control. From what I remembered, that's why they weren't charging borrowers what they used to.

What happened?

I raised my hand just as I was handed a plate of tiramisu. If my dance skills were going to pull them out of this financial pit, I deserved answers. "What made you cut that thirty-dollar rate, anyway?"

"Twenty-nine ninety-nine," Asher corrected.

"I know. I rounded."

"Don't. Thirty sounds more expensive. Twenty-nine ninety-nine was chosen for a reason."

What if I just slapped him? What was the worst that could happen?

"Right," I said, barely holding myself back. "I get that you did this to entice borrowers to come back, but why did they stop coming in the first place?"

Most looks drifted toward the president in the room. Especially Liam, who glared.

"There was an incident," Asher answered sharply. "Any more questions?"

Finally, I understood. The members blamed Asher.

Had he pissed off borrowers somehow? The whole school? The existence of an Asher Price fan club pointed toward other theories, though.

I sunk back in my seat, taking a bite of tiramisu. Despite their finances being quietly controversial, I was thankful, knowing that's why they desperately needed my help. Besides, I couldn't care less about any matter concerning Asher. Otherwise, that would mean I cared. And I didn't.

So.

"Any . . . way," Lenny sang, doing a rewind gesture with a plastic fork. "The formal! Camilo wrote a computer program that helps decide who needs our services the most. Searches for keywords in requests and stuff. Filtering through forty applications shouldn't take long."

I turned toward Camilo, who was spread lazily across a couch. A bottle of orange pop dangled from his inked hand. "Your program?"

"If a request radiates too many out-of-control stan vibes or rants about how much they want to take a hot boy to a dance, my program tosses it," Camilo droned. "If there's a solid reason they want one of us, my program gives it more consideration."

I was too stuck on Camilo being a supergenius coder to move forward. "*Your* program?"

"You already forgot I'm the club's Smart Type?"

"No—just—" I hadn't actually believed it, with how much he screwed around.

"Camilo's skills really are remarkable," Lenny attempted to say through a mouthful of tiramisu. "Some people who only need tutoring end up borrowing him too, since he's not one to volunteer. And then they end up developing a big ol' crush on him."

"Sebastian asked him to create our database as well," Asher added. "It's how we keep track of everyone's borrower assignments. All scheduling and communication between borrowers and boyfriends go through there so no one's info ever gets doxxed."

"That's," I hesitated, "intense."

"We need boundaries," Camilo mumbled. "Believe me."

The club's strongest marketing asset *was* being a group of single attractive guys no one in school could truly have, and that kept customers coming back for more. A system like this could easily spiral out of control.

"Won't everyone know that their date to the formal isn't real, though?" I asked. "That they're just borrowing a club member?"

A unanimous *So?* attacked me from all angles.

Of course, that was irrelevant. Everyone knew they were offering the *idea* of a perfect partner.

Lenny raised his hand. "Are we assigning boys to borrowers for the dance now, Ash?"

Asher took off his Prada sneaker and threw it at Lenny's head.

Lenny ducked just in time, and the sneaker sole slapped against my shin instead. "Asher."

"Not yet," he said. "But we will. Once we add Byrd to our request forms."

The room was silent, only the hum of the fluorescent lights to be heard.

Until Camilo dropped his pop bottle out of shock. The last droplets leaked across the carpet. "You're *sure* he's ready to take a borrower to the dance?"

Asher, still half shoeless, wrote VALENTINE'S DAY FORMAL on the whiteboard. "As you're all aware, I agreed to let Byrd pass the first round, given that he promised to help us win the club talent show in March. This weekend, he also passed our second round by successfully romancing me."

"Whoa, wind that back," Aiden said beside me. "For real?"

"Now Byrd's moved on to the third and final round: Entertain a Borrower," Asher continued, ignoring Aiden completely. "The Valentine's Day formal two weeks from now is an opportunity to see him in action with real borrowers. We'll all be there to monitor his performance."

A heavy wave of dread cast over me. This time I wouldn't only have to entertain my date: all the other club members would be watching too.

But I had to do this. I was so close to being a top guy at this school, to no longer feeling the constant need to turn invisible.

Liam finally paused his video game to laugh at him. "You okay, Asher?"

"Ah, yes, his mind is sound," Everett said, eyes closed.

"Do we have any proof that this guy can dance?" Aiden asked.

I sank even lower in my seat. The distrust in the room was obvious, but who was it fully directed at? The seniors were irritated by Asher, but some were clearly also irritated by me. Maybe because they had already picked up on the truth: I had no clue if I could win them the talent show.

I had to fix that.

"Well, what have you been doing at school dances until now?" I asked everyone.

Most didn't move a muscle. Aiden did a shimmy. Everett bopped his head.

"Okay, stop, stop," I said, gripping my forehead.

These guys knew nothing. In the rom-coms I'd watched, most couples danced together at the end. In the rain. In the airport. Anywhere they could. And the guy always knew basic footwork at least. Even if I had no clue now what this winning choreographed routine would be, these guys needed to learn the basics first.

Time for a lesson! Then they'd see I knew my stuff.

"This formal would be a good opportunity to teach everyone a few moves," I said, tossing my plastic fork around as the excitement inside grew. "Like for fancier slow dances. More like a waltz. Which would also impress borrowers."

Liam snorted. "You think a waltz, something our great-grandparents did, will impress Anita Kömraag?"

My arms deflated on the spot. "Well, we won't be slow dancing at the show, but—"

"*Stop.*" Asher's voice was so loud that everyone jumped. He shot Liam a threatening look before facing me again. "That's a good plan, Byrd."

A flicker of pride lit from within me. "Thanks."

"It's not." Liam leaped out of his seat and pointed a black-painted nail at Asher. "This whole talent show plan's a joke. I signed up to help people with their co-ops and streams and to make some extra cash flirting. Not to look like a complete loser in front of the whole school."

Lenny rose to his feet. "Hold on, Liam—"

Liam ignored Lenny, then stared Asher dead-on. "I should've known this club would implode the second Sebastian handed it down to you. He should've let me take over like I suggested."

"Whoa," said a few in unison.

Liam's voice only grew louder. "This whole year, we've been scrambling to keep up our finances and customers to cover our *president's* mistakes. And he barely goes on dates himself! You think I would've screwed us over this bad?" He scoffed. "You know what? Doesn't matter. I quit."

With that, Liam exited stage right.

Everyone peered at Asher, who stood still as a statue.

"You okay, Ash?" Lenny eventually asked through a wince.

Asher nodded, studying the whiteboard. "I'm fine."

His voice was flat and composed as if he really were. But after having had the need to monitor his impression of me for so long, I'd picked up on many of Asher's tells. For one, his jaw was too clenched, and the usual sharpness to his gray eyes was glazed.

He wasn't fine.

"Isabella, add his name to our watch list. Camilo, remove him as a boyfriend option," Asher said.

Isabella pushed up her glasses, cleared her throat, and wrote in her notebook. Camilo hit a few laptop keys.

I must've looked lost because Aiden leaned closer to my ear. "Most people would never try to expose us to teachers out of fear, you know? Too many of our clients would rip them to shreds if they couldn't borrow us anymore. But we keep tabs on a few outliers who may need a . . . stricter talking-to about the consequences of snitching."

I nodded slowly. I'd known of their financial crisis since day one, but they really were on the verge of falling apart for more reasons than I realized.

How their president remained so calm within the storm, I had no clue.

"We'll all meet two hours before the Valentine's Day formal for our first dance practice," Asher announced. "As for today, Byrd, Lenny, Camilo, and I will stay after to add Byrd to our online form so people can start requesting him. We'll also assign him a Type."

I couldn't believe Asher was standing up for me in front of everyone. Maybe I had misjudged him. "Thank you so much. I mean, for giving me the opportunity to pass the final round."

"This isn't for you." Asher slapped *VALENTINE'S DAY FOR-MAL* written on the whiteboard. "This is first and foremost to keep up club likability and grow clientele. Forty people have submitted request forms. Most of them will be upset to hear they won't be borrowing one of us for the formal, and now we're down a member. A replacement on our request form equals another happy customer. The chance for you to pass your final round is a bonus."

Definitely hadn't misjudged him.

I shifted nervously. "Question. If I don't pass the final round, then what?"

Asher started writing on the whiteboard again.

NO RETAKES.

CHAPTER 14

Camilo needed another orange pop to stay awake, Lenny needed another Snickers bar to lift his blood sugar, and Asher needed a black coffee to "keep putting up with the three of you." We headed into the cafeteria for our various snacks and to brainstorm my *Type*.

Once we settled at a high-top table, which was as chrome and expensive-looking as the rest of the school architecture, Lenny asked Camilo to pull out his laptop. After a few clicks in his browser, a website loaded with their fake logo at the center: the Football and Lamborghini After-School Club's initials in the shape of a heart. Low-resolution animations of Italian flags shook along the sides.

Hello, 2010.

"Nice effects?" I offered.

"Didn't Camilo do a great job at making our site as ugly as possible?" Lenny said across the table. "Teachers assume it's old and no longer updated, so they don't check it."

Camilo scrolled to the bottom of the home page and clicked a small *Terms of Use* hyperlink. Instead of endless paragraphs of boring fine print, a simple pop-up appeared.

ENTER YOUR STUDENT EMAIL
ADDRESS AND PASSWORD

Camilo started typing his *ctorres@heronrivermi.edu* email followed by a password. "This is how we lock out teachers. No one reads a Terms of Use even when they're forced, so no one would ever willingly read one at the bottom of our site. And just in case we have an overzealous faculty member, you have to use a student email to create an account with us. We even have an emergency email that'll pull up a real Terms of Use page instead, in case a teacher forces us to log in and show them." A new page loaded on the screen.

I leaned over Camilo's shoulder to read.

The Borrow a Boyfriend Club Request Form
We serve love!

1. When will you need our services? Please write day/month/year. [Note: requests must be submitted fourteen days in advance to avoid scheduling conflicts.]
2. In less than 250 words, what is the reason for your request?
3. Please select at least two members who you believe would partner with you best. [Note: For school-sanctioned events, any member would suffice.]

- **ASHER PRICE:** Popular Type, Junior
  - Overall use (limited availability)

- **LENNY KAWAI:** Influencer Type, Junior
  - Scene partner, photographer and videographer, brand builder

- **EVERETT MINER:** Psychic Type, Junior
  - Spiritual guide (via tarot and astrology readings)
  - Does not connect with animal spirits

- **AIDEN NGO:** Sporty Type, Junior
  - Accountability coach, game-day support or parental distraction, fitness trainer

- **PASCHA COOMBS:** Musical Type, Sophomore
  - Musician, guitar and piano instructor, songwriting collaborator

- **MAX BOOKER:** Artsy Type, Senior
  - Portrait painter, art model, gallery enthusiast, illustrator (no furries or mechs)

- **CAMILO TORRES:** Smart Type, Sophomore
  - Tutor (anything but Italian)
  - Dessert sampler

4. Please provide your contact information. Data will be kept private.

First Name:

Last Name:

Grade:

Pronouns:

Phone Number:

Hobbies:

5. Would you like to be contacted via email or phone number?
6. Would you like to be contacted anonymously via our safety template? (Ex: Hi, [Borrower Name]. It's [Borrowed Member]! Do you want to start our class project on [date] at [time]?)

Please provide any additional information you wish for us to know.

Thank you so much for choosing us! As a favor, we ask that when discussing publicly, kindly refer to us as the Football and Lamborghini Club to avoid being shut down by administration. You wouldn't want to be the sole reason the whole school loses our services, after all!

A cool draft blew through the cafeteria. Maybe that was the borderline threatening aura radiating from that final line alone. Or maybe because *Liam: Gaming Type* had already been wiped. Either way, I shuddered.

"Wow," was all I could think to say. Despite the dramatic undertones, I was impressed once again at how they'd transformed an after-school club into a legit business.

Asher slapped down a portable whiteboard the size of a textbook. His green dry-erase marker squeaked obnoxiously as he wrote every member's name and Type. He flipped the whiteboard my way, meeting my gaze across the table. "Got any ideas for your Type?"

A group by the vending machines hollered Asher's name.

"We love you!"

"We like your sweatshirt!"

"You should take it off!"

Shushes and laughter.

Asher didn't react. Only studied me hard, which could've been intentional to play into his mysterious persona, but was probably just his naturally bad manners. Lenny took it upon himself to turn on his angelic charm and offer an even flirtier wave back. I almost threw up.

I read over the member Types, then glanced at Lenny. "You want to be an influencer even after you graduate?"

Lenny's beaming grin was brighter than his blue hair. "I have the lead role in the spring musical, Byrdie. I'm moving to L.A. to act."

"You're able to manage two after-school extracurriculars at once?"

"Theater practice is on Tuesdays and Thursdays. The club

meets Mondays and Wednesdays. Camilo does the same thing with National Honor Society and the Politics Club. He's gonna go to Kale Law and become the youngest Supreme Court Justice."

"Yale," Camilo muttered toward his crossed arms.

Lenny furrowed his brow, but there was a buried smile threatening to break through, his cheek twitching. I was catching on that Lenny enjoyed getting under Camilo's skin. Really, he was as capable and intelligent as Camilo, they just had different strengths. I wasn't sure if Lenny always had a joke prepared because he worried about friends like Camilo taking life too seriously, or if, for some reason, he wanted to leave up a wall. He *was* the son of a celebrity. Trust must've been hard to hand out. The world was full of clout chasers.

"You got any ideas yet?" Asher asked.

I bit my bottom lip. Types seemed to lean more toward talents or skills that club members possessed, but other than dance and latte art, my mind drew a blank.

"Um," was all I could say.

That's all it took for Asher to give up on originality. "We can have duplicate member Types too, you know. Let's start with some of the most common Types requested."

I nodded. Whatever Asher wrote down first, I'd claim that Type as mine. It didn't matter if the Type matched my personality. I just needed to prove I was skilled at something. *Anything*.

He wrote the word *Sporty* on the whiteboard in atrocious penmanship.

Camilo snorted.

"I love sports," I lied. "Let's go Detroit Pistons."

"Yeah?" Camilo propped his cheek with a fist, his smirk curling. "Tell me what sport they play real quick, bud?"

Shit. "Baseball?"

"Basket," Asher said. He erased *Sporty* off the board.

I rolled back my shoulders. All good. I'd get the next one.

Asher wrote *Musical*.

I rose right off my stool and pointed at the whiteboard. "Flute! I play the flute!"

Asher snapped his fingers at Lenny. "Get me a flute."

Lenny jogged off and disappeared down the nearest hallway. Camilo yawned and put his head down, one arm stretching across the tabletop like a lounging cat.

Regret washed over me as I sank back onto my stool. I hadn't played the flute since elementary school. Muscle memory existed, right?

Lenny returned shockingly fast with a massive flute case draped over his shoulder. He plopped the whole case on my lap, and I grunted.

Asher crossed his arms in front of me. "Go on."

"Right." I undid the case and opened the lid to reveal the shiny, silver flute.

Except this wasn't a flute. It was quadruple the size of a metal flute and had all sorts of bizarre levers and buttons on the side.

I picked up the instrument. "You sure this is a flute?"

Lenny sat down beside me again, pulling at the tips of his pastel bangs. "I think so. I called out, 'Does anyone have a flute?' and four people ran over with theirs. So."

The world was way too easy for hot people. "And all their flutes looked the same . . . ?"

That's when it hit me. I hadn't played the flute in elementary school.

I'd played a cheap plastic recorder.

I slowly shut the lid of the flute case. "You can wipe off *Musical*."

Asher didn't. Instead, he tapped Camilo. "Pull up the quiz."

Camilo lifted his head off the tabletop lazily. He opened his laptop again. A few clicks later, he passed it my way.

Welcome to
the Borrow a Boyfriend Club's Type quiz!
Please answer the following twenty questions,
and we'll assign you a Type.

I grimaced. This was *so* embarrassing.

"Don't feel weird, Byrdie," Lenny said. "It's tough to know who you are. That's why everyone's so obsessed with Myers-Briggs and zodiac signs. I, myself, am an ENFP and a Sagittarius. See, see?" He wiggled his fingers in front of his forehead. "We all got too much going on up here. But this quiz Camilo made helps you sort that out."

I sighed as I started answering the multiple-choice questions. To my surprise, they weren't prying or deep. Which made sense. Everyone else's branding was simple. Archetypes. One question asked for my favorite color. Blue. Another asked for my favorite hobby. The only option I connected with even a little was watching movies.

I reached the last question and clicked submit. A cartoon image of Camilo sticking out his tongue spun around the screen until the results calculated.

Noah Byrd: Typical Type

I stared at the result for what felt like minutes.

"Ouch." Camilo leaned over my shoulder. "No one's ever gotten the most boring Type before. I threw this one in as a joke."

Everything inside me deflated.

Lenny must've noticed, because he patted my back a few times. "Don't worry. Give the quiz another shot!"

So, I did. Instead of selecting blue as my favorite color, I chose green. Instead of watching movies as my favorite hobby, I chose hanging out with friends.

Submit.

Noah Byrd: Typical Type

I didn't need to glance up from the laptop to know everyone else at the table was wincing. The tension clinging to the air conveyed that well enough.

"That Type will be a placeholder," Asher eventually said, and I swore he sounded a bit defensive on my behalf. "We can spin this for now. You're the boy next door. The wholesome, steady, all-American, friends-to-lovers story personified."

This description *did* strangely dial up my pride. I grinned. "Okay."

"If you do get accepted, then the rules allow us to switch up your Type any time before you're officially added to the club."

Asher drooled over his own club rules, so I knew he couldn't be lying to cheer me up. "Thanks."

"Camilo," Asher said, "update our borrower request form

on our website by tonight. Lenny, spread the news around school that Byrd is a new option and available. Temporarily."

A new option. Available.

The words rattled in my head. Dating meant trusting someone to see all of me, and that was more petrifying than the idea of having to enroll back at my old school.

Calm down. Borrowing was playing pretend. There was no real romance for me in sight.

"What should I do?" I asked.

"Show up on time to the Valentine's formal two weeks from now and prepare yourself well. We're trusting you with one of our borrowers. Don't screw it up."

CHAPTER 15

Don't screw it up in response to *What should I do?* wasn't exactly helpful advice.

Over the log cabin–style countertop, I handed a lavender latte to a rare Saturday morning customer, then scuffed the sticky tile floor with my Converse, pretending I was kicking Asher Price's face. Bitterlake Coffee was hardly busy early on weekends, which was usually nice, but today I wanted to be anywhere but alone with my thoughts.

The last couple of weeks passed in a blur of working even more morning shifts, studying for quarterly exams, and researching how to wow my date at the upcoming formal now that it was already this Friday. Three days away. Even with help from the internet, I wasn't confident on how to make a showstopping impression to pass the final round or what to wear. Especially not when Asher would be a judge. It's not like he'd give me a single hint on his tastes.

Even if he did, I doubted anything in my closet would be appreciated.

My hands were sticky with gross syrup by the time I went on break. The struggles I went through to fund my name change and college tuition. As I wiped the condiment onto my apron, the stuffed deer heads mounted above the fireplace seating area stared back at me. Below them, a pair of girls I recognized sat at a round table.

Snow dusted the top of Isabella's tight ponytail and Constance's highlighted afro. They must've arrived while I was washing dishes in the back.

Isabella was staring into space through her ruby-red cat's-eye glasses. One of her hands, bejeweled with gold rings and chunky bangle bracelets, rested on her trusty notebook. The other gripped a steaming ceramic mug. Constance, in her routine full princess skirt and blouse style, was tapping her forehead with the eraser of her mechanical pencil repeatedly and squinting at her phone.

If I wanted to win the trust of the other members, then I couldn't keep hiding whenever they were nearby.

My feet eventually reached their table, but they remained in trances. An open seat was backed into a corner, a mounted deer head jetting out right behind it.

Summoning my courage, I ducked and dodged the snout to claim the spot beside Constance. Still nothing. Being in charge of a group of boys who secretly dated half the student body must've worn them out.

Be bold, Noah. Be one of the boys. "Hey there, miss—" No. "—Constance. Hey, Chief Financial Offer Constance. And Product Manager Isabella."

Not my best, but that would do.

My voice was like a needle injecting Isabella's face with a reviving serum, forcing a bright smile to the surface. She straightened so quickly that the ballpoint pen tucked into her ponytail tilted. "Newbie Byrd!"

I frowned internally. Another name to add to the list of people who didn't call me Noah.

Constance glanced up from her phone. In the chandelier light overhead, the gold highlighter on her brown cheekbones glittered as much as the rhinestones on the ruffled collar of her lilac poplin blouse. She inspected my torso. "Oh, hey. You have something on your shirt."

I plucked at my apron, where there was a blot of clear and sticky liquid. "It's syrup. Just syrup. I work—" I pointed toward the latte machines tucked in the corner. "Over there."

"Cool."

Quiet indie pop music played over the speakers. The fireplace beside us crackled.

"So, I, uh, wanted to stop by and say that, well, I really hope you'll like what I have planned for the talent show. I'm good at what I do. There's no reason to be suspicious of me. We'll win."

Instead of dancing and cheering, Constance's face fell, and I swore even the rhinestones on her blouse stopped glimmering. Isabella glared at the table again, a shadow casting over her olive complexion and glasses.

"Everything okay?" I asked.

A groan erupted from Isabella so suddenly that I startled, knocking my head against the snout of the mounted deer. I apologized to it without thinking as she tossed the hand gripping her mug. Black coffee splashed into the fireplace with a sizzle. "Why waste my PR face on you? You know our club is falling apart."

"Yeah. Sorry, I didn't mean to bring up any stress."

"It's fine. We're fine. Just busy. I need to finish prepping for the talent show. We need LED lights. Not the lights that stay one color, no; the lights need to flicker to different colors on command, and we'll want to buy a fog machine because everyone loves a fog machine"—hints of an Italian accent were leaking off her words—"but Aiden is allergic to fake fog because he's allergic to the carbon dioxide or the water or something, so I need to get organic fog. We need to stand out. We need that money or everyone else is going to quit the club!"

My mouth hung slightly at the news. "Everyone will quit?"

Constance rested a hand on Isabella's left shoulder pad. "Now that Liam quit, it's only a matter of time until Max follows suit. Everett and Aiden really seem to like serving love, but they're also saving their club earnings for college essentials. The others probably do too, combined with other obvious perks."

"But Mr. President insists cutting our base is *imperative to longevity and success*," Isabella said.

I shifted from Isabella's breakdown to Constance. "Shouldn't you be making financial calls? Not him?"

"I was admittedly the one to suggest this plan when we were dealing with an"—Constance paused—"image decline last semester. But now, no matter how much I tell Asher we can move forward, he won't budge."

"Doesn't he have any guilt, knowing his members need the cash, though?"

"Not when he truly believes borrowers would stop coming," Isabella said. Her face was now planted onto the table, her glasses smushed against her face. "In his eyes, we're still taking this blow to ensure we can keep making a profit in the future instead of never again."

"He *did* claim there's an end in sight to this new policy," Constance offered. "But he's waiting to hear back on something that's taking longer than expected."

"Waiting on what?" I asked.

Constance and Isabella shrugged.

I frowned. "I'm surprised you're willing to stick around for such a prick."

"Well, thankfully," Constance said, "I've never really been in this for the money. But leading the school's most popular club is great for college applications."

Isabella set down her hazardous coffee mug to poke Constance. "That *used* to be Connie's reason. Now she stays because she's in love with Camilo."

Constance's eyes spread wide. "He can't even date anyone because of rules! Whatever. I like all my other friends in the club, too. Can we change the subject, please?"

Happily. I had plenty more to say, knowing now that winning the talent show meant stopping a mass exodus of members. "This sounds like a lot of work for you two."

Isabella's over-the-top smile, which must've been her fabricated PR face, returned impressively fast. "Well, I'm a pro at managing our product."

I shifted uncomfortably on my wooden chair, which sacrificed comfort to keep up the log cabin aesthetic. "What do you mean by product, exactly?" I'd been wondering for the longest.

She pointed a manicured nail at my chest. "You."

"Me?"

"The boys. The boys are all products. I manage the products for consumer use, so I must spend money to satisfy all the needs. Especially fashion. That's why I'm still here instead of applying to all the boutiques downtown. The club is like my passion project." Her eyes narrowed. "I also protect these goods with my life."

"Protect them?"

"You heard me. If any of our classmates ever stops liking us—or even a member of ours—they could report the whole club to administration and get us shut down. Hence, why"— she smiled painfully brightly once more—"I make sure everyone's happy."

Right. The watch list. For people like Liam. And others.

"Camilo's got us pretty protected," Constance mentioned. "We have the secure borrower form and own more Italian flags than Everett owns kombucha. But we've had scares before. Better safe than sorry."

The detail behind this operation never ceased to amaze me. "So, club money partly goes to . . . clothes?"

"Listen, fashion is gospel!" Isabella slapped a firm hand on the tabletop, her rings smacking loudly against metal. A book club made up of elderly men turned our way. I clearly wasn't the first one to question her. "Do you think everyone would be drooling over Asher if he wore camo cargo shorts to school with tube socks?"

I didn't understand why anyone was drooling over Asher regardless, but. "No."

Constance buried her head back in her phone, eerily reminding me of Camilo. Maybe they were a perfect match. "Isabella can usually use Lenny's endless wardrobe. He lets her take anything. But in desperate times—like with Aiden, who Isabella gives dress citations to every day—the budget can handle an H&M trip."

Isabella really did act the part of a jaded New York City designer. Which meant someone like her knew how the Borrow a Boyfriend Club president expected dates to dress for a Valentine's Day formal.

I leaned closer toward her, fearing Asher would walk through that door any minute and ruin my chances at uncovering his secrets. "What are you having everyone wear for the formal?"

Isabella's oversized shoulder pads jiggled as she shrugged. "Depends on the Type."

"Hypothetically, the boy next door. The all-American, I don't know, Typical Type."

Before I knew it, Isabella was lifting my arms out to the sides, and the back of my hand slapped another mounted deer in the face.

"What are you?" she asked. "Thirty-three, thirty-two?"

"Years old?"

Constance snorted.

Isabella rolled her eyes. "Measurements. We want you fitted. A solid, neutral color. You have a suit like that?" She leaned in closer as she patted down my wingspan.

Too close.

I automatically stiffened and balled my hands into fists, so the length of my fingers was unnoticeable. "I've never bought a suit before."

"*What?*" She left my side to pull the pencil out from her ponytail and jot down ideas in her notebook. My whole body relaxed. "You need a clean blazer."

"Okay."

"A sharp pant."

"Okay."

"A crisp button-down."

"Okay."

Isabella ripped out a sheet of paper and slid it across the table. "Lenny's closet won't work. For the boy next door, we need"—she gestured at me—"something more inside the box. Classic Americana. Give me until the formal on Friday. I'll have you covered. Capisci?"

I read over her scribbly handwriting. The estimated clothing prices as well as cost of labor per hour had already been calculated.

For a total, that would drain three weeks' worth of shifts. Renting a generic suit would cost way less money.

I bit my inner cheek. My funds were embarrassingly low in preparation for my name change, but the club's resident stylist dressing me for the formal seemed like a worthy investment. Another few morning shifts would only hurt me. Not kill me.

Anything to cement myself as one of the boys.

Anything to impress Asher Price.

I nodded. "Deal."

CHAPTER 16

Enjoy, O sluttish one!
– Isabella

I squinted at the sloppily written sticky note stuck to the front of my locker. It was seven o'clock on Friday morning.

Furrowing my brow, I plugged in my combination. On the top shelf were a sleek, new pair of oxfords and a thin, cardboard box.

How'd she *break in* here?

I stopped myself. I knew better than to question her powers. The one-minute warning bell rang over the hallway speakers as I pulled out the box and popped open the lid. Several layers of sheer tissue paper protected a folded black velvet blazer, a pair of pleated pants, a white button-down, a textured black tie, and gold cuff links.

Looking back at the front of my locker, I reread the sticky note.

Oh. *O* stylish *one*.

"Sick shoes," someone said behind me. Jennifer Chang from pottery, gliding by and pointing at the oxfords in my locker.

Three seconds in, and I was already receiving a compliment. Isabella was a wizard.

"Thanks!" I called back, then grinned at the box in my hands.

The Valentine's Day formal was a mere ten hours away. Tonight, I had to meet a date for the first time, be dreamy enough to please both them and the club, and, subsequently, pass the final round to finally prove Asher wrong. If I failed, I'd become reject number seventy-nine. With this suit on, I could at least fake it until I made it.

Throughout the school day, my anticipation for the night ahead turned my body into a leg-shaking and finger-tapping machine. Once I finally got home, I stepped into my bedroom as fast as possible to toss on each piece of the suit and inspect my body in a mirror.

My eyeballs bugged at my reflection. Isabella had said I needed a fitted suit. Not one as tight as a latex jumpsuit. The closest I'd gotten to wearing something this tight was my underwear. Tonight was the chance to gain the group's trust, and I'd have to slow dance myself to teach them. In *this*.

Did I even remember something as simple as slow dancing? I *had* learned a bit of ballroom at some point, right?

Watching myself in the mirror, I lifted my arms to hold an invisible partner, one around the hip, and closed my eyes. I put my trust into muscle memory, stepping to the right, then the left, and rotating in a loose circle.

"Look at you!"

I jumped at the sound of Mom's voice. Except she wasn't in the doorway. She was sitting on my bed, watching me, all bundled in a long parka and a knit hat.

"*Mom*, that's so creepy," I whined.

Although a smile tugged at my lips. It was admittedly nice to have an audience again. Dancing felt more real with Mom's eyes on me, like there was a bigger purpose. I'd forgotten that feeling.

But Mom was different than a room full of strangers at a high school formal.

"How long have you been there?" I asked.

"And that suit!" Mom said instead. "When'd you get to be so stylish?"

"A friend helped."

"Prepping to dance with a special someone at your Valentine's night?"

"No, Mom."

"Sure, sure. You're so charming! Can I take a photo?" She was already pulling out her phone from her parka pocket, snapping away.

I offered a weak thumbs-up and even weaker grin as the flash went off.

That seemed to satisfy Mom enough because she disappeared down the hall. "Have fun, be safe, and be home by eleven."

"Okay, Mom," I droned, then glanced at my open closet where the three button-ups she had bought me were hung.

I had no hood to hide my face. No baggy inseams to hide my waist. But I had no choice. No one at this formal would be wearing casual oversized clothes. I'd stand out more if I did. Plus, chances were I'd be stuck all night near Lenny and Asher and Camilo and the others, who'd probably show up dressed for the Met Gala.

My confidence was already bruised considering I'd sent my name-change petition to the city clerk more than a month ago and had heard crickets since. Was I not enough to deserve a name change in their eyes?

While I still had enough adrenaline to give me the courage I normally lacked, I grabbed my phone to send a follow-up email to the city clerk office. A part of me wished Mom or Dad could be my advocate and send the message instead, especially since I dreaded the idea of reading the clerk's response. But their efforts would prove useless quickly. They didn't understand anything about the process.

Once my message was sent with a swishing sound effect, my thoughts went back to the formal. Maybe I could pull this off. I wanted to.

Except no matter what, all I could think was that I'd still look like an abandoned alley cat next to someone as effortlessly gorgeous as Asher Price.

* * *

"Welcome!" Lenny hollered at me in his hot-pink suit. I was right—he was giving Met vibes.

"To Hell," Camilo growled, wearing a patterned dark gray suit with a black button-down shirt underneath. For once, his hands were sans pen ink.

The two stood in the school entryway side by side. Since the school day had ended, Lenny had gotten his hair dyed from pastel blue to fluorescent pink, which perfectly matched Camilo's rose boutonniere.

Words escaped me. They looked great, ten out of ten.

From what I could make out from the gymnasium entrance, chairs had been set up and high-top tables were draped with white lace tablecloths. A *Be Mine* flower wall was set up for photo shoots in the corner, the remaining walls covered with pink and red fabric, and pink heart balloons were randomly scattered along the floor. The school had somehow managed to turn the gym into a five-star ballroom.

There was even a portable stage set up at the very back with DJ equipment and bulky speakers. The rest of the members stood nearby. They all wore dress shirts and ties, and their suit coats were draped over the stage railing in preparation for dance practice.

I started taking off my puffer jacket, but then stopped.

Everyone would see me. *Really* see the entirety of me.

I took a deep breath. *Rip it off like a bandage, Noah. Rip it off!*

In one fluid motion, I yanked the puffer jacket off my body, leaving behind my fitted white shirt and black blazer for all eyes to see. My matching slacks suddenly hugged my legs too closely, and the desire to cover most of my chest with more than this slim tie consumed my every thought. I tried to tune each one out. "How are—"

"Wow!" Lenny rushed toward me so quickly that I swore he was about to smack his lips against mine. I stumbled backward. "Look what you've been hiding underneath those hoodies and sweatpants. You're hot!"

I glanced down at myself. "Oh."

Even Camilo seemed intrigued, one of his thick brows hitching. "Tonight might go better than expected."

The tension in my chest dissipated enough for a small

smile to break across my face. "Thanks. I think. I can't believe there's a stage for this DJ."

Lenny glanced around the room. "Perfect for us, yeah? We can all learn your super-secret dance skills before our borrowers get here."

Right. I just needed to make sure I held up his grandiose expectations.

Lenny rubbed the top of my blond curls, and I wrinkled my nose. "You should go find Asher. He needs to tell you about your borrower." He shoved a palm against my back. "He's messing with the speakers by the stage."

My trip across the gym was like an escape mission. I dodged balloons on the floor and swerved past tables covered with plates full of heart-shaped cookies and pink-colored chocolate drizzled popcorn. The space smelled like a department store perfume section, and I couldn't decide whether that was immersing me in the Valentine's Day ambience or not.

Three teachers I didn't recognize chatted by a drinks vending machine, ready to chaperone and probably live vicariously through us.

I finally reached the front of the gym. No sign of Asher.

Or so I thought until he appeared from behind the speaker system. Asher was nearly unrecognizable as he tried to untangle a clump of wires in his hand. His headful of dark hair was pulled into a bun, a few escaped strands dangling around his cheeks. There wasn't a single expensive-brand logo on his body. Instead, he wore a burgundy shirt tucked neatly into his matching tone-on-tone suit, which had a subtle plaid pattern, and every piece was perfectly tailored to fit his even more perfect figure.

Strange. Asher not wearing a designer *anything* sounded impossible. His belt buckle?

I checked, then realized where I was staring and stopped.

Once Asher sensed my presence, he glanced up from the wires, then scanned me up and down. His face was off. Like he was thrown.

My chest constricted. I crossed my arms over my chest. "Is there something wrong?"

"No—" The clump of tangled wires slipped out of Asher's fingers. He picked them up just as quickly. "No. You, um—"

"What?"

"Nothing." He focused hard on untangling the wires again. "You're barely on time."

"I'm thirty minutes early."

"Should've been an hour like everyone else." Asher pulled his phone from his jacket pocket and scrolled along the screen. He peeked up at me. "You said you don't really know who you're into, right? You'd be cool with anyone for now? Like me?"

My face heated up. "What do you mean, like you?"

"With dating. Relationships. Like with how I am with people."

"Oh, sure! I thought you meant— Um."

"What?"

No way was I about to admit I thought he was hitting on me. *Why* would I think that?

I wasn't sleeping enough, clearly. "Never mind."

"All right." He glanced both ways, then over his shoulder. "Any teachers nearby?"

I shook my head.

Asher flashed his phone my way. The name Rochelle Smith

filled in the chart on his screen. "Keep your voice down, but your borrower tonight is a girl named Rochelle."

"Oh." Right. Why else would he be asking about my preferences? "We aren't actually dating these people, though. Does that stuff really matter?"

"Plenty of people who aren't straight are already pressured enough to pretend they're into people they aren't. My club will never be another one of those places."

I nodded a bit. "That's nice of you."

"No, it's not. It's the bare minimum. If anything changes for you, tell me. We'll edit who can request you."

A few seconds later, my back pocket vibrated.

I pulled out my phone. An unknown number had sent me tons of information about Rochelle Smith. Profile photo, phone number, social handles, birthday, favorite food. Everything about her. She had won several junior poetry contests. A few were even nationwide, and her role model was some social media poet named Jasper Grimes.

She was a literary genius. And I'd received a beautiful B-minus on my *Moby Dick* quiz last Wednesday.

A nervous shiver shot through my spine at the idea of *me* trying to impress *her*. I tried to concentrate on the number at the top of my phone screen instead. "This is your number?"

"No," Asher said. "It's the other invisible person in front of you who's talking about Rochelle Smith at this very moment."

I rolled my eyes and gently shoved his arm in rebuttal, then added his number to my contacts under a very accurate name.

Asher Prick.

"Make sure she gets home safe," Asher went on, but he was distracted by where I'd touched him. Had I been too rough? He met my eyes again. "If she's walking home, you walk her home. If she's driving, get her to the right car. Rule number eleven: borrowers must be walked or driven home to ensure safety. Got it?"

He was oddly stricter than normal. "Yes. Sure. I do."

"Good. All our borrowers will meet us in the lobby in two hours. We got approval from the chaperones to use the stage before things start. Come with me."

I followed him up the metal stairs attached to the portable stage. We joined the rest of the guys.

Well, except for Musical Type—Pascha. He sat with his legs hanging over the stage, strumming an acoustic guitar and singing "Wonderwall" in Italian. To keep up the cover for the teachers watching, I assumed.

Aiden already appeared done with the lesson before it'd begun. "My borrower requested that I pick her up at her house. Now I have to go back and forth."

"Yeah," Artsy Type—Max—said. "I get we're all here to step up our romantic dancing game or whatever, but isn't this counterproductive if we ignore our dates before the dance?"

Pascha was still singing Italian "Wonderwall."

"You're here because Byrd will decide who participates in the talent show by your performances today," Asher replied.

I blinked at him, then at everyone else. "I will?"

"Yep. Choose who you think our best dancers are. Really, our greatest shots at winning. It's only a month away. You shouldn't be wasting your time teaching horrible dancers with no promise. Whoever's picked will have to comply."

Everyone else locked their gaze on me. None welcoming.

"Regardless, all of us should improve our dance skills," Asher kept explaining. "We're invited to weddings and quinceañeras and proms and debutante balls. Learning how to better satisfy our borrowers is essential to being a proper boyfriend."

A few groans came.

"Preachy," someone coughed out. The others snickered.

As Asher handed me a cord so I could plug my phone into the speaker system, I couldn't help but be proud. The most popular guy in my new school trusted me, and I liked the feeling. Even if he was a self-centered nightmare most times.

I found a random pop music playlist and hit play. "Could you all stand in a straight line and face me?" I plucked at my shirt. "And if you don't want to sweat to death, then take off those blazers and roll up your sleeves."

They all did as told, then moved into place on the portable stage and waited for my next command. A tense, prickling sensation took root in my chest as their eyes inspected every inch of me. I had no sweatshirt to cover all five-foot-five inches of me.

The compliments earlier gave me enough of a confidence boost to continue through this stretching session, though. I clapped my hands. "Today, we'll learn the basic form, technique, and posture for a romantic slow dance. As Asher said, this should help you impress your borrowers tonight. Maybe earn you more in tips."

Skeptical faces stared back. In the distance, a shoe squeaked against the cafeteria floor.

"At the very least, none of you will trip and faceplant during the slow dances," I added. "After this, you'll have a general idea of how to guide your borrowers."

"I've only faceplanted once," Max muttered.

"And me twice," Aiden said. "Which is fine when we can just get up and wink the mistake away. We have our hotness to rely on—"

Everett interrupted him by resting a palm on his shoulder. "Our instructor is right. Listen to yourself. The bar is low."

"We'll split off into pairs," I said.

"I call Byrdie!" Lenny stretched his hand toward me and bowed.

Everyone else clumped into their own groups of two, leaving Asher and Camilo without partners in the end. They slowly shifted closer together and formed the final pair.

As I rearranged myself into a traditional slow dance position with Lenny, the tense prickling returned to my chest, stronger this time.

I was about to dance again. *Dance* dance.

Only the club would see me dance. No one else was here. It was fine. I was *fine*.

For now. But what about later?

Once I finished my lengthy explanation of how each person should hold their respective partner depending on if they were leading or following, I moved on to the next step. "Start with a simple stance and movement. Leaders, use your left foot to step to the left, then your right foot to step to the right, and follow that pattern—" A yelp shot out of my mouth as Lenny started swinging me around.

"Like this?" Lenny said. "I'm following the left-right-left-right pattern!"

Then his foot slipped. He tripped forward and smacked right into me. We landed in a heap on the floor, our foreheads clunking.

Asher was quick to kick Lenny's limp body off me. "If you kill our dance instructor, I kill you."

Lenny pouted as he rose to his feet. He brushed off his hot-pink slacks even though there wasn't a speck of dust or dirt on them.

"Lenny had the right idea, though!" I said as Asher offered a hand. As he helped me up, his grip was icy, and yet we weren't anywhere near the snow outside.

Was he always this cold?

I was getting distracted. I let go of his hand. "It's great to improvise. But only once you have the basics down. After that, feel free to improvise spins and dips."

The next half hour passed by fast. As I practiced with Lenny, his steps became more confident as he led, despite him being one of the worst dancers. Camilo kept tripping over Asher's feet, and the former's slicked-back dark hair had completely fallen apart, draping over his forehead in waves. I could tell Camilo was comfortable by the way his feet moved, and it was obvious he was pretending to be horrible so he wouldn't get chosen for the show.

Asher, however, still had an invisible rod stuck up his whole body. His steps were blocky, planned, like he was thinking through each move instead of letting go.

Asher Price, the notorious best boyfriend ever, couldn't dance.

As I slowed to a stop at the hilarious sight, Asher accidentally knocked Camilo in the face with the back of his hand. Camilo's glasses slapped to the floor.

"Get your hand out of my face!" Camilo shouted.

"Get your face out of my hand!" Asher shouted back.

"All right!" I interjected, stepping away from Lenny and rushing toward the front of the stage. "How about we call that a wrap?"

Everyone heaved a sigh of relief in unison, fanning themselves. Fortunately, no one ended up with pit stains.

Lenny walked over to the stage railing and put on his suit jacket again. "Which lucky few are gonna dance at the show, Byrdie?"

Almost everyone sent me daggers. The outliers were Camilo—who was cleaning his glasses with the hem of his shirt under the assumption his "two left feet" disqualified him—and Asher, who had two genuine left feet and assumed the same.

To keep the routine interesting enough, I'd want at least four dancers. The choices for who performed best were obvious. Everett, Aiden, Max, and Camilo.

I started to open my mouth but stopped as a rush of nerves lurched through me. Over the next few hours, every member would assess my boyfriend skills with a real borrower. They would all decide if I passed the club's final round. My fate was in their hands tonight.

And they could fail me simply because they hated me.

"Could I choose who tomorrow?" I asked weakly. "Sleep on it?"

"No," Asher said from across the stage, absently checking his phone.

My heart pounded in my ears, my head, my feet. There were a few select members I trusted who wouldn't sabotage my chances of earning a permanent spot in the club. So I chose them.

I took a deep breath in, then exhaled.

"Lenny. Asher." And there was one member who Lenny could always seemingly keep in check. "And Camilo."

Asher dropped his phone. The sound of cracking glass followed as the screen slapped the floor. He didn't even care enough to glance down. *"What?"*

Camilo had no orange pop to drop today. He made up for it by gripping his forehead and taking a quick stress lap around the stage.

I took one last breath for the final blow. "And me. If I pass the final round tonight and become a member myself, then I'll dance with you all."

Grins swept through the members in a flash.

Aiden slapped me on the back so hard that I lurched forward. "Superior choices, bro."

Everett followed suit with the slapping. "The four of you were totally feeling the flow."

Lenny and Asher were still too stunned to move, and Camilo was nowhere close to finishing his stress laps. The worst part was that I was as stressed as them, even though I'd made the choice myself. How was I supposed to teach these three a winning routine in one month?

Not only that. Asher allowed me to pass the first round because I promised them a victory. Not if I *tried* to. Losing the show meant Asher would definitely null-and-void my membership, even if I passed the final round.

A pit settled deep in my core. Had I just made a huge mistake?

Squeals and shouts echoed over by the main entrance. A

clump of students in somewhat formal attire were starting to show up.

The final round, Entertain a Borrower, was about to start.

"Great job, everyone!" I shouted before quickly ducking down the stage steps in search of the nearest bathroom.

The moment I found one, I rushed inside. A tall guy who looked familiar was readjusting his glasses at the sink mirror. He sat near me in chemistry class, and sometimes he brought an instrument case. I'd clocked him as a band kid.

"Sup," he said.

"Hey. Christian, right?"

"Yep. Your fit's too good. Making me look bad, man."

Man. Just that one word had my spirit soaring. "Nah, you look great."

Christian laughed. I laughed. Then he was out the door.

A normal guy interaction. No mistakes.

I took his spot at the mirror to splash my face with cold water and then inspected what Christian had seen. My curls were looser than usual, falling to my nose instead of my eyes. I'd shaved this morning, so there wasn't even a hint of facial hair around my lips. Over the last few years, my jawline had re-shaped and become sharp enough to slice a Christmas ham, but my face was still on the smaller side. My hands were no better.

Every person at this school was about to see me at this formal. If a single person noticed my face or hands, even my own borrower, everything that happened at Pinewood High would start over. The accidental wrong greeting. The little mistakes. The slipups.

My phone vibrated in my slacks pocket. I pulled it out.

An email from the Ann Arbor Clerk of Court.

Good afternoon, Mr. Noah Byrd,

I apologize for the delay in responding. I can confirm that your name change petition has been received by our office; however, court time is scarce and new matters will not be proceeding until late March at the earliest. Once subsequent dates become available, your documents will be reviewed and approved for filing. You will be advised of your court date at that time.

Sincerely,
Rachel Gonzalez
The Ann Arbor Clerk of Court

My head buzzed so much that I had to read the email twice more to fully comprehend her words. Late March was a month from now, but progress was progress.

And the email was sent to Mr. Noah Byrd.

I grinned at myself in the mirror, puffed out my chest, and gave my reflection a very manly fist bump.

Maybe I was enough.

I was *enough*.

CHAPTER 17

The cafeteria was suddenly overflowing with suits and dresses and hormones.

A DJ had claimed her rightful throne onstage and was blasting a thudding bass. A few brave souls had already wandered toward the speakers to dance while the rest stood around, chatting and eating handmade Valentine's Day–related snacks, which was just normal food dyed pink.

At one nearby table with a girl, Lenny was trying and failing to juggle kernels of pink popcorn he'd plucked from a bowl. Aiden was with another, quite literally feeling her bicep to make her laugh. A third girl was staring passionately into the eyes of Everett, who, between overhearing him say "Your third quadrant matches Millie Bobby Brown" and seeing papers spread across the table, must've been reading her entire life story through astrology charts.

Weeks ago, borrowing boyfriends had sounded ridiculous. But as I watched how happy these members appeared, entertaining their dates and not just the other way around, I had to admit I was getting the hype.

On the other hand, though, Camilo was *not* with a borrower. He stood beside Constance, who wore a beautiful V-neck, ankle-length mesh strawberry patterned dress, taking a selfie with her. Despite the stay-single rule. Was Asher that clueless about them? Or did he . . . have enough of a heart to finally look the other way?

No, that couldn't be right.

"Noah?"

For a split second, I didn't even acknowledge my name being called. It'd been so long since I'd been called my own name aloud. At home, it was N. At the club, it was Byrd.

Once I turned around, a beautiful Black girl with purple box braids approached. Her orange blush gleamed against her deep brown skin and her sleek lavender gown shifted around her figure with each step. She waved with a manicured hand. "I'm Rochelle."

As she spoke, I had to look down at her. Not up. She was five-foot-two at most. In heels.

Feeling a little bold, I waved instead of tucking my hands behind my back. "Hi. Noah."

The girl laughed hard at that. Really hard. Her laugh was cute.

I laughed as well, not knowing what else to say to a genius poet without being labeled a disappointment three seconds into the date.

"I can't believe I'm the first person to borrow you," Rochelle said excitedly. "Every boy at this school has been trying to get into Asher's club since his brother started it, you know? The fact you've already passed so many rounds only a few weeks after transferring here is so—" She made a wide gesture with her hands. "Anyways. I'm Rochelle."

"Right. Noah."

"Yep. We said that." Another laugh. "But I knew your name already. Duh. Everyone knows who you are."

"What?" I glanced around the room at some of "everyone."

"I mean, you're like the hottest new guy. We're all talking about you."

My throat ran dry. "What—?"

Rochelle grabbed one of my hands from behind my back before I could say more and led us to the dance floor, but I was too overwhelmed by what she'd said to move my legs properly. Rochelle had probably been trying to flatter me by calling me the hottest new guy at school.

But if she was telling the truth, then all the work I was putting in since starting at Heron River High was paying off. A piece of me still couldn't believe her, but my chest exploded with hope regardless.

Once we claimed some standing room among the many other dancing bodies, Rochelle's mouth started to move. I couldn't hear a word over the pop song playing on max volume.

"*What?*" I shouted. My new catchphrase.

"Why is Asher considering you so seriously?" she shouted back. "For the club?"

"I applied?"

"That's all?"

I was about to rack my brain for another answer until a familiar face caught my eye. Asher stood off to the side of the dance floor. He had claimed a high-top table with his borrower. Some of his dark hair had escaped his bun after our dance practice, and a bit of his burgundy shirt was untucked from his pants.

My heart pounded as we held each other's gaze.

But then Asher's abruptly found the ceiling instead, followed by the stage, and finally landed on his borrower. Anywhere other than me.

I kept watching him, confused. His stare had been so freakishly intense. Had I already screwed something up? Although Asher's eyes probably had to be on me all night, to judge my entertaining skills.

So, why was he avoiding eye contact with me at all costs now?

The borrower across from Asher said something that pulled him back into their moment. The first three buttons of the guy's collared shirt were left unbuttoned, exposing a ridiculous amount of his chest and collarbone. He kept leaning forward across their table, giving the flirtiest vibes.

His pointer finger inched closer toward Asher's hand. He was getting closer. And closer.

I wasn't the only one showing interest in their table. Clumps of other students peered at Asher and his date from every angle, whispering and frowning. Even a few with dates standing right beside them seethed with jealousy, knowing they weren't the lucky winners of the Asher Price lottery for this year's Valentine's Day formal. I wondered what about his date's application stood out in Camilo's algorithm.

"Noah?"

I flicked my head back. "Yeah?"

Rochelle was shifting back and forth to the booming beat,

her loose purple sleeves swinging to her movements. "When's the soonest you'll officially be on the market? There's a get-together with local poets coming up, and everyone's bringing their partners. It's pretty soon. I may need to cut the line. I'll pay you back any way you want." She winked, her eye shadow shimmering in the cafeteria lights.

"*Huh?*"

Rochelle playfully shoved me on the shoulder. "I'm kidding!"

"Oh." Despite my heart still racing, a small grin broke across my face. "I'm not sure when. But hopefully soon."

The conversation died as quickly as it began again. Thankfully, one of her favorite songs came on, and we could relax without speaking. I knew a good boyfriend always asked more questions, but the pressure had zapped away every topic starter I'd attempted to memorize the night before this date.

One word finally popped into my head, though.

"Poet!" I shouted.

Rochelle's head tilted as her hips rocked. "Excuse me?"

Chill. "You're a poet, right?"

She smiled. "I suppose that's my official title, but I like to say I'm a word doctor."

"Is being a word doctor what you want to do after you graduate?"

"Honestly? No clue. Right now, I'm trying to pass calculus. I call baloney that these formulas are real."

I laughed. "You know what? I hear you."

"Really?" Rochelle's voice dripped with sarcasm. "You're a believer too?"

"Math doesn't exist. You can't touch it, so it's not real, right?"

"Like gravity."

"Yes," I said, grinning, "like gravity."

I was actually enjoying myself. Was this what dating was like?

Maybe it wasn't as terrifying as I'd assumed.

Rochelle moved to the side as the crowd shifted, revealing Asher in the distance once more. I was so wrapped up in my ongoing jokes with Rochelle that I'd already started forgetting he was there. He was staring my way again—but only for a moment. When he realized I was looking back, Asher said something to his borrower without even having the courtesy to meet his eye, and then rushed off toward the stage, alone.

A slow song began to play through the cafeteria.

Rochelle tapped my shoulder. "You okay?"

"Yeah. Great. I'm so sorry, but I need to check on something really quick." I grabbed Rochelle's hand and led her toward Lenny, who was still doing party tricks to entertain his date. "In the meantime, Lenny mentioned earlier that he has a story to tell you."

He quirked a brow, but I zoomed off before he could ask questions.

I followed Asher's trail through the gym and left Rochelle behind, dodging the many high-top tables and balloons filling up floor space, but I wasn't sure why I had such a strong impulse to do so. Tonight was supposed to be about proving myself to her and the boys. Ditching my borrower wouldn't compel them to score me well. And I didn't want to come across as rude to Rochelle, especially when she was someone I'd made such a quick and genuine connection with at this school. But something was obviously wrong with Asher, and that bothered me.

I hated that it bothered me.

By the time I caught up to him, the rosy perfume scent filling the air was starting to get me high. He stood to the left of the stage, shrouded behind the speaker system, checking his now partially shattered phone.

I tugged on Asher's untucked shirt to grab his attention over the music. The slow song that played wasn't as intense back behind the speakers, but something inside me felt the need to fix his shirt regardless. He glanced at where I'd touched him like I'd slapped him.

I instantly let go and took a step back. Now up close, I could tell Asher was running on fumes from his dark circles. Yet, somehow, he still was striking. There wasn't a single blemish on his face, not even a hair out of line around his thick brows. "You're not dancing with your borrower."

Asher huffed. "Neither are you. You've got one more hour to impress her, yet you're here. You dressed up for her all nice tonight and everything."

I peered down at my suit, then at him. "Was that a compliment?"

"You—" He hesitated. "It surprised me, is all."

"How nice I look?"

"Yeah."

Investing in Isabella's handiwork was worth it, after all. I glanced toward the sea of tables, where Asher's borrower was waiting for him. "You don't seem too thrilled about dancing. In general."

"Wow. You're a mind reader, Byrd. You might put Everett out of business."

"Is he even psychic?"

"Who cares? He pulls in all the astrology girls."

We were getting off track. "What's wrong with dancing?"

"Nothing. I just—" Asher slipped his cracked phone into his pocket as he frowned. "I'm bad. At dancing."

A laugh bubbled out of me. "I mean, yeah."

"Then why pick me for the talent show?" Before I could even start thinking up a lie, Asher gesticulated wildly and kept going. "Because I'm the president? The face of the club? My face is going to be flat on the floor, so good luck practicing with me. Have fun. Bon appétit."

Asher was rambling. He must've been stressed. No, embarrassed.

Asher Price was *embarrassed*.

I held my hand out toward him.

He stared at it like I was offering him cat food.

"Didn't you say that this formal was first and foremost to improve club image?" I asked. "If the president continues to dodge slow dances at all these events, then you're going to make us all look bad. How about I try to reteach you the easy move set from earlier? No one can see us behind all this tech junk, I promise."

"You can't teach me in five minutes."

I snatched his hand and pulled him toward me, causing him to trip forward. "You're leading." I slapped one of his hands onto my waist, then my own onto his shoulder, and clasped our other hands together. "Move your left foot to the left. Then bring your right foot over. We should feel in sync. But you first need to initiate it."

He stepped to the left, and I followed. Asher must've gone overboard on the cologne while getting ready for the formal earlier because the rosy perfume scent had vanished from the air now, and all I could smell was a strong blend of citrus and pine.

We hadn't stood this close to each other since we went on that date to the winter festival. When I almost kissed him in front of my apartment.

Focus.

"Good," I said. "Now go in reverse by stepping to the right like you did before."

He did, right on my left dress shoe. I yelped.

"Shit," Asher said, and I swore his face tinged a bit red.

I tried to hold back my wince but couldn't. My foot felt crushed by a boulder. His feet were bigger than my face. "No, no. It's okay. Don't worry if you step on your partner's toes. It's normal to be nervous—"

"I'm not nervous."

"Right."

We kept up our left and right movements as we swayed to the music. Asher was already getting the hang of the steps. I got lost in the moment, so much so that I almost forgot this was supposed to be a lesson.

I even caught myself laughing a bit.

He cleared his throat. "I noticed you dancing earlier with Rochelle. You're good."

My chest warmed. I hated to admit it, but every compliment from Asher felt like a reward. "Thanks."

"When'd you start dancing?"

I hesitated to answer, but after everything I'd confessed to Asher behind the carousel after running from Everly and Jas and Rosen on our pretend date, opening up to him about this was going from a ten to a four. "Young. I danced until I was done with middle school. Ballet. Jazz. Tap. Everything, really. It was kind of my whole life. But then I stopped."

"How come?"

"I just didn't like it anymore."

His gray eyes studied me hard. "Then how come you're smiling so much now?"

My feet froze.

Boys like me can't dance.

Boys like me need to prove themselves in other ways.

I was so tired of keeping my fears of never being enough bottled inside me. But I had to. Every time I revealed more about who I was to the world, to Asher, the more I risked history repeating itself.

For the most part, I trusted that Asher would never expose me to our classmates at Heron River High. He hadn't so far. Despite him acting totally stuck-up about almost everything, my secret was one thing that never made his true prickly colors show. He'd only ever listened and helped. But the tiniest sliver of me doubted him.

No matter how long I'd know Asher, I wasn't sure if that sliver would ever go away.

I let go of Asher's waist, then his hand, and took a step back. "Look at you. I think you're ready to try that dance floor."

"Hey, wait, Byrd—"

I didn't let him say anything else. I dipped back onto the crowded dance floor before giving in to the temptation to burst out everything, my true emotions. The moment I was no longer hidden behind the sound system, Rochelle spotted me and asked for another dance. I agreed, taking her hand.

My time at the formal passed by in a blur. Every time the end of a song faded into a new one, I searched the crowd to see if Asher was stepping on everyone else's toes or falling flat on his face like I expected. But the only familiar person I ever spotted was Camilo, who was always dancing with Constance. Did he even get assigned a date? Asher was nowhere to be found.

"Have you seen Asher anywhere?" I finally asked Rochelle.

"Asher? Yeah, actually. But, like, over twenty minutes ago. I saw him leaving."

"Toward the bathroom?"

She shook her head. "No, to the exit."

CHAPTER 18

As always, I had no idea what Asher Price was thinking, and that was the only thing on my mind as I walked to school Monday morning.

Once my date ended with Rochelle and I walked her home, I texted Lenny to ask where Asher had gone. Apparently, he'd bailed halfway through the formal and had never come back. He'd also had the decency to walk *his* borrower home in the process, but leaving early from an event must've broken at least one of a million rules.

And since Asher had left, there was no way he could've scored my final round. The other members could in his place, but Asher protected this club like a hissing mother goose. He would never put full trust in them alone.

"Hello, I'm Principal Lawson of Heron River High! Come share your opinions with me!"

My feet came to a halt on the sidewalk. Even though I was a whole block away from school, I could hear a confident, feminine voice booming from the back. An announcement was being played over what sounded like a speaker system.

Other students loitering around headed toward the commotion. I followed their lead as we walked the remaining block and rounded the corner, passing by the basketball court, then some outdoor seating dusted with snow beside a pond surrounded by onlooking students. Beyond them blared the announcement.

I wiggled my way through the crowd. The pond was frozen over except for the very center, where a wooden boat with an automatic propeller spun in circles. A massive papier-mâché head tinted ugly green rested on top, looking eerily similar to our principal.

The voice wouldn't stop repeating the same line. *Hello, I'm Principal Lawson of Heron River High! Come share your opinions with me!*

Whispers and snickers came from everywhere at once.

Before the principal and her posse of administrative assistants showed up to shoo us away, I funneled into the school for my first class.

I didn't even need to ask who did this. Only one person would.

But why?

The question lingered in my brain as the day passed. All my classes were probably important considering midterms were coming up in early March, but I couldn't focus. Not when no one would shut up about the pond and the obvious culprit.

"The swim team saw Asher Price by the pond before practice," someone whispered during my chemistry class units-of-force lesson. This made a few others gasp, but I'd overheard this news four times and counting.

"Wasn't the lake frozen over?" another asked.

"I heard he took an axe to it. With his bare hands. No gloves."

"Sounds kind of hot."

My head lifted off my propped fist. An *axe*? *Seriously?*

If I remembered correctly, Asher had terrorized the lawn because of some sidewalk lights. But was that really all this was about? Hadn't he already complained to the office, too?

What the hell was he thinking? He could get suspended.

The black pen in my grasp flew across the classroom.

Mrs. Kamen followed the arc of the pen through the air. "Everything okay back there, Mr. Byrd?"

I nodded, pulling the strings of my hoodie tighter.

Someone tapped my shoulder from behind. Christian, the band kid, holding my pen with a smile.

"Oh," I said, taking it. "Appreciate it."

"No prob."

By the time the final bell rang, I felt like my brain had been cooked in a microwave. As I organized my locker and packed books into my backpack, nerves ate away at every nook and cranny of my body. Asher might've bailed on the formal, but no one had notified me over the weekend if my final round had been voided or if I'd passed or failed.

Now I had to go to the Monday meeting and face my fate.

I slammed my locker shut with the force of a million Newtons.

"Damn, that locker insult your mom?" Aiden shouted from farther down the hall. Next to him were three other guys who matched his meaty muscles, shorter hair, and athleticwear.

Football team bros. Their enormous bodies alone made my anxiety spike.

"Byrd, you know Garcia? Montblanc? Hutchinson?" Aiden turned to pat one of them on the back. "This is that cool new kid I've been talking about, boys."

Instead of shoving me into my locker, they gave me a *sup* in unison.

Someone on the football team referring to me as *cool* left me at a loss for words. "S-sup."

"I'm on my way to the basement," Aiden said. "You coming?"

Aiden and I split off from his teammates as we approached the theater basement. By the time we fought through the costume racks, the other members were stationed around various areas. Pascha and Everett sat on the carpet nearby, practicing their conversational Italian together. Max was with two students I didn't recognize, discussing a shared appreciation for the 2,400-pound cube sculpture downtown that was creatively called The Cube. With how smiley and blushy they were, they must've been borrowers.

Lenny and Camilo hovered around the billiards table, playing a game before the meeting. Lenny's hair was still hot pink, which must've meant this was a long-term change from the pastel blue. He leaned over a corner of the table, cue stick pulled back, armed and ready to smack the ball. He drew back the stick a tad farther before making his move.

I couldn't make out the results, but whatever transpired made Lenny cry out, dying goat style. "This game is rigged!"

Camilo didn't look up from his phone. His turquoise glasses were shoved up into his hair, and his hip rested against the opposite side of the table. "It's just physics, bro."

As Lenny grunted, he noticed me by the costumes. "Byrdie!"

The others glanced over and cheered my name as well.

I blinked at them as the club theme song, background noise at this point, started to play from the jukebox. "Hi."

Aiden fist-bumped me. I bumped back way too lightly, and he nearly squashed my knuckles into meat goo. "Rochelle won't shut up about you, man."

A heavy weight ripped through me. "Like complaints, or . . . ?"

"Complaints? Are you kidding?"

Lenny shook his phone around in the air. "She gave you a perfect five-star review through our website this morning! She says you're a wonderful listener."

A grin rose to my face. If Rochelle and all the club members were this pleased, then this could mean good news. *Perfect* news.

But my victory wasn't sealed until the club president made it official. "Where's Asher?"

"Are you obsessed with me, Byrd?"

I spun on my heel.

Asher loomed over me, another fancy brand logo on his pastel-pink knit sweater and his high-end laptop tucked under his arm. He passed by me on the way to the table without speaking another word. As if there was nothing else that needed to be said.

As if nothing out of the ordinary happened at the Valentine's Day formal.

I wanted to have the impulse to punch him like every other

time he'd acted like an arrogant little worm, but there was only an ache in my chest. I'd danced with him. I'd helped him and *cared* about the rest of his night. Then he bailed and stopped caring about my spot in the club.

"So, was my final round scored?" I asked, struggling to hide the irritation in my voice.

Asher set down his laptop. He undid the bun at the peak of his head, then pulled together the top half of his hair to redo it. "Why wouldn't it have been?"

"Are you serious right now?"

"Sit down, Byrd."

Wouldn't it be fantastic if Asher Price learned some manners? I claimed my usual love seat at the back wall, crossing my arms.

While Asher set up for the meeting, everyone else took seats and floor space. Aiden and Everett sat on either side of me, squeezing our bodies together like sardines.

"We'll now start the meeting," Asher said, standing by the whiteboard. "First things first: those who were selected by Byrd to dance for the talent show need to start having regular practices as soon as possible. The show is officially one month from today."

Of course Asher was going to drag out my membership results for as long as he could. He drank suffering like liquid gold.

"Len," Asher said with the commanding tone of a military officer. "You're the lead role in the musical. Message the director and tell her the football and Lamborghini club will be occupying the theater stage every Tuesday, Thursday, and Friday after your rehearsals until the end of March. We'll have our practices in there."

"Uh," Lenny said.

"Camilo," Asher said, "add our lesson schedule to the on-line calendar."

With a sigh, Camilo yanked a pen out from behind his ear to write a reminder on his hand. His to-do list was so large that he had to roll up his sleeve to access his wrist.

"Byrd, come up with a dance routine. I want to see a draft in my inbox the night before our first Monday practice."

My whole brow popped. That was *next week*.

Lenny thrust a hand into the air. "Wait. If Byrdie's helping us, does this mean he's officially joined our club? Can he dance with us onstage as a member?"

"No," Asher said. "We allowed him to clear the first round in exchange for him promising us a talent show win—there's no reneging—and now he's failed the third. So, he's still helping us, but not as a member."

The room fell silent except for the music. I wanted to stab the jukebox with a knife.

Even if that was our agreement, I couldn't believe he had the gall to start planning the talent show while rejecting me.

"Because you left the formal early, and you couldn't watch me." This time I didn't even care about hiding how pissed off I was. "That's why I failed, right?"

Asher picked up a green marker from the whiteboard and fiddled with the cap. "No. You neglected your borrower for a good thirty minutes. A good boyfriend doesn't ignore his own date."

To dance with him.

To *help* him.

"But you ignored yours too!" There was absolutely no logic to his reasoning, and my burning rage was about to consume me whole.

"Yeah, man." Aiden draped his bulky arm over my shoulder. "No offense, but you dipped from the dance mad early. That's way ruder than whatever Byrd did."

Everett pressed a finger against my temple. "And I sense he performed as best he could."

"All in favor of accepting Byrd into the club," Aiden shouted, "say, *Shut up, Asher!*"

A resounding *Shut up, Asher!* filled the air. Everyone's mouths opened except for Camilo's; he still sat on the carpet, lazily leaning against the couch, beside Lenny's legs. Lenny bopped the top of Camilo's head, but he didn't change his vote.

The tension inside me dissipated. That was a huge majority. Please. *Please.*

But the moment Asher smirked, I knew it was over for me. "See, it's not only me. The decision remains."

A few yelled Camilo's name and demanded answers, but he just buried himself deeper into his phone and mumbled, "I don't think he's ready, all right?"

I sat there dumbfounded. I couldn't believe it. Asher was acting way icier than he'd ever been on our pretend date, or even on the first day I'd met him.

I reflected upon everything that went down at the formal. How Asher had scolded me for arriving thirty minutes early instead of an hour. How I'd chosen him for the talent show and made him drop his phone. How I'd told him more about myself than I'd expected to in private and rushed off. All these offenses seemed minor and definitely not enough to make him go against the majority vote.

Lenny crossed his lanky arms. "You at least have to offer Byrdie the final escape round."

"What's the final escape round?" I asked no one in particular.

"No," Asher said flatly.

Lenny ignored him and turned to face me. "It's basically a round four, used only for emergencies. Before Sebastian graduated, he added a heavy-duty FAQ to the back of our handbook for when super rare conflicts like these come up. Like if the president and the other members don't agree on someone's acceptance into the club. Ties, basically."

Camilo grinned. "I wanna see Byrd get trapped in an escape room. Twenty bucks he won't be able to figure a way out."

"Like that one downtown?" I asked.

Lenny leapt to his feet, knocking a knee against the back of Camilo's head by accident. "Isn't it the ultimate round? Escape rooms are a true communication-skills test. Not to mention they bring out the worst in people. Fights break out. Relationships are tested. It's on par with trips to IKEA."

"Besides, Asher," Aiden drawled, "if you ignore something written in the training handbook, then doesn't that mean *you're* breaking a club rule?"

All the other members nodded in agreement.

Asher looked bewildered and even slightly offended, like a king being challenged by a team of court jesters. But the court jesters were winning.

"This weekend, then." Asher's voice was tense. Dark, even. "At Escape the Circus. If Byrd manages to successfully escape the room with his borrower, then I'll allow the majority vote to win. As long as he agrees to participate."

Five minutes ago, I would've agreed in a heartbeat. Now the president had made it clear just how much he didn't want me around after such a harsh rejection. The last thing I wanted to do was keep helping him.

But I'd be letting down the other members. And the risk of not being in the club, of becoming invisible again, would be way worse than what Asher could ever put me through.

I'd already gotten glowing reviews from my first borrower. Nothing would be different this time around either. "Fine, I agree."

Everyone except for Camilo cheered, and the meeting ended soon after.

As I collected my belongings from the love seat, Camilo hovered over me, his overpacked backpack slung over his shoulder. "Good luck. Double dates are the worst."

I glanced up from my own bag. "Double date?" My heart dropped to my toes when I saw his grin, proof he was hoping for that exact response.

Camilo showed even more teeth. "You don't know? The final escape round is a double date with the club president. He's always grading you."

"Right." A weak laugh left my lips. "I knew that."

I really should've read that damn handbook.

CHAPTER 19

I stared at my open notebook. The clock on my bedroom wall ticked.

This was too much pressure. Too much. Not only did I have to perform perfectly on a double date in a mere twenty-four hours for the tie-breaker round, but I was also supposed to finish brainstorming this whole dance routine for the talent show by Monday.

Fine. Totally fine. Living the dream.

Before I could even start choreographing, I had to decide on the style of dance and a song. When I danced in middle school, I'd no clue what went into the developmental process. Now, one wrong decision and I'd embarrass the popular boys in front of everyone.

My phone vibrated on my desk.

Asher Prick: Don't forget about tomorrow

I groaned and slammed my forehead on the desk.

"You're already here."

I glanced up from my world history textbook at the sound of Asher's voice. His shadow towered over the bench I'd claimed in the Escape the Circus lobby an hour ago. The rare winter afternoon sun streaming through the windows had me lifting my hand as a visor to see him.

My heart lurched. Unfortunately, Asher was one of those naturally attractive people who didn't need to do much to impress. His dark hair was down today for once. He was clean-shaven too, not a stray hair out of place. The plowed snow piles lining the downtown road beyond the windows glistened in the sunlight, and it made him appear almost magical.

He looked good. Really good.

Which meant he was definitely trying to upstage me on our double date. I couldn't make out what he was wearing beneath that peacoat, but he must've dressed up, and for that very reason. My basic collared shirt and cuffed jeans could never compare.

The absolute audacity.

"Early is on time," I said through clenched teeth. "On time is late. So I got here two hours early."

Asher studied the sign above the counter to our right, which had *Escape the Circus* spelled out in an ominous dripping font, then me again. "You're not bored?"

"I brought homework." Which was the most boring activity in the world, so this was technically a lie. But the payoff of seeing Asher's stunned face upon realizing I'd beat him at his own *be early* game was well worth the pain.

I couldn't wait to see that same stunned face again when I performed perfectly today, wowing our double dates. I'd make sure he'd have no other choice but to accept me once and for all, no more flip-flopping.

Asher sat beside me on the bench, pulling out his wireless earbuds. He stuffed them into a pocket of his peacoat. A framed cartoon lion with balloons tied to its tail hung behind him. The two shared an eerily similar mane. "You got my email? With Brooklyn and Anya's info?"

"Yep."

"They're two of our most loyal borrowers. They volunteered to help us out since they're aware of your"—he paused—"unique situation, so don't screw this up."

"Don't plan to."

"Good."

"Great."

Three cars passed by the escape room, sending snowy sludge onto the sidewalk.

Asher glanced at my world history textbook spread open on my lap. The window in front of us. My textbook again. His shoulders were tense. "The Mongols."

"Yep."

"They caused some problems, right?"

"Um, yeah."

Another car. Another sludge pile.

Just as I was about to attempt some miserable small talk about the weather, Asher started to speak as well, and our voices clashed.

"You go," I said.

"No, you go."

"It's fine."

"Never mind."

I cleared my throat. Jeez, this was painful. "We don't have to talk."

We sat in silence and waited for our dates over the next forty minutes. Every so often a group exited the "circus," cheering about how they'd solved some unknown teamwork puzzle. The couples, however, always seemed one insult away from blocking each other on every social media platform. I had no clue what to expect when we entered. I had never been. The building allegedly had more than ten secret rooms with varying themes, which they refused to disclose online.

Asher wanted me to fail this final escape round as much as I wanted to win. Odds were he'd try his best to make me crack under the pressure tonight. I couldn't let that happen.

I had to be a perfect boyfriend.

Snow crunched outdoors as a sleek Toyota pulled up to the curb. The back door opened, and two girls stepped out, one in a fuzzy coat and one without a coat entirely.

Asher left the lobby and stepped outside to greet them, then whoever was inside the car. The two girls rushed up to Asher, slamming into him for the most intense group hug I'd ever seen. One even gave him a kiss right on the cheek.

My eyes sprung wide. According to the club's training handbook, which I'd finally gotten around to skimming thoroughly, "off-limits touching" wasn't allowed between members and borrowers. Kissing *had* to be off-limits.

But Asher didn't shrug the girl off. Even more shocking,

he was smiling, which looked more genuine than the one he reserved for Ms. Vora.

That thoroughly pissed me off. Asher could beam at two random borrowers and even let them douse his cheeks in kisses, but he could barely spare me a single smile?

As the car drove off, the three stepped inside.

"Brooklyn here's with me," Asher said to the coatless edgelord. She was as pale as the snow in contrast to the other's light-brown skin, and even though her sheer black tights must've helped combat the cold somewhat, there were plenty of rips exposing her bare legs.

That meant the one wearing a baby-blue hijab and fuzzy coat was with me. The smile she gave was as warm as sunshine. "Anya."

I smiled back. "Noah."

Brooklyn, however, frowned at me through her black lipstick, stuffing her hands in her plaid miniskirt pockets. "Thanks, I guess, for hanging with us."

I didn't understand why I was being thanked. They were the ones doing me a favor.

Before I could respond, Asher showed me an infuriating smirk. "Ready, Byrd?"

With that, they approached the lobby counter, and I trailed behind. A receptionist blasted us with a confetti popper. We jumped. "Welcome to the Circus! How many?"

Asher held up four fingers.

While the receptionist took our coats, Asher placed five twenties on the counter.

"Whoa." I pulled my wallet out of my back pocket. "I can pay for myself."

"You're a prospective member," Asher said. "The rules state that the club must cover the necessary costs of a member's required rounds."

I frowned, even though this was a bizarrely thoughtful gesture. "Last I heard, the club's fund is empty. That's why, you know, I need to teach you all how to dance and win that talent show next month? Until your members start getting paid more again?"

"Good thing my personal funds are still alive and kicking, then."

I glanced at his crumpled stack of twenty-dollar bills again. "Your funds? Not your mom's?"

"Yeah. Well. My mom forgets sometimes."

"To, what, give you money?"

A hint of a grimace showed on Asher's face. It was just enough to convey he'd meant less about the money and more about himself.

It left me at a loss for words. A swarm of staff members snuck up behind us and wrapped blindfolds around our eyes before I could think up a response. Another staff member introduced herself to us as the circus ringleader. She made us follow her into a room much colder than the lobby. After a minute of walking, a door slammed shut behind us.

"You may now take off the blindfolds!" the ringleader announced.

I ripped mine off.

A clown stood a mere inch away from my face.

Asher screamed at the top of his lungs, and I jolted. He tripped backward and away from a *second* clown. His back slammed against a wall.

Brooklyn and Anya laughed, unafraid.

A grin rose on my face. "You good?"

Asher searched wildly around the escape room, presumably for the nearest fire extinguisher to knock every clown over the head. Eventually, he composed himself well enough to come over to our group again.

Maybe I was eviler than these killer clowns for finding humor in Asher's freakout, but I couldn't help it. Asher Price was practically squirming.

Asher Price. *Squirming.*

"Welcome to the Clown Car!" the ringleader said, standing on a crate. "You have one hour to figure out how to escape from the clowns who have kidnapped you."

As she explained the rules, I inspected the area. It was no bigger than the theater basement's tiny interrogation-style room. The bloodstained walls were curved, metallic plexiglass windows and side doors lined the sides, and realistic passenger and driver seats were installed at the front, complete with a dashboard and gearshift.

With the rules defined, a digital timer on the wall started counting down from sixty minutes, and our mission began. The four clowns still stood before us. Three of them stared while one honked a horn.

Asher's mouth twisted.

"You're really not a fan of clowns, huh?" I asked.

"Love clowns," he lied.

"Then you'll love the next fifty-nine minutes."

"Sure will."

I laughed, but the hilarity of the situation dwindled once I reminded myself why we were standing in this killer clown car in the first place. Escape rooms brought out the worst in people. To pass Asher's final test, I had to escape this room while acting like a perfectly poised boyfriend. These three weren't going to help with that. Especially not Asher.

But I still had to try to work alongside my date the way a good partner would, so as calm and collected as possible, I started walking toward Anya.

"Byrd, get over here!"

Asher hovered over the dashboard and gearshift, searching for clues.

Or not. My brow furrowed.

Brooklyn and Anya were cheering on the clowns, who had shifted to popping balloon animals. They were clearly too preoccupied to help, so I joined Asher instead.

He attempted to shove the fake gearshift into drive, only to realize there were no keys in the fake engine. "We need keys." His voice was quick and tense.

"You really want to get out of here, huh?"

"Shut up."

I checked the tattered fabric seats. No keys on the driver or passenger sides. No keys on the dashboard either. No keys on the ground. I swiveled around to face the four clowns again; a key ring was attached to the back of one's fuzzy belt.

I walked over to the clown on the very left, grabbed the key ring, and returned to the front of the room. Once I stuck the keys in the fake ignition, the fake dashboard lit up.

Asher went for a high five. "Good one."

My stomach flipped at the praise. I hesitated before high-fiving him back. "Yeah."

Now that the keys were in, he reached for the gearshift again.

"Wait!" I grabbed his hand to stop him.

The touch made Asher flinch, like I'd shocked him with a clown's joy buzzer. "What?"

"What's your logic behind putting the car in drive?"

"It's something. And it's there." His logic was compromised from wanting to escape as fast as possible.

"We'll still be stuck with the clowns in the car with us, though." I pointed at the door-lock controls beside the dashboard. "Why don't we first try to unlock the four doors and leave through one? That's low-risk."

I had no clue why I was challenging Asher Price. Trying to change his mind was as easy as getting a legal name change.

"Sure," Asher said, and left it at that.

Not what I was expecting. It even felt like we were working together.

I pressed all the unlock buttons as suggested. A clicking sound effect played over the ceiling speakers. The four doors must've unlocked.

Asher immediately headed toward the door aligned with the driver's seat.

Except there was no way we'd already successfully escaped the clown car. It'd only been a few minutes, and fifty more were left on the timer. Nothing was ever that simple.

"Hold on!" I chased after him. "I'm guessing only one of these doors will lead us the right way. There must be a longer puzzle to know which one."

"Or we could open all of them and see."

"But there might be something bad behind the wrong—"

Too late. Asher was already opening the first door he'd set his sights on.

A whipped-cream pie slapped him right in the face.

The clowns in the killer clown car cackled. Their ringleader cackled. Brooklyn and Anya cackled. A fifth clown emerged from the door Asher had opened and cackled the hardest. The sound would probably give him nightmares.

I walked up to Asher. "Want to try a different door?"

Even though his face was covered with whipped cream, I could sense him glaring at me.

To keep working as a team, I had to lift his spirits. So I started walking toward another door. "Here. I'll take a pie for the team, too."

I reached for the handle.

"What? No!" Asher rushed toward me, bits of whipped cream dripping off his face and onto the floor. But the door was already opened.

Two of the clowns pressed their palms to our backs, then shoved us through the door and into a dimly lit room the size of a closet. They locked the handle with a click.

"Oh no!" the ringleader exclaimed outside the door. "The killer clowns now have two prisoners. The others must help them escape!"

Muffled sounds of Anya's and Brooklyn's jabbering followed.

Asher and I stood there in the empty room. Totally still.

Until I finally broke the silence. "My bad."

CHAPTER 20

I expected Asher to tell me I'd screwed up big-time. That if only I'd had better boyfriend skills—listening, communication, foresight, *something*—we wouldn't be locked in a room without our dates. And now that Brooklyn and Anya were our last hope at escaping, which was not going to happen, my last chance at becoming a member of the Borrow a Boyfriend Club was over.

Asher just sighed. He sat on the concrete floor, up against the wall, and let his head fall back. Big chunks of whipped cream clung to his hair.

Not knowing what else to do, I joined him on the floor. The space was so cramped that our shoulders touched.

Asher glanced at them uncomfortably.

"Sorry," I blurted. "Should I stand, or—?"

"You're fine."

A loud thud came from behind the door. Brooklyn and Anya yelped in the distance.

"I thought off-limits touching wasn't allowed between members and borrowers," I said.

"Huh?" Asher was untucking his baggy sweater from his belt so he could wipe his face. The hem was lifted toward his chin, revealing his bare stomach. Which was toned. Very toned. As he cleaned up, he accidentally knocked an elbow into my chest. "Sorry."

My whole body tensed, and I flicked my gaze away. "You're good. Um. Brooklyn touched you, like, a lot. And kissed you on the cheek when you first saw her."

Asher stopped wiping his face and pulled his sweater back down, allowing the weird tension in my chest to dissipate. "Anya and Brooklyn are exceptions."

"Why?"

"They're together. A couple."

"Okay."

"And Brooklyn's parents believe God forgives murderers and cheaters and liars as long as you're straight."

"Oh."

"They borrow me and Lenny from time to time to keep Brooklyn's parents from learning the truth. According to them, Brooklyn and I have been dating for over a year."

"A year?" I asked. "But the thirty-dollar base rate existed then."

"Twenty-nine ninety-nine."

I chose to ignore that. "Sounds super expensive for them, right?"

He hesitated. "They've always been an under-the-table situation with me."

I wasn't expecting that. Asher had *never* charged Brooklyn and Anya because he felt . . . sympathy?

Sympathetic. Asher. Was that why he wasn't asking borrowers to pay anymore too?

There was so much about him I didn't understand. Like why he told the school to go screw themselves over outdoor lights. Or why he'd let me sail through so much of the membership process when more than seventy others had failed, only to reject me after I killed round three and when everyone else wanted me to join. I didn't understand his logic behind anything.

I wanted him to make sense for *one second*.

It seemed like we were going to be stuck together for a while. Now was a convenient time to dig in. "Is the school ever going to install those outdoor lights?"

He smirked at the dusty floor, but it held bitterness. "You heard."

"Overheard. You were in the office, and I sort of—"

"Spied on me?"

I started to form my rebuttal, but Asher kept going. "They told me they won't consider the matter further because of my"—he lifted air quotes—"attitude. Whatever that means."

"Well. You defiled the lawn. And the back pond."

"They didn't catch me axing up the pond."

I frowned at him. "So? You could've hurt yourself."

"Whatever. I'm going to the news next, so the lights will be installed one way or another. It's just taking longer than I thought. Then everything will be right again."

Longer than I thought. That sounded familiar.

"Constance mentioned you've been waiting on something

to happen before you start charging borrowers again. Does it have to do with the lights?"

Asher didn't speak for a moment. "Did you hear about that student who got mugged around the corner from here? Last October. On a Thursday night."

The news sounded vaguely familiar. I couldn't place it among the many monthly robberies and pickpocket stories that happened in downtown Ann Arbor.

He didn't wait for me to answer. "A freshman was near Heron River High when he got held up by someone with a switchblade, who took all his stuff. He managed to get away, but the school didn't even want to install some measly lights afterward."

"Why not?"

He shrugged. "Lack of funds. Lack of time. Lack of giving a shit. Ever notice how adults never care until it's too late? If he'd gotten stabbed and died, there would've been streetlights and security cameras up the next morning."

"How come you care so much?"

"I don't. Forget what I said."

A buzzer went off beyond the door, signaling a mistake made. A metal pipe running along the ceiling shook and rattled.

Then it was quiet.

"He was my borrower that night," Asher mumbled. "The incident was my fault. So was all the damage control we had to do."

"What?"

Asher scrubbed his face. "He ended up transferring schools. Didn't feel safe at Heron anymore. I should've walked him home from the Homecoming dance. Driven him home. Something. Not let him go off by himself."

"Hey, whoa. Wait. You can't blame yourself because someone got mugged by someone else."

"That's not just it. I also blame myself for making the club look bad. Everyone at school knew I was his date and bailed. They blamed every member. It's taken months to get back so many borrowers."

"Well, you still have a whole fan club. You're regaining everyone's trust."

"Gradually." He huffed. "I mean, our requests were down for the Valentine's Day formal. That's why I refuse to let us charge lately and rely solely on tips. I've been trying— failing—to make up for my mistake."

Asher always came off as strict and icy, but as he discussed the possibility of the club crumbling, he was igniting into a raging fireball fueled by enormous dedication. He worked so ridiculously hard on this club.

Why?

If the guilt haunted him, why hadn't he just quit?

Another glob of whipped cream fell off Asher's forehead and onto his jeans. "Dammit," he hissed at his lap. "Where does this stuff keep coming from?"

A short chuckle bubbled out of me. I pulled my shirt cuff over my palm and reached for Asher's forehead to wipe off the residual whipped cream. "There."

"Thanks." Asher let himself laugh a bit too. The rarest sound in the universe. My stomach leapt at how twinkly and high and oddly innocent it sounded.

Our faces were close. Inches apart.

Asher studied me in the dim light, and my whole head

flared with heat. His gray eyes traveled from my eyebrows to my nose to my cheeks, inspecting my every imperfection.

Our faces were cast in so many shadows that I didn't mind. Still, I could see when his gaze landed on my lips. And when his hand drifted toward me, closer and closer, until the warmth of his palm moved to my thigh.

My heartbeat pounded everywhere through me. A strange pull in my chest tempted me to close the distance. I started to lean forward.

"Byrd—"

The door whipped open on its hinges and slammed against the wall.

We jumped and split apart. Fluorescent lights from the killer clown car blasted into our tiny closet and nearly burned our eyes out of the sockets.

A clown stood in the doorway with hands on its hips.

Asher startled so much that he screeched and knocked his head against the wall. Again.

Brooklyn rushed over. "Get out! We have fifteen seconds left before they eat us alive."

"Did you save them?" Anya hollered behind her shoulder.

My blood pumped so loudly in my ears that I could hardly hear them, my whole body tingling and burning. "Yeah. Yeah, you saved us."

Asher stayed silent. Too silent. He rose to his feet and returned to the clown car room. Like nothing had ever happened.

By the time I returned as well, the digital countdown clock on the wall had already been replaced by a single phrase written in red.

YOU FAILED.

CHAPTER 21

Asher Prick: Have you finished the dance routine draft?

My heart jumped at the sight of his name on my phone as I lay in bed on Sunday. I'd only woken up ten seconds ago, but the time stamp on his message read three in the morning.

Why was he messaging me in the middle of the night? Why was he thinking about me instead of sleeping?

A moan released from my deepest depths as I stuffed my head in a pillow. Tomorrow. I had until tomorrow to choreograph a routine for the club talent show happening a mere three weeks from now. That was our agreement, and I still hadn't chosen a song. I hardly cared now, though. All I felt was mortification after nearly kissing Asher again.

That *was* what had happened, right?

There was no way I'd meant to. I'd just wanted to wipe whipped cream off his face. Or I'd fallen forward because I was passing out in fear of the killer clowns. Fear can be contagious.

I didn't *like* like Asher. I didn't even like Asher.

I hated Asher.

After a few groans, I grabbed my laptop. Until the meeting on Monday, I wouldn't know my true fate. For now, I had to focus on what would win a talent show.

Not ballet. Too personal. Not a waltz. Too slow. And if we were being judged by a Tony Award winner, a story needed to be told. One that would stick out among the competitors.

I forced myself to spend my Sunday morning watching trending dance-routine videos in bed. Each sparked something in my brain. It was one thing to watch and learn how to perform. But choreographing was the equivalent of a professional racecar driver attempting to build a car with spare parts in his garage. An entirely different skill.

And I hadn't danced in four years. Not seriously.

Once I'd digested enough inspiration, I picked up all the dirty clothes off my floor, tossed them into the hamper in my closet, and stood at the center of my bedroom. The door was shut. Mom or Dad wouldn't catch me this time.

Breathing deeply, I watched my reflection in a wall mirror do the same warm-ups my teachers had made us do at my old studio. My fingers could barely touch my toes. Great start. Then I watched the slowed-down movements of a viral tutorial. I could do that.

Replaying the video, I danced along at a normal speed and did so fine. Naturally.

It was strange. Different. In middle school, I'd loved the way dance was so expressive. But I spent a lot of time thinking about how my body performed each movement. A surface-level joy fought against an icky dread residing deep within my own skin. Emotions had raged a civil war inside me, clashing their conflicting desires like swords.

This time, at nearly seventeen, there was no dread as I watched my reflection in the mirror. No ick. I cycled through the steps again, trying to make each movement feel like they had in middle school, but more confident—until I rammed my toe right into my bed frame. I yelped, hopping around until I landed on my desk chair.

Okay. This was going to take way longer than I'd already assumed. I didn't only need to figure out a story to this dance, I needed to remember *how* to dance.

Picking my phone off my desk, I pressed on Asher's name and sent a message.

> **Noah Byrd**: can I get an extension?

He answered three seconds later.

> **Asher Prick**: No

I was about to beg him for mercy and tell him I'd do anything he wanted when another message buzzed on my phone.

> **Asher Prick**: Unless you tell me I'm the best club president in the whole wide world

Was he joking? I rapidly typed my response.

> **Noah Byrd:** No

Then I slammed my phone down.

Another vibration. With a huff, I peeked at the screen.

> **Asher Prick:** Don't worry. You're going to do a great job

My insides flooded with butterflies, and I instantly slapped my stomach to make it stop. What the hell was going on with me?

Still, it was nice to hear he believed in me. That anyone did. I picked up my phone one last time.

> **Noah Byrd:** thanks

I sighed at my desk. If I didn't get my act together, then showing Asher this mess of a routine would be as mortifying as the time I hummed "The Borrow a Boyfriend Club Theme Song" in front of his house.

Tilting my head, I glanced over at my laptop. My cursor blinked in a browser search bar, still waiting to be told what song to play during our performance.

Everyone *did* know the club's theme song.

I tripped on a costume rack as I stumbled into the Borrow a Boyfriend Club's territory.

As I regained my balance, I hiked my backpack higher on my shoulder, trying to play it cool. Of course, I couldn't walk straight. I'd pulled an all-nighter trying and failing to think of a story to tell through a short performance, using the club's nightmare of a jingle. Now my stomach was in knots, knowing I'd only been able to choreograph a painfully normie routine concocted from a mix of dance trends.

If I wasn't even impressed, then would the other members be? Would Anita Kömraag?

Beside the Sebastian Shrine, Lenny had stopped mid-lifting a keyboard onto a stand to flick his head my way. I assumed Asher hadn't told them how poorly I'd done at the final escape round since Lenny had so much twinkling hope in his eyes. "There you are!"

The keyboard slipped from his grasp and slammed onto the carpet in a chorus of clashing vocal synth sounds.

"Pascha's gonna slice you," Camilo droned beside Lenny. Then he sent me a clear "thanks again for choosing me for the talent show, asshole" glare before going back to his phone. Likely texting Constance.

Asher sat on the bright-red love seat at the very back wall, an army of heart-suit kings and queens and jacks surrounding him. He didn't even care enough to lift his eyes from his laptop. Beside him, the club's music played from the jukebox, as always.

"Asher told me to stop by after your meeting," I mumbled, ignoring the ache in my chest. "To talk more about the show?"

Lenny's eyes zipped to Asher, who still didn't glance up from his screen. Not surprising.

"Thank you for coming," Asher finally said.

He spoke the words casually. Calmly. As if today were any other Monday. Like we *hadn't* been locked in a room together and nearly kissed.

Fine. If Asher was playing this game, then I would, too.

I'd act just as obnoxiously calm. He'd see.

As I walked toward them, I purposely kept my steps as loose and carefree as possible, but my mind still wouldn't stop gaslighting me. Maybe Asher had gone home and chugged a fifth of his mom's vodka to forget about the moment altogether. Or maybe he'd genuinely forgotten about it because our double "date" was *that* unremarkable.

I super casually claimed the available seat beside Asher, his cologne filling the air around us. The familiar pine and citrus scent tickled my nose, and another unexpected rush of nerves lurched through me.

I didn't like him at all. I didn't.

Asher shut his laptop. "I appreciate you three staying after school to meet up. Byrd's here because—"

"Is he a member or not?" Camilo interrupted over by the keyboard, which Lenny was still trying and failing to fix.

My heart sank as I faced Asher. "You didn't tell them yet?"

"No," he said.

Lenny and Camilo stared in anticipation.

Finally, Asher took a deep breath. "He's in. For now."

My brow furrowed.

But we didn't escape the room. . . .

Lenny raced over and practically jumped into my lap, his lanky arms gripping me by the shoulders as he shouted congratulations in my face. I even caught Camilo grinning before he realized what he was doing and switched back to a frown.

"I said *for now*," Asher practically shouted. "Byrd failed the final escape round."

The celebration ended as quickly as it had begun.

"However, I'll offer him a special deal," Asher went on. "Byrd had a point at the Valentine's Day formal. If he dances with us at the club talent show, that'd be a huge advantage for us. Only thing is, if we're performing as the Football and Lamborghini Club, then the student body will assume he's our newest official member. So, I might as well add him to the roster. And per our original agreement, if we win, he can stay. If we lose, he'll be kicked out."

This didn't sound like an award. Not even a deal.

This was another manipulation tactic. Asher was bending rules and giving me chance after chance just to ensure I help secure them the five-thousand-dollar prize. But all I felt was disappointed that Asher feared I'd turn my back on him.

At least now I knew the truth. The moment Asher and I had shared in that escape room had meant nothing to him.

I could refuse his deal, but this club was still my best ticket to proving who I was to the school. The boys also needed me.

More importantly, Asher didn't hold all the cards.

"I'd like to negotiate a better deal," I announced.

His brow hitched. "Excuse me?"

I squared my shoulders in my seat. "Instead of getting kicked out right away if we lose, I at least want my membership to run until the end of term."

Nerves crept up my chest the longer our staredown lasted.

Eventually, he grumbled, "Fine."

He'd agreed.

He'd *agreed*.

I was so proud of myself that I had to hold back a grin. "Good."

Tension hung thick in the air, the fluorescent light buzzing above our heads.

Lenny cleared his throat, shifting his gaze between Asher and me. "Congrats?"

"First dance practice is tomorrow," Asher announced. "Meeting dismissed."

With that, Lenny and Camilo collected their belongings and disappeared through the costume racks.

I picked up my own backpack off the couch and started to follow.

"Byrd."

My legs froze. I glanced over my shoulder.

Asher was focused on me. "Stay back for a second."

I eyed the empty cushion beside him. Earlier I'd felt fine sharing a small couch while Camilo and Lenny were in the room, but now doing so seemed wrong. Especially after what we did in that closet and how coldly he was treating me. If we sat too close, he would probably shove me right off the seat.

I needed to act like I didn't care about Asher as much as he obviously didn't care about me. I coughed. Sniffed twice. "I actually have plans."

I started to head toward the exit.

"Wait!" Next thing I knew, Asher was chasing after me, seizing my wrist to spin me around. His mouth opened and closed a few times. "About what happened between us . . ."

My heart pounded. If Asher was trying to forget about our near-miss mouth smushing, then he was doing an impressively subpar job. "What about it?"

"We're cool, right?" Asher's voice was low, and his gaze

drifted to the frilly Victorian dresses hung beside us instead of looking at my face. I'd never seen him so unsure before.

"Why wouldn't we be cool?" I asked.

"Well, you know that I find you attractive, for one."

The words slammed into me so hard that I nearly toppled over. Asher *hadn't* chugged a fifth of vodka to forget about our time locked up together? There was no way he didn't feel my pulse pounding.

I had so many questions, but one shone in my mind the brightest. "*Me?*"

"Um, yeah." Asher's focus bounced all around the basement walls. This wasn't the bold and overbearing Asher I knew. Maybe this wasn't him. The idea that I was hallucinating made much more sense. Too many reasons why Asher Price shouldn't even glance my way swarmed my brain, too many insecurities that I couldn't fully admit to myself.

"But I'm five-five."

"And?"

"That's short."

Asher smirked. Literally *smirked*. "Short guys are hot."

Spit caught in my throat. I coughed to save myself in time. Asher just stared at me as if he totally didn't just indirectly call me hot.

"Sorry," I managed to get out. He went to pat my back, but I waved him off. "I'm good."

But barely. No one had ever said that to me, and now my stomach was doing weird twists and flips. The wall I'd built up to protect myself was breaking down terrifyingly fast. A part of me was horrified that a jerk like him had this effect on me, that maybe I'd joined the Asher Price fan club. But another part wanted to keep pounding down this wall to see what would happen next.

"I suppose," I mumbled, "I find you attractive . . . as well."

The stiffness in Asher's shoulders and face released all at once. I had that effect on him? He even let out a small sigh of relief. "Cool. Glad we got this out of the way."

He grabbed his tote bag and turned to leave, conversation done.

I furrowed my brow. "That's all?"

Asher stopped to glance over one of his unfairly broad shoulders. "Aren't we on the same page? I just needed to check that you didn't have, like, real feelings for me or something. Club rules and stuff. Members must stay single?"

A second slam to the chest. Except unlike last time, Asher's words felt less like a blast of butterflies and more like being kicked to the ground. He didn't have real feelings for me, and that realization hurt.

Shit. Why did it hurt?

Did *I* like *like* Asher?

Not possible. During our Modernism unit, our English teacher, Ms. Gao, taught that Ernest Hemingway was a pretentious asshole, yet he was also ranked online as the hottest dead author of all time. Asher Price just suffered from the Hemingway Phenomenon. He happened to be an obnoxious human being who I found attractive. That would never become anything more.

I shifted, the Victorian dresses scratching at my arms. "Right."

Asher raked a tense hand through his hair. "Look, there's

a reason why my brother put these rules in place. He always knew how to protect the club. And he knew how to market it perfectly. My brother's right about everything. Always."

I hated to agree with Asher on anything, but I got where he was coming from. The club's reputation and marketability were based on each boy being single, attainably unattainable. Let's just say Asher and I lived in a reality where we were madly in love like in those rom-coms. We couldn't be together. Not as long as we both refused to walk from the club.

Neither of us would ever want that reality, anyway. He was Ernest Hemingway. Hot, but insufferable. And I was Noah Byrd. Quiet and polite. Well, at least compared to Asher.

"So—" I hesitated. "We're . . . friends?"

"Friends?" Asher repeated.

"Yeah?"

"Right." His mouth quirked up as he considered, and my whole body heated. He hadn't possibly always been this attractive. He *hadn't*. "Friends."

Except even if we were just friends, that didn't erase the obvious chemistry between us.

Chemistry. Me. With someone else. The day I never thought would happen in a million, bazillion years.

How would this *not* be the most awkward month of our lives?

CHAPTER 22

"The sky is falling! The sky is falling!"

Lenny's voice echoed through the theater a few octaves higher than usual. He stood onstage holding a script and was flimsily tossing his arms through the air. Beside him, that same girl I'd seen rehearsing lines about an alien invasion on the first day I'd ever stepped into the theater asked why he thought the sky was falling.

Lenny hopped and shuffled to the left. Instead of answering the girl like a normal human being, he broke into a song and dance about how a little chicken like him knew aliens were taking over the world.

So, the school was doing *Chicken Little: The Musical*. And Lenny played Chicken Little. Coincidentally.

I wanted to laugh, but my stage fright wouldn't let me. In twenty minutes, I had to show the guys a bland, directionless dance routine. While I waited, I watched the musical scene unfold from the lower-bowl section of the audience, biting my hangnails to shreds. Lenny kept attempting a mess of spins and pliés as he continued to sing. It was ballet alphabet soup.

None of those moves were right. At all.

I lifted my head, an idea striking me.

Lenny knew musicals. Weren't musicals just stories set to dance and music?

Maybe he could help.

The drama teacher sitting in the front row called out a sharp "Cut!" then made some end-of-the-day announcements.

Lenny walked offstage and toward the row of seats right in front of mine to collect his belongings. His rainbow tank top and lime-green leggings clashed with his hot-pink hair. Lenny had probably bought them at some designer women's shop when visiting Los Angeles. As always, he could wear clothes "only for girls" and still get called a guy.

"Byrdie!" he called, spotting me. "How'd you like my performance?"

I considered telling him the truth.

"Stellar," I said with a thumbs-up instead.

Lenny suddenly lifted a black shih tzu puppy. A sleigh bell was attached to the puppy's red velvet collar and jingled as Lenny bounced her in his arms. "An honor to receive such praise from the dance master himself!"

I blinked at the puppy. I hadn't picked up on the presence of a furry mammal chilling near me this entire time, but looking closer now, I could make out a pink, fuzzy dog bed.

Lenny glanced down at her in his arms. "This is Poochie! Have you met Mrs. Jacobson yet? She let me bring her for a project on natural selection. Isn't that right, Poochie?"

Poochie stuck out her tongue.

"Nice to meet you," I told the dog, then checked a clock on the wall. Five minutes until practice. "Can I ask you a question?"

He nodded, hiking Poochie higher on his waist.

"So, the routine is in great shape," I said, like a liar. "But to stand out to Anita, I want to add something compelling."

Lenny gasped. "Emoción."

"R-right," I said. "The thing is, I'm probably not as good of a storyteller as you. Since I'm newer around here, can you think of anything that could relate to the Italian club? You know, to really sell it?"

"Storywise?" He pondered until his mouth formed an O. With a free hand, he dug a stack of laminated booklets from his backpack.

"What are those?"

"Our emergency supplies." He displayed the booklets with brown covers first. "These here are pocket-sized Italian dictionaries." Then the blue ones with fancy cursive titles. "These are old Italian folktales. Handy little things. When we meet outside the basement and need to pull off our guise, we whip these out."

Folktales. That idea had potential.

I had no clue if the stories inside them would actually help, but I was out of time. If I had to wing this lesson today, then this was my best bet. "Can I borrow one?"

Lenny randomly picked out and offered me a booklet. "The pages have an English translation side. Oh, and if you need to re-work any choreo, my musical brain might be able to help ya out."

"Thanks," I said, shoving the booklet into my back pocket.

"Um. Could you keep this from Asher? That I asked for your help?"

Poochie yapped as Lenny zipped his smiling lips with his free hand.

"Stop harassing our dance instructor with your dog," Asher interrupted from the main door. He stood beside Camilo, who wanted to be anywhere but here.

My eyes spread looking at Asher, or, rather, what he was wearing. He was in an outfit that I never imagined I'd witness on his body: a plain white tee and sweatpants.

His arm muscles shifted visibly as he stretched. "Everyone onstage. It's already two minutes past four."

I flicked my gaze toward the stage floor marked with scrapes and gaffer tape, the domed ceiling, anywhere other than at him. Surviving today would be hard enough knowing I needed to teach three left-footed boys how to dance to a barely completed routine. Hiding that I kept mentally replaying that scene of Asher and me in the escape room—and what would've happened if we'd kissed—would make this way harder.

No one could ever find out about that moment, but *especially* not Lenny and the other members. Not when they were being forced to follow the first rule of the club.

I shook my head to knock some sense into myself. There was nothing real between me and Asher, so there was nothing to worry about.

Lenny set Poochie back in her fuzzy dog bed, then led the way up the left side of the stage. The rest of us followed. As we placed our stuff onstage, the *Chicken Little* musical cast filtered out of the theater, giving us looks for invading their territory.

Once I started playing a pop-music playlist on my phone, the three boys formed a straight line. Time for warm-ups.

And I was in a sweatshirt. With only a simple black tee underneath.

I froze. The realization that I'd be sweating at practice hadn't occurred to me when I'd gotten changed this morning. The shirt I was wearing came nowhere close to the looseness of even my collared shirts. I'd be on full display. But I couldn't suffer through this practice in several layers, sweating the whole size of Lake Michigan.

Chill, Noah. It was just Asher and Lenny and Camilo. It was fine. I was *fine.*

Before pulling off my sweatshirt, I checked the audience for any nosy bystanders, then the backstage areas on both wings. The coast was clear. Taking a deep breath, I yanked my sweatshirt off and tossed it aside on the stage, leaving me in the black tee.

The sensation wasn't as bad as I thought. I actually was a bit relieved.

"There are three weeks left until the talent show," I said after warm-ups, whipping the booklet Lenny gave me out of my back pocket. "Good thing is, I hold the key to our success in my very hand."

"One of our emergency supplies?" Camilo muttered across the stage.

"Art needs to tell a story for it to be impactful, right? That includes dance. Especially when we need to impress a Tony Award–winning actor. She'll eat this up."

Lenny nodded with so much vehement passion that his

pink hair flopped against his forehead. Beside him, Asher, however, watched me, scrutinizing my every word.

The pressure of pulling this off had already formed knots in my stomach. "We'll act as characters from an Italian folktale while dancing to 'The Borrow a Boyfriend Club Theme Song.'" Or. "Even better . . . the Italian version! Anita will love the dramatics. Teachers won't question anything since we're the Football and Lamborghini Club."

Stares were the only response. A draft blew, curtain rigging squeaking backstage.

I smiled with a shrug.

"Genius!" Lenny finally announced unnaturally loudly, elbowing Asher and Camilo. "A wonderful, unique idea! A lot of borrowers in the audience should find it funny too, knowing it's the theme song Pascha wrote for us, yeah? Since it's always playing in the basement whenever borrowers come in."

Camilo slowly nodded. "Isabella could make us some sick costumes."

Asher still hadn't given up on his scare tactic stare. "Which folktale did you choose?"

"Oh." I flipped the cover over to see which one Lenny had given me. "*The—*"

My mouth froze as the title slapped me in the face.

Was I reading this right?

Camilo walked over to inspect the front cover. There was a delayed reaction before he spoke too. "*The Ass That Lays Money?*"

Lenny winced, then mouthed a *sorry*.

"Correct." I forced a bright smile, but on the inside, I was sobbing.

"The folktale is about—" I speed-read the cover's summary while simultaneously keeping a calm aura as if I'd been preparing for this since the womb. "A widow and her only son. Right. She . . . sends him off to ask his uncle for money to keep from starving, and he gives them . . ."

"A little ass that lays money," Asher finished. "I'm familiar with the story."

"*Ass* better mean *donkey*," Camilo said with a hitched brow.

I lifted a defensive hand. "It does! It does. We can speak some of the folktale dialogue during the performance to really drive home the theme. We'll represent the son, the uncle, the landlord, and the . . ."

Everyone traded looks with one another.

"We should assign roles based on Types," Lenny suggested, bending over to readjust his green leggings. "The donkey is the main character, so our club president should—"

"I'm not being a donkey," Asher said, arms crossed. I once again forced myself to ignore the flex of his muscles.

"I'm the evil landlord," Lenny went on anyway, "Camilo's the rich uncle, and Byrdie's the honorable son who owns the donkey."

They turned toward me, waiting for my gavel to fall.

I shrugged again. "We can try it out?"

Though I still had no clue if we were about to go onstage and become a laughingstock (complimentary) or a laughingstock (derogatory).

An annoyed huff came from Asher, which we took as a yes. I asked Camilo for a link to "The Borrow a Boyfriend Theme Song: Italian Version" to pull up on my laptop, then started to teach my basic routine.

Secretly tweaking the choreography based on *The Ass That Lays Money* proved to be a harder challenge than every genetics square I'd solved that semester combined. Blocking, for one, had to completely change. The beginning of the folktale included everyone except for Lenny's character, so he plopped down nearby to write us a script. Meanwhile, I worked on Camilo and Asher, whose characters had to unfortunately dance beside one another.

Camilo was a natural as usual, but Asher still acted lost in a corn maze. Every few minutes, Camilo shouted "Dude!" in his face, and Asher replied with some variation of defensive profanity. The longer that practice continued, the more I thought the two would break into punches and kicks.

I eventually walked over to tap Camilo on the shoulder. "How about you help Lenny with our dialogue?"

"Finally." Camilo trudged over to Lenny.

When Asher met my gaze, his expression quickly flipped from pissed off to embarrassed. "I don't know why I can't—"

"You can," I interrupted, standing beside him perfectly parallel. "Follow my lead. We'll start with the footwork."

He swallowed, his Adam's apple bobbing. "Okay."

I walked him through the moves. Step three times—right, left, right—then jump with both feet out in slow motion. His movements were choppy, and he kept staring at his feet like he was terrified of making a single mistake. He silently counted each step.

I stopped and lifted his chin with a finger. "Hey, look at me."

He did. Instead of his typical coldness, Asher's face was soft. This Asher had no smirk to give. No condescending eyebrow to raise. This Asher was a nervous wreck.

My chest went all fuzzy and warm. I'd told Asher to look at me, but I hadn't thought that through before I'd spoken at all. He was looking at me. *Really* seeing me. And I felt exposed.

But him watching me was clearly helping. On the second try, his steps were more fluid.

"See?" I said, trying to keep my voice calm. "That was the problem. You're in your head. Let your body take over and do whatever it wants."

Asher's gaze studied my face, dropping slowly toward my lips.

My heart leapt. We were nothing. He felt nothing. I must've been overreacting.

We passed by Camilo and Lenny. Both were examining us closely. *Way* too closely.

Red alert, red alert.

"You suck at this!" I suddenly blurted so loudly that Asher startled. "You're annoying and an asshole, and your feet are like flippers."

His thick brow shot up. "Excuse me?"

"Yeah." My focus drifted back to Camilo and Lenny, whose stares now signaled that they were witnessing wild animals fighting in an alley. "You're the worst!"

Asher was quick to get the hint, clearing his throat and coming back to reality. He brought up a smirk that was laced with venom. "As are you, Byrd."

Lenny and Camilo traded *yikes* faces while keeping up their improvisational spins.

The tightness in my chest dissipated, an excited trill quickly taking its place. The fact that I had this secret with Asher was a rush I couldn't ignore.

Extremely piercing alert of all red alerts.

"Now let's add in the body and arms," I said, much quieter this time. My heart was pumping hard, and I couldn't tell if that was because Lenny and Camilo had been eyeing us or because Asher's body was inches away from mine. "I'll do the same thing, so mimic me."

Asher frowned.

I took that as a yes. "Shake your shoulders and turn your body as you do. Your hip will go to the back and chest to the front. Hip, chest, hip, chest."

As I counted the beats up to seven, Asher did everything he was supposed to. But on eight, he tripped and slammed against my chest, wrecking-ball style.

I let out a choking sound.

"God, man. I can't—" Asher stepped out of my hold, ready to give up.

I pulled him right back into me. "Again."

Without any warning, I twisted his body forward to restart our steps. We moved quicker than last time and eventually fell in sync.

"Good!" I twisted him back for another go.

We did this for a few minutes, expanding further with the head tilts and curling hand waves. Asher had hardly any skill, and I'd forgotten most of mine over the years, but whatever we were doing was working. We could call this dancing.

I was really dancing.

Huh. I missed this.

I laughed as we slid to the left together. "See, you're doing great."

Asher chuckled a bit, too.

Clapping started from the lower bowl of the audience. The alien girl from my first day stood at the bottom edge of the stage. "Wow! I didn't know you guys were learning how to dance."

My limbs locked. My heart stopped.

Someone had been watching. Was I too small to this stranger in a tighter shirt? Asher was a whole head taller than me. His shoulders were broader, and his neck was thicker, and his hands were double my size. Was all of that obvious?

I shoved Asher away from me as fast as I could. He shuffled to catch his balance. The desperate need to grab my sweatshirt consumed my thoughts.

As Lenny started telling the girl about how much fun he was having and how great of a dance instructor I was, I grabbed it and tugged the cotton fabric over my head. Had I covered myself up before anyone saw too much of my body?

"Byrdie?"

Lenny's voice broke me from my daze, but I remained too frozen to speak. Too terrified. A mumbled excuse about needing to leave for dinner left my mouth as I snatched up my backpack and rushed out of the theater.

CHAPTER 23

I wandered the sidewalks that surrounded Heron River High School in a daze.

Boys like me couldn't dance. Boys like me wouldn't be taken seriously doing a musical.

Maybe boys like me could never be enough.

But I wanted to be.

"Byrd!"

I spun around. Asher was jogging toward me. His coat was unbuttoned, revealing his gray sweatpants and a pastel-pink sweater I'd seen him wear in the halls, which he'd thrown on over his plain white tee. His typical tote bag covered in environmental iron-on patches bounced at his side. Everything about him was becoming familiar, and I didn't know what to think about that. "Hey. Hey. What happened back there? You all right?"

I stood still, taking in the way the dull winter sunset turned his complexion warmer than usual. The way his heavy breaths wisped through the air, and the way his chest rose and fell like it had when we stared at each other in that escape room.

"I don't know if I can do this," I finally said.

Asher frowned. A couple with a stroller passed by, followed by a group of Heron River students wearing tie-dye Chess Club shirts. Maybe they were practicing for the show too. He pulled us under the awning of Whimsy Bookstore. Miniature evergreen trees camouflaged us, which were drowned in holiday lights despite it being March. "What do you mean by 'this'?"

"Be the club's instructor."

His shoulders lost some rigidity as if relieved. I assumed he'd be pissed at me until I realized he'd thought my weirdness was somehow his fault. I threw my hands up. "Not everything is about you. This whole dancing thing—"

"You looked like you were having fun."

"I was."

I *was* having fun, and I hated that. Because I was supposed to run away from dance like I did with long hair and pastel sweaters and silver rings and lime-green leggings—

"Then what happened back there?" Asher asked.

"It's just different," I said. "Dancing in front of others. *People* seeing me dance. I'm scared they'll—" I was revealing too much, and the bottle cap keeping all my fears contained threatened to pop.

Surprisingly, Asher's forehead creased with worry instead of annoyance. I tried to ignore the burning desire to tug my hat low enough to cover up my soft cheekbones and long lashes and the baby facial hair on my chin—

Asher grabbed my wrist before I could. "If you want to talk, you can talk to me."

Our touching hands had my chest fluttering. Even through the thin fabric of my gloves, I could feel his icy fingers in the cold.

His touch was enough to unscrew the cap.

"I'm scared they'll figure it out," I muttered at the cracks in the sidewalk. "Start doing what everyone at my old school did to me. They'll make mistakes here. Slipups. Which is why I transferred schools."

"There's nothing to *figure out*."

"You know what I mean."

Asher didn't respond, his grip on my hand loosening. But still there.

I tugged pine needles off the mini evergreen beside me as I began to regret bringing up this conversation. A dead-eyed leprechaun toy perched above me started to yodel about gold, and I startled.

"Why did you quit dancing?" he asked.

His abrupt question threw me more than the leprechaun. "I told you. I didn't like it anymore."

"And I told you I didn't believe that."

"Boys don't dance." The leprechaun wouldn't stop yodeling. I glared at it.

Asher snatched the toy by the neck and chucked its flimsy body down the sidewalk. My eyes widened. "Lenny and Camilo and I are taking dance lessons from you," he said.

I sighed. "How do you feel knowing you're wearing pink right now? Or that your hair has grown out a little long?"

He plucked the front of his light-pink sweater. "Am I supposed to feel something?"

"Exactly. You don't. Guys like you get to have long hair

and wear pastel colors and still be seen as guys. I need to have short hair, and a super manly voice, and super manly clothes, or else people won't think I am one."

I'd never been so honest. Mom and Dad had no clue about this. Neither did the two psychologists I'd been forced to speak to before my top surgery. I couldn't tell them. How would they take me seriously if they knew I was angry that I had to run away from anything remotely feminine? These boys didn't think like that.

Life was unfair. Lenny could dye his hair hot pink or pastel blue and model his mom's makeup line for her viral videos, and Asher could grow his hair to his shoulders, and no one would make a *little mistake*. If I didn't want anyone to make a mistake, then I was stuck with oversized sweatshirts.

I was so *tired* of sweatshirts.

"You're a boy," Asher said suddenly.

My breath caught. "What?"

"What?" Asher shivered as he said it.

"Nothing. Just." I blinked once. Twice. "No one's ever told me that before. At least, not that directly."

"Well, no one's ever told me that I'm a boy, either. Because it's obvious."

My head buzzed too much to form a single coherent thought. If this was so obvious, then why couldn't I see what Asher did?

Maybe I was being too hard on myself.

Asher's shoulders trembled again. He shoved his bare hands in his pockets. His long hair looked scraggly from dance practice, draping over his face in waves, but I could make out the rosiness of his cheeks. He'd never learn how to dress for the snow.

I took off my knit hat with a grin, stepping closer, and pushed it onto his head. "You're the worst."

A hint of a smirk rose to his face as well, which morphed into a soft chuckle that left his lips in a foggy wisp. "As are you, Byrd."

My whole body froze. Too close. *Way* too close.

My phone buzzed in my back pocket, and I pulled it out. Mom. I answered.

"Hi, sweetie," she said. "I spotted you a second ago while leaving the boutique."

Her words were also drifting our way from the sidewalk.

Furrowing my brow, I stepped out from behind the protection of the evergreen trees and away from the bookstore.

"*N!*"

Mom stood beside a shop a few feet away. Of course she'd called for N instead of Noah.

All that warmth from Asher slipped away. "Hi, Mom."

Mom tucked her phone in her purse. She was lugging a plastic bag full of plantains and an enormous jar of chocolate protein mix, bought for Dad. She wore massive faux-feather earrings and a stopwatch necklace that came to her stomach.

"So glad I ran into you. Dad says boxer briefs are two for one at Walmart and is wondering if he should pick some up for you—" Mom's gaze drifted toward my left as Asher joined me on the sidewalk. She scanned from his expensive sneakers up to the hat she'd knitted me that was now on his head. "Who's this?"

I prayed for a passing car to swerve my way and hit me dead-on. None did. So I awkwardly gestured at Asher. "This is my— Uh, Asher."

"*Your* Asher?"

Asher extended an arm for a handshake. "Nice to meet you, Mrs. Byrd. My name is Asher Price. Your son's in my after-school club. I'm the president."

He was strangely more polite. Each word had a bit more energy to it. Like he was on edge.

Mom's eyes practically twinkled. "N didn't tell me which club he'd finally decided on."

Asher opened his mouth, but I cut him off.

"Yep!" I said. "It's an Italian language and culture club. Asher talked me into joining on my first day!" I nudged Asher. The absolute last thing I needed was Mom figuring out I was joining a secret club for borrowing boyfriends. "Right?"

He shifted his gaze between Mom and me. "Sì."

"Wow," Mom said. "Asher, you must be phenomenal at Italian if you're the president. Your club meets quite late, though, doesn't it? It's almost six o'clock. Your parents must want you home earlier than that. N's nearly missing dinner!"

Asher cleared his throat. He must've also sensed the subtle jab Mom was trying to make. "My mom's been out of town."

Mom clapped her hands, causing Asher and I to flinch. "Well, I would love to hear all about this club over a hot meal. I'm assuming you don't have dinner plans if your mom is out of town? Our family has weekly burger nights." She pointed over her shoulder. "There's a place right around the block."

Forty seconds into this conversation with Mom and Asher,

and I had already experienced enough embarrassment to last me a lifetime. There was no way I could survive an entire meal.

"Actually," I interrupted, "I was hoping burger night could be the three of us."

Mom pursed her lips. "Don't be rude, N. You don't want to have a date night?"

My mouth dropped. Never mind—enough embarrassment to last me in the afterlife. *"Mom."*

Asher stared somewhere farther down the sidewalk like he was paranoid someone would overhear the word *date* and bring down the club on the spot. He snapped his gaze back to Mom and smiled. "Thanks, Mrs. Byrd. I'd love to."

But his voice was still off.

Mom didn't notice. "Excellent. I'll call my husband and tell him to skip the boxer briefs so he can meet N's new"—she glanced at my knit hat on Asher's head again—"friend."

CHAPTER 24

When Mom said she knew of a "burger joint" right around the block, she meant one block *closer* to the school. Not one block *away* from it.

I'd never noticed this restaurant before. Most likely because it was in the opposite direction of home, but also because it looked like a five-star banquet hall reserved for people who draped cardigans over their shoulders and purchased yearly yacht club memberships. Uncomfortably romantic jazz music played from above, candles flickered on each table's center doily, and everywhere smelled like roses. The place was giving less "fast food" and more "vital nourishment delicately ice-picked from ancient Antarctic glaciers."

The waiter popped over fast, tapping a spiral notebook with a pen. Instead of saying we were waiting on another guest, Mom said, "I know my husband wants the black bean burger. What are you thinking, Asher?"

"I'll eat anything," he said, but whether that was the

truth or solely for our impatient waiter's benefit, I wasn't sure.

"N always goes for a boring and typical plain burger, so please don't be shy about ordering a stacked bacon cheeseburger. That's what I'm getting."

Boring. *Typical.* Thanks bunches, Mom.

Once Asher settled on the same burger as Mom, the waiter walked off.

Dad stepped through the door soon after and claimed the seat beside Mom. He hadn't changed clothes after his shift at the gym he managed downtown. The tie-dye shirt clinging to his body was so tight that I could make out every curve of his arm muscles. His presence alone dropped the elegant restaurant ambience from a ten to a one. "Hello, hello, greetings! Sorry for the delay. Walmart was like a zoo. But I scored the pack of dinosaur boxer briefs for N." He chuckled to himself.

Dad thought he was a comedian, and of course he had also called me N. It was Noah. Say *Noah.*

Could my name-change court date come *any* sooner? The government clearly had to make things official to them.

I swallowed my irritation. "Hi, Dad."

As Mom and Dad caught up about work, the romantic music continued to swirl around us. Wineglasses clinked at a table beside ours. Laughter.

This was nothing like our weekly burger nights despite what Mom had insisted. This very much gave "double date with my parents."

I sank lower in my chair. We just had to survive an hour. One.

For the most part, Asher and I listened to my parents'

conversation until our food arrived in red baskets. Everyone reached for their burgers and fries except for Asher, who sat silently with his hands on his lap. He looked too terrified to move.

Dad gestured at Asher, then at his bacon cheeseburger. "Dig in."

"Thank you, sir," he said.

"Sir!" Dad beamed in his striped tank top and camo shorts. "What a compliment. But please, call me Josh."

Asher's mouth squirmed. He definitely would not.

At least this got Asher's limbs moving again. He picked up his fork and knife with the posture of a royal prince, his silver rings glistening in the overhead lighting. Instead of picking up his burger with both hands, he started cutting it into perfectly even pieces.

Dad stopped chewing his burger and stared.

Mom took a long sip from her white wine, her chunky charm bracelet clanging against the rim of the glass, and cleared her throat. "So, what's one funny thing that happened to everyone today?"

Dad was quick to tell a story about how he slammed himself into a glass door that had been freshly cleaned at the gym. The two gradually disappeared into their world again, leaving Asher and I trapped in a more intimate silence.

As I racked my brain for a conversation starter, I watched Asher tap his rings against his fork. Most had elaborate logos engraved on the silver bands. The band on his right ring finger, though, was way chunkier and more oversized. The center mimicked a tigereye gemstone but was rosy pink, and a few silver butterfly wings protruded off the sides.

"Big ring," I said quietly enough to not interrupt Mom and Dad.

Asher stopped tapping on the fork. He glanced down as he leaned close to my ear. "Anteros."

"Sorry?"

"One of the seven Greek winged love gods. The design's supposed to represent him."

"Isn't it heavy?"

"Not really." He popped the band off his ring finger. "Wanna try it on?"

"Proposing to me right in front of my parents, huh?"

Asher smirked at that. "I'm as daring as Anteros."

All the spit drained from my mouth. Asher must've noticed because he coughed awkwardly, and any hint of that daring personality he'd bragged about disappeared.

"Excuse me for a moment," he announced to the table. His voice sounded as smooth and unrecognizable as it had earlier outside with Mom. With that, he stood, courteously pushed in his chair, and headed toward the bathroom.

Mom played with her necklace as she watched Asher walk away from the table. "Isn't Asher the most well-behaved boy?"

A nervous laugh tickled at the back of my throat. I picked up my glass of ice water and took a sip.

"Seems so," Dad said. "I'm glad to see you're meeting new people—"

Two familiar figures passed by the window. One had circular turquoise glasses. The other had fluorescent pink hair and held a black shih tzu puppy.

I choked on my water as Lenny and Camilo walked past.

Poochie jumped out of Lenny's grasp, and he hollered something that looked like *Come back, Poochie!*

Camilo followed Lenny past the window, gripping his forehead.

They passed the restaurant in a flash.

I released the biggest exhale of my life. What luck. No one from the club could spot Asher and I sitting in a sultry restaurant together, but especially not Camilo and Lenny, who'd just seen us sparring at practice. All sorts of theories could sprout in their minds.

Dad was continuing to ramble about the gift of human relationships, but my whirling thoughts drowned him out. We had no reason to worry about being seen together. Everything was fine. *Fine.*

Asher reclaimed the chair beside me. He undid the fabric napkin to the right of him, which was folded into some type of bird, and spread it across his lap. "Did you know that the urinals in there are shaped like pickles?"

Lenny scooted by the window again. Poochie was slapping her paws against Lenny's face in an attempt to break free from his hold. Camilo came to Lenny's aide, trying to rip Poochie off his face.

I instantly reached for Asher and shoved his head underneath the table. His head clunked against the underside.

Mom's and Dad's eyes spread wide.

Lenny and Camilo finally crossed the street, heading up the hill that led toward Rich Bitch Street.

I yanked Asher's head out from under the table. His dark hair was a frizzy mess now, and his stare was as wide as Mom's and Dad's. Once he glanced out the window, his jaw tensed. He must've seen Camilo and Lenny in the distance as well.

A nervous laugh burst out of me. I elbowed Asher's arm. "That's something Asher and I do sometimes. Dunking each other. You know, boys being boys!"

Mom and Dad smiled, confused.

"Well, I certainly don't get it," Mom said, wiping her hands with her napkin.

Dad grinned, which meant a very not-funny joke was coming. "Feel free to give his head a good shove underneath the table too, Asher. Love is a battlefield."

"*Dad,*" I practically shouted.

Mom whispered into Dad's ear, and then Dad made a surprised face. "Sorry. Friendship!"

Asher didn't say a word. His jaw remained clenched, his gaze glued to the window. Probably regretting ever agreeing to be my "friend."

CHAPTER 25

Asher had apparently walked to school that morning because his ancient Mustang was in a repair shop for a broken muffler, so we drove him back to Rich Bitch Street after dinner.

As we both climbed out of the car, I told Mom and Dad to leave without me and that I'd endure the twenty-minute walk home, and then I followed Asher up to his porch. I needed to talk to him alone. To no surprise, the windows of his house were dark.

Asher pulled out a jangling set of keys and twisted the door handle. He glanced over his shoulder. "Inviting yourself over, are you?"

"I want to talk," I said.

"Sure." Asher stepped into his dark home, leaving the door ajar.

There was a click, and then a burst of light streamed through the home.

"So?" Asher's voice echoed from somewhere inside. "What are we talking about?"

Awkwardly readjusting my knit hat, I entered.

Beyond the door was the type of spacious foyer I'd seen in movies: fancy tiled floors that could be put on display in a museum and no furniture except for an antique bench against the far wall, sandwiched between two staircases, one on each side. Above the bench hung a collection of artwork showcased in ornate, brass frames.

The squeak of my Converse against the tile bounced around the walls and domed ceiling, where the fanciest chandelier I'd ever seen was hanging. Gold flowers decorated the twisty candle cups, and teardrop crystals dangled off the bottom.

Over by a closet overflowing with winter clothes, Asher peeled off his coat.

I kept mine on. My nose still felt like a chunk of ice in this hollow foyer, which was marginally warmer than outside. Maybe Asher never dressed properly for the winter because he lived in the cold.

Burger night had turned into disaster night, and there was so much to say, but only one word came to mind. "Sorry."

"Nah." Asher's voice was a little more at ease than at the restaurant. "Your parents are nice."

"They aren't perfect."

"They're around."

"Right. Sorry. They'd just called me N a lot during dinner is all."

Asher waited for more.

My honest thoughts kept slipping out around him. "My

mom and dad. They've called me that my whole life. N. Never Noah."

"Isn't N still the first letter of your name?"

"But N is also tied to someone else. Noah is who I am. It makes me wonder if they're thinking about that other person. Wanting that other person. I don't know." I shuffled my feet.

He leaned a hip against the closet, rolling his sweater sleeves up to his elbows and then crossing his arms. Which was distracting, to say the least. "What about Byrd?"

I tilted my head. Despite the club unanimously giving me the nickname, I'd never actually questioned why that didn't frustrate me like N. "No one's ever called me Byrd before you and the others."

"Really?"

"Yeah, but a lot of guys call each other by their last names. So. It's sort of nice."

He nodded a couple of times like he hadn't considered that before, either.

"I didn't mean to make this about me," I said. "You're right that my parents are there, and even though they're weird, I like to think they try."

Asher wandered toward the antique bench at the rear foyer wall. The bloodred cushion upholstery and gracefully curved wood framing reminded me of something found in the theater basement. I wondered if the Prices were so rich that Sebastian had transported some of this luxury furniture into a public high school, and their mom hadn't blinked.

He took a seat and scrubbed his face. "No, I'm sorry. Wasn't trying to make this a contest."

"I know." I stood motionless in front of the door, unsure

where else to go. If there was proper protocol for entering a mansion, Asher wasn't letting me in on the secret. All I could speculate was he didn't want me to. "Do you know when she'll be back home?"

"Don't know. Don't really care."

The air between us was too thick, too suffocating. I studied the artwork hung above Asher instead of looking at him. A staircase packed with bustling crowds, a crashing wave beside Mount Fuji, and one I even knew the name of. *The Last Supper.* Jesus and his apostles were the focal piece of the wall, dining on bread loaves in the largest and most exquisite frame.

Below still sat a silent Asher, legs spread wide and gaze cast toward the floor.

My throat burned. "We shouldn't be friends, should we?"

He let his head hit the wall, stuffing his hands into his sweatpants. "If anyone gets any ideas about us, then the club—"

"Why do you care so much about the club?" It came out so strong that it reverberated through the whole mansion, and I instantly regretted it. "I didn't mean—"

"No." He wasn't as defensive or grumpy as I thought he'd be. "I'm not oblivious. I know that on the surface it looks like we're all about rising to the top of a gross high school popularity food chain or whatever. So, I get it."

"But you *are* popular."

"What?"

"That's your Type. Popular."

Asher smirked. "Popular was my brother's Type. The members decided for him back in the day. I carried the title over to myself, I guess."

"You're not your brother, though."

"I know. Trust me, I know."

"That's not what I meant. I meant that you're your own person."

Asher didn't respond.

The other members didn't bring up Sebastian often. Really, only when they made offerings to the Sebastian Shrine. I wasn't sure if that was a coincidence or there was something Asher wasn't telling me.

"Does it have to do with your brother?" I asked, approaching him until we were only a few feet apart, but I remained standing. Sitting beside him felt too close. Too intimate.

He peeked up at me through a dangling lock of hair. "Does what?"

"The club. Why you care so much."

"Thought we were talking about our Types."

I didn't care about that anymore. All I could think about was why Asher was acting strange. I stared at him and waited for answers.

Asher sighed, his gaze fixed on the chandelier. "My brother's at Yale's School of Management. Camilo's planning on applying there because Sebastian wouldn't shut up about it over winter break. He's started a company, too. On the side. He's already made half a million."

"Seriously?"

"Yeah. First Daticating? First Datecation? Some app that fuses dating and traveling. All I know is, it's successful enough for my mom to fly to Yale every time his business hosts an event or wins an award, even though she didn't fly in for my birthday back in October." He spun his Anteros ring around his finger. "Sebastian's set up to make millions, and I can't even run his high school club, the business that jump-started his career. I'm basically a failure."

"You haven't failed at anything."

"One month into being president, one of my borrowers got mugged. Then the whole school blamed us. Me. Now we're down a member and running out of money to grow the business because I'm not like Sebastian."

"No," I said, "because you've stopped your rates while working hard to convince the school to install those lights. To make things right. You'll bounce back, don't worry."

He kept picking at his ring.

"You said that's what you've been waiting on," I added slowly.

"I know. I know." He paused. "But."

"What?"

"How am I supposed to charge our borrowers in good conscience when I don't have a clue what I'm doing?"

I wasn't sure how to answer. Logic had been chucked out of Asher's brain. "You're not the only one running this club, you know. You have Constance, Isabella—"

"If Sebastian were still in charge, all the members would be happier." He wasn't listening to me. "None of this would've happened. If I'd just—"

"Just what? You've always followed every single one of your brother's rules." I bit my bottom lip. "Even when you were tempted not to."

A strong gust of wind blew against the house. The windows creaked.

"What are you trying to say?" Asher asked, quiet.

"I'm trying to say that maybe that's the problem. The rules."

Asher scoffed.

"I'm serious," I said. "From the moment you took over as president, you've been following *his* plans. Not yours."

"So?"

"So, the club is struggling regardless! Maybe that means it's time for the new president to change things."

Asher shook his head, his dark hair grazing his cheeks, his gaze wandering somewhere deeper in the home. "Sebastian's rules aren't wrong. I'm what's wrong. I'm the one who's not executing and implementing them right."

I knew Asher believed this club had to be perfect. That was why he was so strict. He wanted, *needed*, his members to be perfect too.

Because if the whole club was perfect, then so was he.

"We just have to win the talent show," Asher mumbled to himself as he inspected the chandelier. "You'll help us win, and it'll all be okay." His face was flat. Empty. He looked exhausted.

Maybe I was a cause. Asher had given me so many chances. And I still hadn't passed. I wasn't good enough.

I thought I had been. I should've been.

A mixture of regret and embarrassment churned inside me. "Should I have passed the first round?"

Asher finally looked right at me. His eyes were so blazing and severe that my breath seized. "Of course."

My heart pounded as I held his gaze. Doing so took all my willpower. "You only let me get this far because I made you a deal."

Asher shook his head.

"That's not an answer," I said, struggling to contain the frustration in my voice.

"You probably shouldn't have come in." He gestured at the door. "Go home."

The audacity he had to constantly order me around. To order *everyone* around. "You do realize that if I become a member, you won't be following the rules. You'll be accepting someone who bribed you into getting another chance." I stepped closer. "How come you're fine following certain rules and ignoring others? Are you sure you even *care* about the rules?"

This awoke something in Asher. My question was vague, but we both knew what certain rules I was referring to. He rose off the bench, leaving barely any space between us. "Don't talk about stuff you know nothing about."

"What don't I know?"

"I'll give you till the count of three to leave."

"Are you serious?"

"Three."

Panic bolted through me. I didn't know what would happen when Asher stopped counting, but I stood my ground.

"Two."

"Whatever you want to do to me, just get it over with. Ban me from the club. I'll find another way to prove I'm—"

Asher grabbed the collar of my coat in both hands, shoved me against the wall, and crushed our mouths together.

My eyes shot open, and my lips hardly moved. The world melted around us, becoming a white, static nothing. The realizations came one by one, that his warm chest was pressed against mine, that his lips were on my own and making my insides burn. That this was the threat.

That I wanted this. Really wanted this.

My mouth caught up to my brain, and my wants overpowered all my rationality. I let my tongue meet his. My brain melted to slush. I had never kissed anyone before, but I never expected it to be like *this*.

Asher took this as a cue to go further, his fingers digging into my hips as he lifted me up in one swift motion. My legs wrapped around his waist, and he pinned me against the door, closing any space left between us. "Is this fi—"

I pressed my mouth over Asher's before he could finish, draping my arms over his shoulders, threading my hands through his hair and tugging at the roots. I kissed him until I felt like we'd suffocate each other, until I hoped we could forget the hundreds of classmates who expected us to stay single for their pleasure. For a moment, I selfishly thought about ours, his and mine. Asher gripped my thigh harder as his head dipped lower, kissing underneath my jaw and neck.

My gasp turned into a chuckle. "So, I take it you're fine with breaking a few more rules?"

Asher stopped and lifted his head. He looked transformed, with his dark ruffled hair and flushed cheeks, like a boy I wanted to kiss until sunrise instead of the raging jerk I wanted to punch in the jaw. I let myself stare into the intensity of his deep gray eyes, at his swollen red lips. I felt like I would die if I couldn't go back to kissing him.

But then Asher set me back down.

He swore under his breath and stumbled to the side, dazed

and disoriented like he'd snapped out of a trance. He pulled out his phone. "I'll call you a car."

"What?"

"A car."

"No, I heard you." I just couldn't believe what I was hearing. "You're serious?"

"You can wait here, or . . ." He gestured loosely around the foyer, taking another step back like I was some rabid rodent.

I stared at him, my mouth hanging open in disbelief.

Unbelievable.

No, it was believable. It really, really was.

"I'm done waiting," I said right to his face, and without a second thought, left his house and slammed the door.

CHAPTER 26

Once upon a time, I'd assumed that if someone kissed the life out of you, they'd start paying attention to you more afterward instead of less. But this was Asher Price I was dealing with. I knew better than to expect predictable behavior.

What I hadn't expected was how differently Asher would act compared to after we'd almost kissed in the escape room. After that day, he'd transformed into a tiny fifth grader attempting to give a speech for the first time whenever he'd spoken to me, his voice shaking and eyes darting all over the place.

But now, he was flying right by me on his way to talk to Camilo and Lenny at our dance practices held twice a week. And during our five-minute break, he only asked them specifically if they wanted anything from the vending machines.

My fury convinced me to tap him right on the shoulder. "Let's practice the end where you and I dance together."

"Sure."

That was all he said.

We practiced in silence. Asher didn't show a single awkward face, didn't act remotely uncomfortable moving his body so close to mine. He seemed bored. Indifferent.

After our double-date disaster at the escape room, Asher had at least actively avoided my presence because it mattered to him. *Affected* him. Now my presence didn't matter to him at all. He never ended up answering my question that night in his house—if we should still be friends—but now he was clearly answering with actions instead of words.

We weren't even friends.

We were nothing.

* * *

Weeks of Asher ignoring me turned into a month.

Midterms were taken, weekend morning shifts at Bitterlake Coffee weren't filling up the name-change piggy bank fast enough, and weekly burger nights were nearly impossible to endure, with Mom asking about Asher regularly. Aiden started asking me to sit with him at lunch, and soon, Everett and half the football team were circling the table too.

Liam's absence led to Constance asking me to take on requests at Bowling Lane City and the Holi festival in Detroit. Even though the idea of finally entertaining borrowers without other members judging me should've calmed my nerves, I was only more on edge.

Performing perfectly was the expectation now. What if I didn't match my date's energy? Or shared an opinion that made them chuck water in my face? Or didn't look as manly as they hoped?

But once the dates started, my borrowers' laughs and stories quieted those worries. I was too focused on them to care how I looked or talked. Dating was never as scary as I thought it would be, as long as I was myself.

So, by the time our eighth practice came around, I didn't even bother trying to snag Asher's attention. I did my job as an instructor and left him alone.

Halfway through the session, a group of Asher's fans snuck into the back row of the lower bowl. They laughed and shushed each other like they didn't want to be detected, but the way they were pointing their phones toward Asher to take pictures was a much bigger giveaway.

Instead of overlooking his adoring fans like usual, Asher waved at them.

He *waved* and showed the tiniest hint of a smirk.

I stopped dead in my tracks while dancing with Lenny. Lenny said something, I thought, but it sounded like distant, garbled nonsense in my head.

Asher could show that much kindness to classmates he barely knew, but none to me.

Something inside me cracked.

The rest of the hour passed by in a fog. Once six o'clock struck, we started packing up our things. Asher's fan club was quick to swarm him onstage. *Are you really dancing at the talent show, Asher? You look great in those sweatpants, Asher.* Asher said something that made all of them laugh. Whatever he said was probably as funny as a doorknob.

Irritation shot through me. I wanted to shout that Asher couldn't care less about them. I needed space. I needed air.

I swiped my belongings off the stage and left. My backpack clunked roughly against my spine as I slid down to the floor outside.

Every day, I was trapped with Asher. Two hours every Tuesday, Thursday, and Friday for dance practice, and another two hours every Monday and Wednesday when the club met. There was no escape from witnessing him speak to everyone except me, from this overwhelming pain in my chest whenever he proved how fine he was with whatever we had being over.

How could I survive this for another week, let alone until the end of the school year, just to keep trying to prove myself? Sure, I'd never have to worry about the little mistakes and slipups starting again. People respected those at the top of the social hierarchy. But then this game with him would keep on going.

And going.

And going.

I didn't know which situation sounded worse.

It was a ridiculous thought. An embarrassing one. Proving I was enough should've been more important than anything else. Especially more important than my mess with Asher. No little mistakes had been made for months now, but that didn't mean anything to me yet. Not when, if I failed at becoming a member, the whole school could assume I wasn't a good enough boy. They'd change on me in a snap.

Especially if they found out what my old classmates knew.

Although Asher had found out. He'd never changed. But what were the odds that'd be true for the other four hundred students here?

Aiden, Isabella, Constance—everyone else at the club—I believed in them. Rochelle at the Valentine's Day formal. I believed in her. There were some good people here.

Lenny passed by the hall, looking like a Big Bird cosplayer. His coat was triple his size and decked out in yellow fuzz patches, and a matching yellow velvet beret was tilted along his head. As he accepted a box of chocolates from a girl and thanked her, he noticed me, wallowing on the ground. "Whatcha doing down there, Byrdie?"

I glanced around the sterile tile floors engulfing me as I searched for a response. "Meditating." Then I gave his coat a good up and down. "Nice coat."

"Thanks! I'm trying to do as much Method acting as I can for *Chicken Little*."

"Ah."

Lenny studied me with a crease of worry on his brow.

He offered me a hand. "Wanna hang out?"

*   *   *

Almost everything in Lenny's house was pink, and I wasn't sure if this was due to Reina's influence, Lenny's, or both.

The walls were pastel pink, the floors and ceiling were dark pink, and the toilets were the hottest hot pink of all. The only breaks from pink were the kitchen cabinets and appliances, which were a pristine and shimmering white, and Lenny's two younger sisters I briefly witnessed wearing patterned velvet tracksuits while running upstairs.

I silently picked at my nails on their living room couch. On the far wall, an oil canvas painting of Poochie, who wore a pink bow tie and a matching party hat, watched my every move.

The real Poochie chewed loudly beside me. Lenny was feeding her bone treats from a cup that seemed to be made of rose quartz. The fact that Reina Kawai claimed she was giving Lenny and his two younger sisters a *normal teenage experience* by having them live in the biggest, pinkest house in Ann Arbor made me wonder what their home in Los Angeles must've looked like, and if it was next door to all the top one percent combined.

"What a good face!" Lenny scratched Poochie around the neck, who now had puffy chipmunk cheeks from all the treats. "Could you take a picture, Byrdie?"

I pulled out my phone. One percent battery. "I can take one with yours?"

"Ah, that's okay. I don't have mine on me."

"Oh. Why?"

He hummed. "I try to limit how much internet I take in unless I have to post stuff. Makes me foggy with all the hate and other not-so-fun things."

I didn't want to pry, but I also wanted him to trust me a little, especially when I was armed and ready to trust him with why I'd been spiraling earlier. "Your mom's videos?"

His expression sunk the slightest bit. "People are just nosy."

"In the comments?"

"*Why are you putting makeup on your son? He's fine looking like a girl?* I'm not a girl, thank you very much. I'm just very pretty." Lenny showed a proud, goofy sort of grin.

I wondered if it was forced. Hearing him talk about such similar fears as mine struck me hard, especially when he was someone I'd looked up to since switching schools.

"What's with that face?"

I snapped back to focus. "Huh?"

Lenny's eyes widened. "You're sad."

Lenny was strangely perceptive. The knack made every humiliating moment from the last few weeks replay through my mind. The almost-kiss between Asher and me during the escape room double date, the disaster burger night, the even more disastrous talk in his empty house.

Asher ignoring me at every single dance practice.

A tight ball of anxiousness settled in my stomach. Lenny had been best friends with Asher since freshman year. He understood Asher more than I did. More than anything, I wanted to vomit out the chaos swirling inside my head and ask how to stop caring about Asher the way he'd so effortlessly stopped caring about me.

"Asher kissed me." The words burst right out of me, sizzling on my tongue as they escaped.

The truth was out.

Lenny's mouth hung open like this was the most jaw-dropping news of his life. Although if I'd told him I'd dropped my peanut butter and jelly sandwich in the snow, he would've reacted the same way. Had to appreciate an active listener. "When?"

"Almost during our escape room date," I said. "And then for real in his house—"

"There are *ands*?" Lenny shrieked. Poochie yapped twice and jingled.

The story of Asher and me had been attempting to crawl out of my body for weeks. Now that the truth was revealed, all I felt was relief. *Finally,* someone else knew. "Weird, right?

When he kissed me, it made no sense because he's been on my ass about every little thing since I met him. Not passing most of the rounds. Not arriving to meetings on time. And after he kissed me, he pushed me away because he didn't want to keep breaking the rules and have you find out. Or Camilo. Anyone."

Lenny pouted. "Well, that was pointless because I already knew."

"Wait, what?" Mortification crashed through me. I grabbed the nearest pink pillow to stuff my face in. "Oh God—"

"Oh, no, no, not that you smooched! Only that he *really* likes you."

I peeled my face off the pillow. "He told you that?"

"No. Never. But I've never seen him go out of his way to ignore someone the way he's been ignoring you."

I wasn't sure how to react to that.

Lenny fed another bone dog treat to Poochie on his lap, and the corner of his baggy leopard-print cardigan sleeve slapped her against the eyeball. She grunted.

"If it helps any," Lenny went on, "I think everyone in the club has a secret thing with someone. Of course, nothing official, since Asher would kick them out."

"You really think Asher would kick them out if people dated for real?"

"Well, it's happened before. Sebby kicked out Stand-Up Type last year."

"Stand-Up as in, he does comedy?"

"Did comedy." Lenny's voice dropped low. "He hasn't since."

"What happened?"

"Getting kicked out broke his soul, Byrdie. Sebby screamed

at him in the middle of the Homecoming dance for having a girlfriend. Everyone saw. No one has seen him laugh since that day."

The retelling seemed a bit too intense to be real until I remembered who I was talking to. Lenny was a good actor for a reason. He was the most melodramatic man on the planet, but I did ask him for help for that very reason.

"Sounds like he should be on your watch list," I muttered.

His somber gaze flipped back to a grin in a flash, which confirmed my suspicions. "Oh, he is, he is. Most would never try to shut us down, of course, but if they were peeved enough . . . Anyway! Some still take the risk with secret dating. You didn't notice Constance not-so-subtly spending the Valentine's formal with Camilo? They've liked each other for the longest time."

"But they don't do anything about said feelings, right?"

He paused like he was considering how honest he wanted to be with me before finally indicating that they, in fact, had done many things together.

It was a lot to take in at once. "This is happening with everyone?"

"Oh, not me, no. I would never break Asher's rule."

"You mean Sebastian's rule."

"Asher's the president now, and he hasn't changed the rule. So, it's his now, isn't it?"

"I guess," I said. "You've really never been interested in anyone?"

"Well, my heart got wrapped up in some messy stuff before I joined as a sophomore, but that's a long story for another time. See, the thing with Asher is—" Lenny twisted his mouth as Poochie continued to munch on his lap. "He's just. Sort of. *Bad*. At this stuff. Romance stuff."

My laugh came out sharper than I intended. "Asher's the Borrow a Boyfriend Club president. He's literally supposed to be the best at romance stuff."

"But Asher's the only member who's never dated before. *Truly* dated."

The words short-circuited my brain. "Everyone's always trying to get with Asher. People give him freaking origami tulips. Why wouldn't he see anyone?"

"He's never seemed interested before. Well, until you. And now, he has no idea what to do with these feelings."

My face heated up. I stared pointedly at the oil canvas painting of Poochie on the far wall. Asher, like me, had never dated anyone before.

I had come to Lenny for advice on how to get over Asher, but that was now the last thing I wanted to do. I wanted more answers.

"Is Sebastian really as perfect as Asher thinks he is?" I asked.

Lenny sighed and hung his head; his beret slipped off. As he slapped it back on, Poochie tumbled off the couch. Her bell collar jingled as she trotted away. "Sebastian is impressive. The club was so much different under his command. He ran it strictly like a business. Much less casual."

What I'd seen was casual? "That's why Asher's so obsessed with making sure the club runs perfectly and stays afloat? So that he can be like Sebastian?"

Lenny pressed his lips tightly together before responding. "I don't really think he wants the club to stay afloat because of Sebastian or the business, even."

"Really? Why, then?"

"Asher's house is always empty, Byrdie. But the basement is always full."

CHAPTER 27

Waking up to an email from Sonny, the school's administrative assistant, telling me that I'd been added to the *Football and Lamborghini After-School Club Membership Roster* was a dream that I'd been waiting on for months. But all I did was roll my eyes and toss my phone aside.

With the talent show happening tomorrow, I'd been expecting to be added. Asher had wanted me to be an official member to dance alongside them. Since I had no clue if I'd stay on that roster next year, or if my heart could bear sticking around as long as Asher and I weren't speaking, dread washed over me.

The other unread email beneath it, however, wasn't as expected. A message from the city clerk office stating my name-change petition had been approved. My court date had been scheduled for this Friday at one o'clock. Two days away.

Two *days*.

I leapt right out of bed, feeling on top of the universe. As fast as I could, I gathered the pound of name-change paperwork off my desk, rushed down the hall and into the kitchen, and slammed everything down on the table in front of Mom and Dad.

Mom glanced up from her spring crochet magazine spread along her crossed legs, a mug held in her hand. She lifted her reading glasses, which were attached to a gaudy beaded necklace only her Avocadia boutique would sell. "What's all this?"

"My completed petition. My court date was moved up to Friday. Can I skip school? They scheduled me for one o'clock." Before they could respond, I fanned out my paperwork. "Here's my student identification card. My proof of home address. My medical records from the last three years. My primary care, my two psychologists, my surgeon. It's all here."

Mom shuffled through the paperwork on the table briefly before setting it aside. "Proud of you for getting all this information in order, sweetie. Sounds good." She patted my hand.

That was supposed to be a compliment but didn't feel that way. It would've been nice if they'd checked everything over a bit more. What if I missed something? "Thanks."

"I agree with your mom," Dad said, even though he hadn't looked up from his phone. His short hair was sticking up every which way, and his band tee appeared to be drenched with sweat. Must've been from his usual daily post-morning workout. Every day, I swore his arm muscles got bulgier.

"So." I hesitated. "Would you be able to come with me?"

Mom and Dad glanced at each other across the table.

"Sure," Dad said, deciding for them both. "We'll figure out work. Everything still good at school?"

We were already switching topics. All right.

I knew what Dad was really asking. *Was history repeating itself at Heron River High?*

"Nothing's happened," I said.

"Your club going okay?" Mom interjected. "Asher's doing bene?"

End me. "Yes."

"Classes too?"

"Yes. All A's except for Algebra II."

A dribble of sweat dripped off Dad's forehead and landed on the kitchen table. I made a mental note not to eat on that side of the table for a while. "Good, good. Don't forget to mention if you ever want us to contact the school, N."

Noah.

My name's Noah.

Two days away from a legal name change, and they still couldn't get my name right. Maybe I should've called them M and D since full names were such a hassle?

They still didn't understand why contacting the school would never work either, even after my old one had said to their faces that little slipups couldn't be helped. Sure, nobody had yet to bother me at Heron River High, and my guard was admittedly lowering, but my parents still should've known better.

I said a quiet thanks and headed into the bathroom to get ready for school, but I could hardly concentrate on brushing my teeth and washing my face. When I'd first scheduled this court date, I'd expected to be overcome with excitement as the day came close. But all I was now was stressed. Impatient. Friday was in a matter of days, but it felt like a year away.

Soon I'd be seeing my name officially as *Noah Byrd* and brimming with joy.

Soon.

*　　*　　*

I had to rework half of the freaking dance routine.

We had one dance practice left until the talent show, yet Camilo, Lenny, and Asher hadn't mastered any of the difficult moves in our mini musical. Which was why I was stepping through the theater doors an hour before our final Wednesday practice to figure out what changes needed to be made to ensure a win.

I just hadn't expected Camilo to be here early, too. He sat at the center of the stage, his black hair styled back perfectly, as usual. His laptop and a splattering of notebooks were piled around him.

I froze in my tracks by the main door. The two of us trapped in a theater alone for the next hour didn't sound ideal. Between his continual eye-rolls and frowns directed at only me, it was clear that I'd never be forgiven for choosing him for the talent show. Or for, like, existing.

Before approaching the stage, I drifted over to the vending machine in the hallway, bought a bottle of orange pop, and stuffed it into my backpack. Just in case apologies were in order. I must've done something more to irritate him than just choosing him to dance in the show. Then I walked toward the cross-legged super genius and cleared my throat.

Even before Camilo could process who was trying to grab his attention, he was already glaring over his turquoise glasses. Once he took in my familiar face, the glare softened into a blank stare. A ballpoint pen was tucked behind his ear, and the homework on his laptop screen looked like alien language. His notebooks were all labeled *Calculus I*.

He was doing calculus with a pen. And he was a *sophomore*.

"Hi," I said quietly.

"Hi," he said. Also quietly.

I cleared my throat again. "I was wondering if—"

"I've stopped writing people's essays. I'm too busy."

"What? No. I wanted to rework our routine before practice started. Hopefully to make it a bit easier for you all."

Camilo wasn't stabbing me with his pen yet. So far so good. He sighed and waved a hand toward nowhere in particular. His inked to-do lists of the day had bonus drawings of skulls and thumbs-downs surrounding them. "It's a public space."

Despite needing to set up my own laptop and rework my ideas, I sat in front of him, the stack of calculus work separating us. "You don't like me."

"I don't like anyone."

"But you *really* don't like me."

"Do you actually want to know why, or are you trying to annoy me more?"

I blinked at him and waited.

Camilo pulled his pen out from behind his ear. Instead of stabbing me in the chest, he twirled it between his thumb and forefinger. "It's less that I don't like you and more that I think you've been flying through this membership process way easier than I did, bro."

I never expected anything other than cutthroat bluntness from Camilo, but it still stung to hear his truth. *"Easier?"*

"I'm sure you've heard that I failed my first round with Sebastian just like you did with Asher. But do you know how long it took me to even get Seb to hear me out a second time?"

"Well, Asher only looked at me again because I made him

a deal. I would've never passed all three rounds without that. You're all perfect."

Camilo narrowed his dark eyes behind his glasses. "I could waste my time explaining how you're wrong. But as you can see"—he circled his pen at the textbooks and test packets swarming him—"I'm busy."

I reached into my backpack, pulled out the orange pop, and slid it over.

He inspected the pop a moment before grabbing the bottle and twisting open the cap. He took a long sip. "What's this for?"

I had to keep him talking. I shrugged. "Had an extra. So, you and Constance."

"What about us?"

"You seem good together."

Another narrowed look. "Who told you?"

"I didn't have to ask. You two just have a lot of chemistry."

A slow grin broke across Camilo's face.

Angels came down from the sky, singing and celebrating my name. Finally, I'd made the unpredictable super genius smile.

"She's worth breaking the club rules for," he said, but quietly, like Sebastian was already flying back to Ann Arbor to make him the next Stand-Up Type. "Anyway, about what you just said. None of us is perfect."

I scoffed. "On your borrower request forms, Asher's marked as Popular Type. Lenny's Influencer Type. You're Smart Type. And you all look like—" I gesticulated in his general hot direction. "And I look like—" I pointed at my chest. "So at least compared to me, you're perfect. I'm Noah Byrd, the Typicalest Typical Type—"

"Bro," Camilo interrupted me. "Hollywood sounds cool, but Lenny will flop a lot at first. Same for me. The Supreme Court isn't exactly the easiest goal to aim for. There's law school, and being a clerk, and networking, which is not easy when you hate everyone. And Asher. Well."

"He's a prick?" I offered.

"I assumed the same before I first joined the club," Camilo went on, tapping his pen against his temple. "Thought he was trash."

I peered at the mountain of calculus work separating us again. "You don't seem like someone who'd be interested in a Borrow a Boyfriend Club. Don't you have Politics Club and National Honor Society too?"

"Yeah, well, I'd heard Sebastian accepted the best of the best. And I always had been—you know—the best."

I stared at him. He'd seen the club as a challenge. "You're serious."

"Of course I'm serious. I had the best grades. The best everything. I low-key planned on quitting once I got into the club. I just wanted to prove I could. But then Sebastian failed me. Not gonna lie, it was the first time someone had failed me in my life. And, God, I wanted acceptance more after that." Camilo played with the pages of his open notebook. "I don't know why I'm telling you all this."

I only had an hour left to rework our routine before practice started. But after months of glares and smirks, we were finally talking, and I couldn't let the opportunity go. "I mean, you can tell me. If you want."

Camilo yawned, and he didn't even bother covering his mouth. "Long story short, once Sebastian finally let me try again, he went harder on me and made me disclose everything about my life. I had to tell him all about my parents and the reasons why they still don't love my grades." He rolled back his shoulders to push away that memory. "At first, Sebastian said I failed again because his club wasn't around to prove a point to parents. We were here to *serve love*. For a profit."

I winced. "Sorry."

Camilo shrugged. "Nah. It worked out because that fired up Asher. He interrupted and said something like, 'Not everyone has the luxury of getting their parents' approval automatically.' Cue the most intense brotherly staredown of the century."

"For real?"

"Dude, there was Western standoff music. A tumbleweed rolled by."

"Who hit who?"

That pulled another grin out of Camilo. "Neither. Sebastian put his weapon away and told me, 'Fine. You're accepted.' And then left." He casually leaned back on his palms. "That's when I realized how cool Asher is."

I nearly choked on my spit. "You? Think *he's* cool?"

"There's no way I would've made it in without his help. He understood me. And he stuck up for me, so I didn't quit like I'd planned. Don't tell anyone I said this." Camilo hid his yawn this time around, better showing off the scribbles on his hand. The only legible ones were *chapter 12 study guide* and *practice second chorus footwork*.

Footwork. For the talent show.

As if my choreography were important enough to enter his sacred hand to-do list.

A grin rose on my face; I couldn't help it.

His brow hitched. "What?"

"Nothing, nothing."

Camilo kept up his curiosity a moment longer before shrugging it off. "My bad, by the way, about the cupcakes. And whatever else I did to you that I probably forgot about." He did a "cheers" with his orange pop. "And thanks for the drink, bro."

* * *

My three dance companions formed a line for warm-ups onstage.

"I changed the routine," I said.

"What?" Asher snapped.

It was the most he'd spoken to me all month. Despite his voice cutting through the air like a dagger, I couldn't deny how strangely comforted I was hearing it.

"The show's tomorrow," I said. "And at our last practice, you were all still flopping around the stage like fish."

Which I'd been afraid of since the beginning. I'd selfishly chosen who I thought would least likely sabotage my chances of getting into the club. And at this point, it was too late to swap them out for members who could perform better.

But hope hadn't run out yet. Asher and Lenny were two of the most popular boys in school, with Camilo following close behind. They basically all had hot powers. No matter how bad things got onstage, they would at least have freakishly symmetrical faces to fall back on.

Lenny pouted. His hair was now a deep red, the color of the basement couches and club logo. Even hair could secretly promote the club. "We've disappointed you."

"No!" I said. "No. I've just changed the routine a bit to stop us from panicking."

Asher crossed his arms. He was dressed in his usual dance practice outfit. I'd gotten mostly desensitized to his muscles and collarbone showing off in his plain white tees, but that immunity was crumbling as he looked my way for the first time in forever. "As long as we win."

I nodded. "We will win."

"Good."

"Great."

"Awesome."

Lenny coughed. "Places?"

So, I taught them the simplified routine for the first half of practice, then told them to get into places for a preliminary run-through.

"This time, I won't be dancing with you," I said at the front of the stage. "I'll only be watching for mistakes to make sure we're perfect. Got it?"

They shared a few nervous glances, but nodded.

I watched as they danced and recited their lines from *The Ass That Lays Money* in time to the music. On my end, it was a lot of shouting to keep the arms extended and fluid and to stop having staring contests with their own legs. To smile, to smile, to smile. Every moment felt stressful and repetitive, yet an unexplainable confidence still thrummed through my veins.

Lenny and Asher were at least better than they had been a month ago. Camilo was still a natural, who I assigned the most impressive moves to on purpose. As the best dancer, he stuck to all the right timing even though his steps were a little rough and arms a little flimsy. And everyone remembered to say the right character dialogue.

Please. *Please, theater gods. Give them the memory of a spelling bee champ.*

And yet, after two whole hours, none of them could make it through the whole song without screwing up. Camilo was one run-through away from dicing Asher's and Lenny's bodies into bite-sized chunks.

The auditorium doors swung open with a loud bang.

An elderly custodian stood there with a cart. "School doors close any minute, kids."

We were out of time.

Lenny instantly rushed toward the custodian. He flipped on his Lenny charm by sweeping up the elderly custodian's hand and smiling like an angelic cherub. "A beautiful woman like yourself would let us stay ten more minutes, right?"

The custodian made a strange face. "You have five minutes," she called before leaving.

Lenny groaned and plastered the back of his hand against his forehead. "My powers. They've failed me."

We exchanged defeated looks.

Tomorrow, the club would be on the line. As well as my membership. And, like Asher, the thought of losing everyone who filled that basement with joy and broship every day hurt my heart.

Lenny was still groaning by the time I came up with a new-new plan.

"Calm down!" I shouted over him, making everyone flinch. "Emergency meeting at my house!"

CHAPTER 28

Camilo and Lenny stepped through the front door of my tiny apartment like there was nothing odd about them coming over for an emergency dance practice. Because there wasn't. Not really. Though this was the first time since last summer vacation that I had friends over.

Meanwhile, Asher entered my apartment like he would a haunted house. His eyes darted all over the entrance hall, waiting for a chainsaw-wielding clown to chop his head off.

Lenny scrubbed my head with his fuzzy yellow mittens. *Chicken Little* musical rehearsals clearly weren't over. "Your apartment is so cute!"

Cute sounded like *nowhere near Rich Bitch Street*, which more or less ripped out my soul, but at least Mom and Dad weren't home from work yet to embarrass me further.

Camilo yawned as he took off his peacoat, revealing his dress shirt with the collar folded up instead of down, his rich-uncle vibes already there. "How long will this take?"

"As long as it takes." I held up my phone. The screen lit up with six o'clock. "Even if that means we need to practice from six to six."

"*Six* in the morning? Dude, I got a bio test coming up," he replied, holding up a particular part of his hand scribbled with *KILL ME BIO TEST*.

"None of you knows the routine by heart. If we don't practice all night, we're going to bomb. And that's unacceptable. We need to be perfect."

Camilo and Lenny stared like I'd transformed into a lion before their very eyes. Even Asher offered a rare glance in my general direction. But there was no time to waste. I wasn't about to let these three guys make fools of themselves under my watch and destroy my dance routine in front of Anita and all our classmates.

"Well, I for one am ready!" Lenny shouted.

Camilo lifted a much weaker thumbs-up behind him.

I led them into my living room and started shoving the chairs and tables against the walls. The old wood floors creaked beneath our feet, and the lavender essential oil diffuser Mom had set on a shelf on the wall made everything smell like Tide Pods, but it would have to do.

I set up my laptop, hit play on the music, then approached Asher and Camilo across the living room. My stomach twisted and curled. I hadn't bothered with trying to dance with Asher for weeks, and now our hands were about to be weaving around each other's bodies. Brilliant.

The first run-through breezed by. I was strict with my words but still supportive enough, making sure none of them lost their steam. Asher's moves were getting better.

Another run-through. Better.

Another. *Better.*

But toward the end of our fifth run-through, as the final chorus played, Lenny stopped in his tracks. He stomped over to my laptop and paused the music. "Stop, stop. This is no folk tale!"

Asher and I froze.

Lenny thrust a finger my way. "You, the son, beat up the evil landlord"—he pointed at himself—"me, with a stick for stealing the donkey"—then at Asher— "you! You two should be celebrating, not acting like you want to run in opposite directions."

Was the tension between us really that obvious?

"Asher's the ass," Lenny explained further. He should've been sitting in a director's chair, wearing a bougie beret. He might not have had rhythm, but he had vision. "He's your ass."

"I know," I said. Asher rolled his eyes.

Lenny rewound the song, so the chorus played from the beginning. "So, act like it. Speak your lines with resolve."

I started my left, right, left, right steps and arm twists to the beat. "Now we do not need anything more. I have an ass that lays money, a—"

"Ride him!" Lenny shouted over the accordion solo.

"W—What?" I shouted back.

"I said: ride him!"

"Okay, okay!" I slung one leg over Asher's back in a panic; Asher was so overwhelmed that he willingly bent down without any complaints.

"Not *literally*." Lenny's leopard-print cardigan sleeves

dropped down his lanky arms as he massaged his temples. "Noah, stand behind Asher. And Asher, keep the same hand choreo, but do it on your knees. The audience needs to be able to see Noah."

We followed orders until seconds of the song remained.

Lenny clapped three times for his final command. "You've saved the day, so end the dance together! Lean over your ass, son!"

My knees slammed against the hardwood floor as I threw myself over Asher's shoulders and wrapped my arms around his neck.

The song ended.

Lenny held up a fist full of pride. "Magnifico."

Asher and I sighed simultaneously, our eyes meeting. With an awkward throat-clear from us both, we rose and parted. Just the memory of my body on his had my nerves shooting a whole level higher.

"That was good," I said to him, smiling. "I mean, you were good. At changing up the choreography so quickly."

Asher lifted his gaze from his feet in surprise. Finally, he showed his own dimples too. "You're a good teacher."

A whole swarm of butterflies blasted through me. Not only was that a full sentence, that was a compliment.

Finally, we were getting along.

After weeks. After so many disasters. *Finally.*

But whatever this was, it didn't feel like friends getting along. There was something more in Asher's eyes as we stood so close. A longing to say something more, *do* something more than smile. I didn't know whether to be thrilled or worried.

The front door opened right outside of the living room.

Mom and Dad stepped through, each of them holding takeout cartons of sushi.

"Hi, honey!" Mom said, closing the door behind her. "We got your message about your friends being over, so we stopped to—"

Dad and Mom came to an abrupt stop once they saw the current state of their living room. Water bottles and chip bags scattered along all the furniture. Chairs shoved against every wall. A new black skid mark lining the floor from having shoved so much stuff around.

Then there were the three boys standing beside me. Lenny, with his red hair and leopard-print cardigan. Camilo, with an outfit that made him look like a retired premium golf club member. And Asher, the familiar face from the disaster burger night.

"Goodness," Dad said. "Your Italian club has quite the cast."

"Asher! *So* good to see you again," Mom said, grinning.

All I wanted to do was shrivel up into dirt and become one with the earth. Before my parents could embarrass me any further, I raced over to the entryway, set the sushi spreads on a side table, and dragged my parents into the living room by the wrists. I sat them down in two cushioned chairs that faced the living room.

"Mom. Dad," I said. "I need you to watch us do something."

Before they could decline or ask questions, I faced Lenny, Asher, and Camilo. "We're going to perform our routine for my parents. Pretend they're the audience we'll face tomorrow. Taste that pressure. Do you taste it?"

They stared blankly.

I summoned as much courage as it would take to boss around the most popular guys in school, then barked, "I SAID, DO YOU TASTE THAT PRESSURE?"

A resounding and panicked *yes* shot out of their mouths.

"Good," I said. "If you perform the routine perfectly, then we can all be done."

Lenny nervously lifted his fingers to his mouth. "And if we don't?"

I pointed at the stacks of sushi by the front door. "No food."

Lenny gasped.

I clapped. "Places."

Once I handed Mom my laptop and told her to hit play, I got into place with Asher while Camilo and Lenny grouped together on the opposite side.

A beginning mandolin solo of the club's Italian theme song played. The living room was cramped even with the cleared furniture as we danced, but we managed to dodge one another as we slid and jumped and spun.

Camilo kicked up a foot as he offered Asher the donkey to me. It was pointed. Good.

Lenny stuck his arm back as I fought him for stealing my ass. It was straight. Good.

The routine was going well. Going perfectly.

I was too distracted with monitoring Lenny and Camilo while keeping in sync with Asher all at once to look at Mom and Dad. But I desperately wanted to. I wanted to know if they were impressed because we were doing as well as I thought we were, or if they were repulsed because the folk tale was too strange, or if they were confused because we kept saying *ass*.

Or if they were shocked because they were watching me dance for the first time in years.

Toward the end, I stood behind Asher. This was the best I'd ever witnessed him dance before. I got lost in the steps, and I threw in a few improvisational moves that led me around his body. At the end, I recited my line about how happy I was to have him back and draped myself over him once more.

The song ended. Heavy breaths heaved out of both of us.

I checked over to my left. Camilo had nailed his final pose as the uncle, a hand straight up, and Lenny was splayed out dramatically on the floor in defeat as the evil landlord.

We'd *done* it.

Relief shot up into my head and down to my toes. I glanced up at Asher, who I was still draped over, and found him smiling over his shoulder at me. Like he was as proud as I was. Like we were going to win this talent show and save the club from falling apart.

The longer we stayed that way, all I could do was pay attention to the way his dark hair messily draped over his face. The way his smile tilted to one side more than the other. The way his usually sharp eyes had softened on me. He was turning a shade of red.

He was nervous. All because of me.

It made me too elated to think, to breathe, and had every ounce of logic inside me disintegrating into nothing. I grasped Asher by the cheeks and pulled him into me.

And I pressed my lips to his.

It was sudden, reckless. But Asher didn't pull back. He leaned deeper into the kiss, gripping my arm with a firm hand, his pine and citrus cologne dulling the lavender air fresheners in the room. The living room melted around us.

But not for long. My eyes split open as I violently broke away from him. Asher blinked like I'd hit him over the head with a hammer.

What had I done?

What had *we* done?

In front of my *parents*.

Asher's attention drifted toward the right of us. I followed his gaze. Lenny and Camilo were frozen in place. Staring at us.

I glanced to my left. Dad was in the middle of pulling his wallet out of his cargo shorts and passing a ten-dollar bill to Mom. Mom took the bill without giving it a glance.

I'd made a huge mistake. The biggest mistake.

A loud laugh burst out of me. "That's an Italian thing!"

"Your club is very authentic," Mom said, enjoyment in her voice.

"I thought Italians kissed each other on the cheeks," Dad said. Potentially genuinely.

Lenny leaned closer toward Camilo's ear. "Have we been practicing wrong?"

Camilo pinched the bridge of his nose.

Asher still looked like a toddler lost in a mall.

"Okay! Nice job, everyone." I clasped my hands together and stepped far, far away from Asher. I couldn't bear to look at him. My heart couldn't possibly sink any lower into my stomach. What did Lenny and Camilo think? Would they tell all the other members and get Asher thrown overboard? "Time to celebrate with some food!"

"Actually," Camilo said, grabbing his bag, "my dad messaged that he wants me home for dinner soon." But then he pulled out his phone to check the clock for the first time all night.

"Same here," Lenny said. "Sorry, Asher and Byrdie. Seems like it's just you two!"

CHAPTER 29

At least there wasn't any romantic jazz playing during this double date with my parents.

Mom turned on the speakers beside the microwave and selected an Italian pop playlist on her phone that "fit the mood of the evening." I had an inkling Mom and Dad had already figured out I was never in the Italian club. This must've been an inside joke that thrived off the expense of their child's shame.

As I collected a bunch of antique plates and cups from the cabinets to set the kitchen table, Asher hovered awkwardly beside me. At first, I assumed he was being weird because I'd kissed him in front of everyone and wouldn't want to be anywhere near me. Especially not trapped in this apartment with my parents for a Wednesday night dinner. But if that were true, why didn't he leave with Camilo and Lenny?

I gestured my handful of chopsticks and forks toward the kitchen table. "You can take a seat."

"Which one?" Asher's voice had changed to that slightly higher-than-normal tone again. The on-edge one he'd also used during burger night.

Maybe he was afraid of someone spotting us through the kitchen window. Or of someone hiding inside the pantry and snapping photos of us through the door. Or of me planting another kiss on his lips.

"It doesn't matter," I said.

"Really?"

"Yeah, why would it?"

He wandered toward the wicker chair to my right and sat down. "My mom has assigned seats for the dining table. When she's around."

"Seriously? Isn't it just the two of you?"

"She likes order. Or something. I don't know."

The memory of Asher's hollow foyer flooded back. The way our voices echoed, the way the chandelier had nothing to shine upon except for a measly bench and some overpriced paintings. I wondered if his dining room was just as empty— one long table with chairs for Asher, his godlike brother, and his busy mom—and if he still sat in his assigned seat when they were gone.

Mom and Dad claimed the two other chairs at the table, leaving the last open space beside Asher. I took the seat and opened the box of assorted nigiri as Mom undid a box of avo- cado and cucumber rolls. Dad accidentally broke the plastic bowl of edamame instead of opening it like a normal person. His muscles made this a usual occurrence.

At least Asher was bold enough to reach for some food

without permission this time. Once again, he used his fork and knife.

"Is your mom back in town, Asher?" Mom asked, doing her best not to stare at the chunks of avocado roll he was cutting up. "I remember you saying she was away."

The question made Asher stop sawing the roll briefly, but he resumed soon enough. "Not yet, ma'am, no."

Mom's pointed expression communicated that she'd be asking a list of questions about Asher's home life later, then she went back to him. "Bummer. I bet she'd love to see you dance at this talent show you've all been preparing so hard for tonight."

Asher gave a weak smirk.

"You know," Dad said suddenly, "we have the biggest, most comfortable blow-up mattress stuffed away in our bedroom closet. It's really such a shame to have a comfortable mattress not being used at all."

Mom fought off an obvious grin. "Yes, so comfortable."

Everything inside me fought the urge to bash my head into my plate.

Asher's focus was still on his own. He wasn't picking up on a single word being said.

"*So* comfortable," Dad repeated louder this time.

"Dad," I hissed.

Asher abruptly lifted his head. His eyes were wide. Panicked even. "I'm sorry. Could you repeat the question?"

Who *was* this?

I leaned closer toward his ear, and his cologne overpowered the smell of soy sauce that had been dominating my nose for the last hour. "My parents offered to let you stay the night. If you ever want to. While your mom's gone."

Asher blinked a few times. "Really?"

"Yeah."

"Thank you, Mrs. and Mr. Byrd. I really appreciate the offer."

"Clara," Mom said.

"Josh," Dad said.

A hint of a relief spread along Asher's face. "Clara. Josh."

Finally, his voice was back to normal.

The remainder of the night wasn't as much of a total disaster as last time, but it still wasn't the most comfortable experience in the world. Asher started engaging in the conversation, answering Mom's and Dad's prying questions about his classes and if he had any hobbies—Asher's mom forced him to take harp lessons every Sunday until he was fourteen?—but I wasn't helping the conversation flow in the slightest. All I could think about was how I'd kissed Asher in front of everyone and he hadn't pulled away, only to then glitch out like a phone slamming against concrete afterward.

Once dinner was over and I'd cleaned the table, I led Asher toward the front door. As he threaded his arms through his wool peacoat, I walked him onto the snowy porch of my townhome apartment building.

"Thanks for dinner," Asher said under the glow of the porch light. "Again."

I shivered as I stood before him and crossed my arms over my shirt. I should've put on a jacket since I had so many questions. "Is this the part where you tell me you're filing a restraining order against me?"

"What?"

"Or should I stop trying to be a member of the club? Would that be easier?"

"Hey. Whoa." Asher leaned lower to my height, strands of his long hair draping into his face. The small bun at the peak of his head had wilted after a long day of dancing. I wanted to reach out and touch his hair but kept my arms against my chest. "I don't want that."

"Then what do you want? Because you ignored me for weeks, and then I kissed you, and you didn't pull away, but then you didn't stop acting like you were on edge all night."

"Was I on edge?"

"You were cutting your food into perfectly square chunks again."

Asher's face contorted. Then he sighed. "I never want to screw anything up."

"With me?"

"Your parents."

I relaxed a little. "It was just some sushi."

"Yeah. I get that now." He ruffled the back of his hair. "My mom is a lot different from your parents. Your parents are, like, parents. Like ones I've seen in movies. But with my mom, I don't know. I think of her the same way I do my algebra teacher."

I nodded a few times, failing to understand.

Asher must've been able to tell because he kept talking. "Or, like, a boss. She tells me what to do. If I act out of line, if I make a wrong choice, if I'm not on time—she yells at me. She's never around otherwise."

My heart grew heavier the longer he spoke. I should've

known this was how Asher's mom acted, from what he'd mentioned in the past. Especially since every time I visited him, all the rooms in his house were dark except for his own. Every day, he wandered that house alone. But from the way Asher was describing his mom, it sounded like he preferred loneliness over being stuck with her anyway. "Right."

"Parents make me nervous. But I like yours. I do. And when you"—he gestured at my mouth vaguely—"did that, we were right in front of them. They were so chill about the whole thing. And even without the club rules, I just don't know."

"Okay."

"I want to get to know them," he said. "I might take them up on their offer sometime. To, you know, let me stay."

"You could stay tonight."

"Huh?"

I gestured at the dark street beyond the porch. "You of all people know walking home at night isn't the safest idea."

He glanced back at my apartment, me, my apartment again. "I could get a rideshare. I don't want to intrude."

But I was already opening the front door and leading him back into the living room. He followed without arguing for once in his life and sat himself on the couch.

"I'll get you some clothes to borrow," I said, hovering in the hall. "Then grab that mattress my dad mentioned, okay?"

He just nodded. I started toward my bedroom.

"Noah?"

I froze in place. *Noah*. Not Byrd.

I spun right around, my stomach flipping at the sound of my name on his tongue for the first time. Asher's hands were folded loosely in his lap. For someone with such a typically overbearing presence, he was nothing but small as he sat before me now.

"Thank you," he said.

My heart beat fast. Too fast.

"You got it." With a smile and a finger gun, I retreated to my room as fast as possible.

As the door shut, I gripped my head. I was a mess. A lovesick mess.

By the time I returned to the living room with clean clothes, blew up the mattress, and started to put the blankets on it, all my conflicting emotions toward Asher had bubbled to the surface. Our conversation had given us no closure. No answers. I had to say something.

Asher grabbed at the sheets in my grasp. "Let me help."

"No, no, you're the guest," I countered, shuffling farther away.

"Come on." He yanked a bit harder, then too hard. I tripped over the air hose that fit on the mattress corner.

And my face slapped right into Asher's chest.

I whipped up my head, my cheeks burning so hot that I feared I'd branded his skin. The English language evaporated from my brain.

Asher didn't move away. A low chuckle came out of him. "This is kind of weird, huh?"

"Y-yeah," I said. "Little bit."

"I can still go home."

"No, no."

"You sure?"

I nodded, then realized most of my body was still stuffed against Asher's chest. I scuffled backward. "This *would* be less awkward if you hadn't been ignoring me for a month."

Asher sighed and took a seat on the unmade mattress. He was quiet.

"Asher?" I eventually said.

"I didn't want to ignore you." His voice cracked, stunning me. I'd never heard him speak so passionately before. Frustrated, yes. Passionate, never. "It's complicated."

This wasn't the flat-out rejection I'd anticipated. But I still didn't know where Asher truly stood, and that hurt. Because Asher Price wasn't Ernest Hemingway. He wasn't just some prick to me anymore.

I trusted him to see me for me.

I had real feelings for Asher.

I set down the sheets and sat beside him on the mattress. "You're not allowed to say *it's complicated* now. You were allowed to say it the first time, but not the fourth, or fifth, or however many times we have these conversations."

"I know. I know."

"I don't think you do," I said. "Maybe it's easy for you to keep kissing me and walking away, but I can't keep—" I was sounding too vulnerable, too broken, so I cut myself off.

Asher met my eyes again, his expression pained. His mouth hung open like something was on the tip of his tongue, itching to be said. More than anything, I wanted him to finally say that he didn't want to keep pushing me away.

But the vulnerability on his face vanished just as quickly, leaving behind hardened gray eyes that studied me. The freckles on my nose, the blond baby stubble on my chin that

I never bothered to shave, the edges of my face that I wished were as sharp as his.

Even through my hurt, I still wanted Asher to see me. He was the first person I'd ever let inspect me like this. Who I *wanted* to inspect me like this. I wanted the world around us to disappear, leaving us behind, so that all he could do was keep looking.

After tonight, I knew longing for that was a mistake.

"If things were different, I . . . I wouldn't be walking away," Asher finally said. "I'm sorry."

CHAPTER 30

The library was so noisy during lunch that I assumed the student body had usurped the librarian and thrown her body in a ditch. In actuality, the talent show happening later that night had intoxicated everyone else with a uniform giddiness, librarian included.

I'd hardly slept with the knowledge of Asher being in my own home, so there was a chance my brain was overreacting to my five senses. Now he was somewhere in this building too, wearing clothes I'd lent him before Mom and Dad drove us to school.

I scooped my belongings off a library table and into my backpack with a huff, then meandered toward the auditorium to escape. On the way to the backstage basement door, some students practiced monologues in the lower bowl. They momentarily stopped faking their emotions to wave at me.

I glanced over my shoulder. No one else behind me. I waved back with a smile.

By the time I fought through the costumes and sunk onto a couch in the back room, lunch was already halfway done. From my backpack, I grabbed the Ziploc bag with my peanut butter sandwich and ripped the sandwich into pieces on my lap.

As I lifted one piece toward my mouth, the billiards table caught my eye. The one I once set a tray of cupcakes on to ask Asher on a date.

A pang struck my chest, and the chunk of sandwich fell from my hand. I had left the library to clear my head, but the basement wasn't better. Every hearts-suit playing card and talent show flyer on the walls reminded me of Asher, if we would win the five-thousand-dollar prize tonight to help the club, and if I'd become a full-time member after all this time.

Tonight, I had to dance with Asher. In front of the entire school.

A groan droned from my mouth as I covered my face with my palms. At least the basement was deserted and quiet.

A piano chord struck so loudly on the other side of the room, I startled.

Pascha Coombs, Musical Type, was at the electronic keyboard tucked beside the Sebastian Price altar, his head hung so low that his ashy blond hair draped over his face. A light, melancholy melody seeped off his fingertips.

Squeaking hangers and footsteps came from the costume racks.

Aiden emerged soon enough in a pair of pants Isabella had flung at his head once, carrying a mound of mozzarella sticks and chicken nuggets on a tray. He went still at the sight of my near-dead body on the couch, then glanced over his shoulder. "Guess who flew in?"

"I sense a familiar dejected aura," Everett's muffled voice came from the costumes. Once he joined Aiden on the fuzzy red carpet, he gasped at me.

So, I radiated as much misery as I felt.

I activated just enough energy to wave at them.

"Yep." Aiden pointed toward the keyboard. "And Pascha's playing *the* song."

I traded looks between the two. "The song?"

"'The Borrow a Boyfriend Club Theme Song (Emotional Piano Version),'" Everett said.

Pascha struck the keyboard with all his might and threw his whole body back. His eyes were closed, lost in the music.

"The song is for when we entertain borrowers," Everett went on. "Especially when we divulge emotional stories about the times we've overcome all the odds."

Aiden bro-fisted the air. "Like when I scored the winning touchdown at last year's Homecoming game a month after getting diagnosed with my diabetes."

Everett nodded and pulled a string-cheese stick out of the plastic wrapping. Instead of peeling the sides, he chewed the whole thing like a block of beef jerky.

"*Move!*"

Isabella blasted through Aiden and Everett, and they tripped and tumbled around her. Carrying fabric rolls as tall as she was, she darted toward a sewing machine on a folding table where more embellishments and buttons littered the floor. I hadn't even noticed the new setup.

Aiden gripped a rack to recalibrate his balance. "You could've, like, not done that."

Isabella slammed her fabric rolls down on the table. Everyone flinched.

"Oh, really?" she wheezed. Her Italian accent was thicker than I'd ever heard, and her slicked-back ponytail was replaced by frizzy curls left down that hid most of her flushed face. "Since I got word about the talent show dance being inspired by some folk tale only this week, I have eight hours and twenty minutes left to design costumes and props that will make everyone drool while on a budget of fifty cents. And you dare imply I should calm down?"

Aiden stepped back to shield himself behind the protection of the costume racks. "No, Isabella, ma'am, I'm sorry."

I wanted to laugh at their usual ridiculousness, but I couldn't. Too much was at stake tonight, and not just for me. The whole club could fall apart if we lost. How were they joking around?

The couch shook beside me. Aiden had claimed the other cushion with his leaning tower of mozzarella sticks and nuggets. "I take it you're freaking about tonight?"

The show *was* also on their mind. Maybe they were nervous too, but they just weren't showing it. Because that's what bold, masculine, perfect boys were supposed to do.

I was too embarrassed to nod.

Aiden sighed over the sounds of the sewing machine and sad piano music. "Were you not listening to me just now?"

"Huh?"

"I told you. Pascha plays the theme's piano version to accompany our *overcoming the odds* stories. That means you'll kill the dance tonight." He patted my back so hard that the sandwich chunks on my lap fell to the carpet.

"Pascha isn't psychic like Everett."

Everett plopped onto the couch armrest beside me. He pressed on a temple and closed his eyes. "You will kill it."

A severe lack of effort seemed to go into that reading, but I still nodded again.

"Even if you don't," Aiden said, his voice soft, "who cares?"

"Everyone cares," I said. "The club—"

"Is our home."

"Huh?"

He sunk deeper into the couch, folding his meaty arms behind his head. "I mean, think about it. Lenny and Asher? Barely got any parental supervision. Part of me is jealous, but that must get pretty bleak for them sometimes. Or look at Camilo. He's mad-busy studying. We're the first friends he's ever gotten the chance to make. No matter what we're dealing with, though, the basement is always here."

"What about you? Don't you have the football team?"

"Gotta admit, I don't really care for those guys. Most of 'em are major douchebags. Especially toward women. The club has taught me a lot about respect."

"Oh," I said. "That's cool."

"Yeah. Y'all are my true bros." He pounded his chest with a sturdy palm. "We got the smartest, most talented students at school in our club, and we won't go down without a fight. Just worry about nabbing that membership for yourself tonight."

The words were such a relief to hear that I smiled for the first time all day. The combination of carrying both the club's future and my own on my shoulders had been weighing me down more than I'd even realized.

"I am unsure about that analysis, Aiden," Everett said through bites of cheese stick. "Even if we all care, we are still severely down in borrower numbers from the previous year; furthermore, I sense Asher remains nowhere close to charging—"

Aiden threw a chicken nugget at Everett to shut him up, and it hit him in the face.

Never mind, then.

Even if Everett was right about this show being the club's final shot to survive, it was at least nice knowing that the members had so much belief in me.

I just hoped that belief wasn't a mistake.

* * *

Stepping into the theater for the club talent show was like entering a mega shopping center the day after Thanksgiving. Clumps of students funneled through the doors to buy tickets.

Some early arrivers held signs in the audience like we were at a boy-band concert instead of a public high school, already cheering for their favorite clubs. A poster toward the back left had *PERFECT BOYS DON'T EXI*— followed by a picture of Lenny holding a rhinestone thermos and sticking out his tongue in the junior section of the parking lot. Brooklyn and Anya came with a poster of Asher and me holding *WE GOT EATEN BY CLOWNS* signs we'd been forced to pose with after our double date.

Five other club members were here too, including Constance. They were the most noticeable, waving tiny Italian flags as if they were at the Olympics.

All phones were out. Nothing had begun yet, but everyone in here knew what was to come. A battle among students performing as eccentrically as possible to gain the attention of a Broadway star.

I was about to *dance* in front of the whole school.

Lenny sighed beside me backstage. He was peering through the curtains at the poster of him holding the rhinestone thermos. "They could've chosen at least ten better photos off my website, but they always go for the thermos."

Someone busted out of the basement door. We all turned to see Isabella with layers of clothes slung over one arm, a fistful of props, and her smile bigger and bolder than ever.

"Finished!" She scurried over to pass out our costumes. Or, rather, our suits.

I held up different pieces to my chest. First, the snug leather pants with gold chains dangling from the waist. Then the even more snug suit vest and blazer with tassels trailing up the chest. On the back, rhinestones formed *FALAC* inside of a heart.

I'm not sure what I expected, but it was not this body-hugging.

Isabella's smile burned a hole through our brains as she inspected our reactions carefully, waiting for feedback.

Camilo and Asher peered at their suits in a similarly confused fashion. The club logo was on their backs too, but Asher's blazer and vest were brown, and Camilo's should've been owned by a Wall Street accountant. Lenny was the only one who seemingly didn't notice the jarring tightness of the fabric, humming the club theme song as he buttoned his red and black suit made for an obvious villain. His didn't even include a vest, his bare chest out loud and proud.

Eventually, Camilo was brave enough to clear his throat and open his mouth, inspecting the rhinestones on the back of his suit. "Did rhinestones exist in peasant times?"

"You said the folk tale was only a theme," Isabella snapped. "I went liberal with it."

"Very liberal," Asher mumbled.

"Listen." She flounced up to Lenny, who had dressed himself in the full PG-13 attire, and yanked on the collar. Lenny let out a yelp as he got dragged down. "You will be hot up there in suits. Even if your dance routine sucks, maybe you'll win for sex appeal."

Camilo grimaced. "I don't think Anita cares about that . . ."

As I put on my suit, I glanced toward the audience beyond the curtains again, where chants of our individual names were going strong. The people who were about to make out every curve and dip of my body. "Sounds like we have a lot of fans out there."

"We have a lot of *borrowers*," Camilo said on my other side.

Asher walked up behind us to peek through the curtains as well, now in his own suit. Unfortunately, Isabella was the most powerful product manager alive, so even a brown blazer with fuzz on it fit him in all the right places. He'd chosen to roll up the sleeves too, which bunched tightly around the elbows and pronounced his forearms more.

I glanced away deliberately. *Not the time, Noah.*

"Welcome to Heron River High's annual club talent show!"

The audience cheered at the sound of a woman, who now stood in a sleek dress at a microphone stand at the center of the stage.

"I'm Anita Kömraag, two-time Tony Award–winning actress, and I'm honored to return to my high school." She gave a gushy speech about how school clubs are a safe haven for the fostering of creativity and friendships, how she took part in theater and improv while her parents were working, and how, without these clubs, she wouldn't be where she is—on Broadway. Then came the club names in order: chess, photography, jazz band, French, classic literature, football and Lamborghini, and, finally, film.

Of course we were toward the end. That way we could enjoy simmering in our nerves even longer.

As the others were called to perform, one by one, we sat together backstage in silence. Asher and I kept a very wide, very intentional distance between us.

Anita eventually called our name through a microphone. "Next, please welcome the Football and Lamborghini Club!"

"All right," I said, facing the guys. "If any of us screws up footwork, try to distract from it. Blow kisses. Remove an article of clothing. Something, okay?"

They nodded.

We all rushed onstage. Camilo, playing the uncle, claimed the left side while Asher and I claimed the right as son and donkey.

Lenny jogged over to the microphone stand, the red and black suit fit to his lanky body, and waved to every section of the bleachers. His matching red hair was even deeper in the overhead lights. "Hi, hi, everyone. Hello."

The sound of Lenny's voice alone made everyone scream at the top of their lungs.

"Thank you so much for watching our performance this evening! This routine wouldn't exist without our newest member."

All eyes were instantly glued to my body. My curls, my shoulders, my arms, my face, my legs, my tight suit.

My heart pounded as I wondered what they saw.

It didn't matter. It shouldn't matter. But—

"So please," Lenny went on, his voice rising, "let's hear a word from Noah Byrd!"

Then he was shoving the mic right in front of my mouth.

"Uh" blurted out of me. Was I supposed to look at the lower bowl? The balcony? "I'm Noah. The inspiration for this piece is a famous fairy tale called *The A*— Can I say this here?"

Lenny nodded. "It's art."

"*The Ass That Lays Money.* I hope you like our performance?"

He took back the mic. "Let's give Noah Byrd a round of applause!"

Cheers exploded from everywhere at once, crashing against me like a wave. *We love you, Noah*s. It took a moment for the reality of their excitement to sink in.

A grin slowly lifted on my face.

That was a lot of *Noah*s. No *Byrd*s or *N*s to be heard.

I soaked it in before remembering that every single person at school was about to witness our little musical. All our bodies.

"Thank you so much! We really"—Lenny grabbed a tissue out of his blazer, dabbed his left eye with it, then sniffed twice—"really want to be the best club for you all."

Everyone lost their goddamn minds.

Lenny rushed away from the mic stand and stopped by us on the way back to Camilo, nudging my arm with an elbow. "What'd you think of my crying improv?"

"Go." Asher shoved Lenny's back to make him keep jogging across the stage, and Lenny stuck his tongue out at him.

As I got into place beside Camilo and Asher, my thoughts consumed me. Maybe Asher feared that by dancing this closely in front of a crowd, we'd be revealing everything that had gone on between us. After the awkwardness of our conversation last night, it was hard enough to look him directly in the eye.

"The Borrow a Boyfriend Theme Song: Italian Version" played from the speakers. Fog machines turned on from each side of the stage. LED lights lit up around the perimeter.

The performance began.

"We are dying of hunger, uncle!" I shouted at Camilo, shifting my hip to the back and chest to the front, then side-stepping. "I am too small to find anything."

Camilo's footwork and arm movements were flawless during his solo. "I will give you this little ass that lays money. Don't leave this animal with anyone."

Asher broke through our bodies with a body roll. We nailed the rest of the first chorus, then made our way toward where Lenny stood in his ominous landlord suit.

"Give me a lodging," I announced as the second verse began, "but look! My ass spends the night with me."

Lenny and Asher began their duet, mirroring one another as they depicted the landlord stealing the donkey by hiding Asher behind him. We had reached the halfway mark, and the routine was going perfectly.

I caught a glimpse of the lower bowl. They were cracking up and flinging around their phones to find the precise angle to take videos and photos.

And there were cheers. Lots of them.

The most shocking part was how I felt about everyone watching my every move. I wasn't terrified at all. It was a thrill—going back to my theater roots. No more *ick*.

I was a boy, dancing with other boys.

"Landlord!" I shouted even louder than before, swinging my hands back and forth to the beat and spinning twice. "Where is my donkey?"

Lenny nailed every move as he reached for the stick at my belt. He lifted it high in the air with a spin, acting like he was about to hit me.

"Beat, beat, beat!" I chanted in his face.

In a combination of spins and kicks, Lenny began to smack himself as if the stick were enchanted. "Save me, boy, I am dead!"

"What!" I threw my hands high over my head and slid them back and forth, stepping to the right, left, right, and left again. "Give me back my property—the ass that lays gold."

Lenny kept beating himself up as Asher and I went into our final chorus. He slid in front of me while leading into a bend.

A screeching bird noise came from somewhere behind us.

I glanced over Asher's shoulder. Lenny with a stick. Tumbling. Falling.

My eyes spread. "Look out!"

Lenny's shoulder slammed right into Asher's back. The domino effect sent them both stumbling forward and toppling into me. We all crashed onto the stage.

As the weight of each body rolled off me, the last part of the song played. Laughter echoed everywhere through the theater, bouncing off the walls.

"What the heck?" Lenny shouted. "What were you two doing?"

Asher was still sprawled on top of me, his dark hair scattered across my chest, and I tried very hard to ignore that. If Asher heard my racing heart, I prayed he blamed the choreography.

He finally gained the strength to lift his head, his legs twisted in mine. "The routine. What were *you* doing?"

"Getting beat with a stick!" Lenny said.

I scrambled to push myself up and deliver my last line toward the hollering crowd. "Now, we do not need anything more! I have an ass that lays money and a stick to defend me from whoever annoys me."

The song came to an end.

That was that. We'd been prepared to play off fumbled steps, but not total wipeouts. There was no way we'd be voted the winner by Anita.

I wouldn't be a member next year.

But . . . after tonight, did I even want to be in the club anymore?

CHAPTER 31

The thought came out of nowhere and stunned me still.

Strangely, I wasn't scared of the idea of losing. The whole school had just seen me perform with a group of guys. I had fully *felt* like a boy, doing something I'd always loved. And everyone had cheered me on.

The animated audience distracted me again, and when I found Aiden, Everett, and the others, they weren't cheering like everyone else. The realization why hit hard.

What would happen to the club?

Maybe winning didn't matter because this *was* a family. But could it end here?

Anita took an excruciating fifteen minutes to call every club to the stage for the results. Behind her was a screen that projected *RESULTS* in a bold, intimidating font. She dragged on even further by explaining how she, a Broadway sensation, donated a whopping five thousand dollars to encourage teens to express themselves, even though we all knew the biggest reason was to be put on a pedestal by her hometown and get the theater named after her.

Lenny stood beside me on the right of the stage, gripping his arms like he was freezing.

Camilo had brought an orange pop with him, and in his other hand, he was messaging someone. There was a slight smile on his face. Constance must've been trying to cheer him up. I spotted her in the crowd, texting too.

Asher was to my left, but I had no clue if he was anxious like Lenny or defeated like Camilo. I couldn't force myself to meet his gaze to find out. I'd promised to make sure the club would stay alive.

I had promised Asher. Everyone. And I'd failed them.

My friends. They were my *friends*. Now the idea of losing everyone, that camaraderie found in the basement, left me crushed.

"We will now reveal which act will be receiving the five-thousand-dollar prize." Anita gestured toward the screen behind her.

The winning club name appeared: *THE FOOTBALL AND LAMBORGHINI CLUB.*

I stared at our name in shock. This had to be wrong. A technical error.

But it wasn't. Anita cheered "The Football and Lamborghini After-School Club!" a second later, and everyone in the lower bowl section stood and shouted our names.

Classmates screamed "We love you!" and "Kiss me on the mouth, please, God!" from several directions. In the third row, the other members blew party horns and threw confetti into the air.

Lenny screeched at the top of his lungs, breaking me from my trance.

"What the hell," Camilo murmured beside me.

"See that? See that?" Lenny said, punching up and down Camilo's arms. Camilo swatted him away, but a wide grin spread across his face.

"Hey, he's happy!" Lenny shouted. Camilo flipped back to a frown.

"A moving performance," Anita announced, wiping a fake tear. "An interpretive narrative about survival—about dreaming for a life of gold and success, and the struggles of falling down. Tonight, this club will receive such a dream themselves and be uplifted!"

Lenny moved on to me next, tackling me with his gangling arms. "We knew that you'd pull this off, Byrdie!"

My head buzzed from all the praise. "But we screwed up."

"Our routine was supposed to be weird, though, right?" Camilo said. "Maybe Anita thought the fall was part of the routine?"

"Nuance!" Lenny exclaimed.

Camilo ignored him. "Either way, we were perfect until the last chorus."

I still couldn't believe we won. Once I finally faced Asher, I expected his gaze to be glued to the projector screen like mine had been, or that he'd maybe even be letting out one of his twinkly laughs from the disbelief.

Instead, he was looking right at me. Wearing a small smile.

And something inside me shattered. We'd saved the club, so I was a permanent member. And now, every day, I would be around the boy who would never feel the same as I did about him.

Soon enough, the audience funneled out the theater in a cloud of chatter, and all the competitors followed suit through the backstage door, including us.

The moment our club stepped into the hall, classmates blasted out more compliments and selfie requests. With this many fans, I wouldn't be needed for twenty minutes at least. I headed for the dressing rooms.

Until my name shot through the crowds, startling me to my core. A group was calling me back over. Most I recognized from my classes.

I pointed at my chest, confused.

"Yes, you!" one shouted, already rushing up to me. She dragged me to them by the wrist. "I gotta ask—you guys were being funny with that whole routine or whatever, but you could actually dance! Are you a professional?"

"Gotta be one of Lenny's influencer friends," another person commented.

"Um, no," I said through a small laugh. "I really liked experimenting with all types of dance growing up. That's all."

"So sick," another said, shoving her phone into someone else's hands. She bumped us together for a pose. "Get a pic of me and Noah!"

At first, I was so taken aback that I almost forgot to smile, but soon my whole face was lighting up in ways I couldn't control. I'd admitted to caring about something guys weren't stereotypically supposed to do, but I wasn't scared. Not around them.

This school really did feel different. It was different.

"Hey."

Liam had approached the club, too. He looked the same as the day he quit, his outdated hipster frames shoved into his orange curls, plus a graphic tee likely gifted to him for a streaming sponsorship that advertised a game I'd never heard of called *RAID: Shadow Legends*.

For once, he wasn't holding a game console, so he was able to outstretch one hand toward Asher. "Good job, man."

Asher didn't move a muscle. "You watched us?"

"Yeah, I mean, I was hoping you'd all win."

Beside me, Camilo shot a nasty glare over his glasses. "Are you actually attempting to get back into the club now that we have money again?"

"Even if you hadn't won, I still wanted to talk!" His forehead was wrinkled and tense, like he really was sincere. "I'm sorry, okay? For real. I really do miss my boys."

Asher was supposed to throw an uppercut on Liam and send him flying into a brick wall, but he didn't. Instead, he took Liam's hand into his own and shook it. Even more unpredictable, he said, "Welcome back, Liam."

A few blinks and stares were shared by all.

Eventually, Aiden broke the silence by punching Liam lightly in the stomach. Liam winced, but then Aiden offered a bro handshake and a muttered, "Missed you, clown."

Camilo tilted his head with a fabricated cluelessness. "You missed another member? And here I swore you once claimed to only be in this for the money too."

A choking noise shot out of Aiden, but he quickly turned into defensive linebacker mode, shoving fists on his hips. "Money's *nice*. But money can be replaced. Unlike you guys."

Pascha hummed while fiddling with the handwoven guitar case strap hung over his shoulder. "I agree. Don't you, Camilo?"

Camilo's mouth squirmed. With a head flick, he muttered, "I suppose."

The conversations surged again. Some members teased Liam while teachers trapped others, like Ms. Gao and Mr. Alberich, who claimed it was refreshing to see an *academic club* put on such a high pedestal by students. Although they shared a laugh as they did, and I overheard them muttering "Can't imagine why . . ." as they left.

But then I caught a glimpse of Asher. The commotion bustling around me faded, leaving only him behind. He was beaming nonstop as club members high-fived and thanked and hugged him amid the celebration. His dimples were already so rare to spot, and even rarer for them to show for more than a second.

And his eyes were full of pride.

Ms. Vora came over to give her congratulations, breaking my mesmerized state, and the other teachers patted her on the back, complimenting her ability to sponsor a club outside of her comfort zone. Sonny, the admin assistant, who was busy speaking to a younger man nearby, also stopped to toss me a thumbs-up.

The man Sonny was speaking to turned to face our circle as well. He pulled a hand out of his sweatpants pockets to wave our way. "Could I bother you all for a photo, too?"

A single name resounded around me so loudly, the heavens shattered above.

"*Sebastian!*"

As the other guys swarmed the slender man in a flurry of bro handshakes and hugs, I squinted at him from afar. In the framed photo worshipped so regularly on his shrine, Sebastian was dressed all professional in a designer suit, effortlessly fitting the millionaire businessman mold Asher had talked about so much.

But not today. Today, his thick, dark brown hair matched Asher's in color but was cut shorter, and the top stuck up like he'd buried his head in a pillow during the show. His only prestige came from his Yale sweatshirt, but it was in severe need of an iron.

He was the dictionary definition of underwhelming.

As Aiden wrapped an arm around Sebastian's shoulder, Sebastian focused on a spot past me. "You have quite the moves, Ash."

I glanced over my shoulder. Asher was a few feet behind where I stood, his expression indiscernible. Flat, empty. "We had a good instructor," he said.

"I heard. Lenny gave such a moving speech about him before your dance started. He's a new member you accepted?" His eyes trailed over to me.

I considered bowing or greeting the club's divine creator with a *your excellency*, but Asher spoke up again before I could. "Ann Arbor is far from New Haven."

Sebastian laughed. It sounded nothing like Asher's high and twinkly one—more a low chuckle that matched his deeper voice. "When Camilo messaged me saying my club was taking part in renowned actress Anita Kömraag's club talent show, I couldn't resist making the trip."

Asher glared at Camilo, who returned a comparable nasty look.

Sebastian raised his arms in a sweeping gesture to signal everyone's attention. "Who wants to catch up at our place?"

CHAPTER 32

Asher looked like he was about to throw up.

Whether that was because twelve people were occupying the Price estate's back patio table while Mrs. Price was forever away on business or because his older brother was hanging out with the very club he'd painstakingly run to impress the guy, I wasn't sure.

Even though the patio was insulated with temporary plastic walls to keep out cool March weather, we were still outdoors. At least Lenny couldn't accidentally knock over any vases, and Camilo couldn't purposely chuck them at walls.

Unfortunately, that didn't stop Asher from monitoring everyone else, who were drinking spiked lemonade and asking Sebastian questions about Yale and the East Coast. Asher sat there in his fuzzy brown suit, arms firmly crossed, just waiting for us to destroy something his mom would yell at him for once she returned.

Of course I'd gotten stuck sitting beside the grumpiest ass

in the land. The stress seeping from his pores kept poking my shoulder and distracting me senseless. I even caught myself feeling bad for him until I remembered where we stood.

A voice inside me whispered to go home and crawl into bed, but my curiosity over Sebastian Price, the living legend himself, had me here with my hands politely folded. For so long, I'd wanted to know who had a monstrous grip on the most popular boys at Heron River High—and especially the president who reigned over them all.

If Asher was a prince, Sebastian was the king. Tonight, I would find out why.

Across the marble tabletop, Sebastian slid his glass of whiskey, which he'd at some point snuck into the house, toward his brother. Pretty sure whiskey wasn't supposed to reach the rim. "Need a sip, mate?"

Asher stared emptily at the single ice cube bouncing in the fancy crystal glass. The combination of the glowing full moon and flickering heat lamps cast an array of shadows across his face, making him even more intimidating than usual. "Mate?"

"Sorry, that means *friend*."

Asher's hands, still slightly buried into his crossed arms, clenched tight. "I know."

If being forced to spend more time with Asher wasn't going to kill me, then the tension between these two would.

It was strange to witness brothers so similar in appearance wear such different expressions. They had the same bigger nose with a subtle bump on the bridge, the same thick eyebrows against their lighter olive complexions. The difference was their eyes. While Asher's were rounder and almost more hollow, Sebastian's were angled like the rest of his face, all sharp edges and lines. I couldn't tell if that was because Sebastian was two years older or because young millionaire businessmen had to look the part.

A corner of Sebastian's mouth hitched as he held a stare with his younger brother across the table. "Apologies. *Mate* was a slip of the tongue. I flew straight here from Oxford. I was there for the week, meeting with some research partners for First Datecation."

Some intrigued *oohs* floated around the patio.

"Get any British girls?" Aiden asked, and Isabella smacked him on the arm. "What? Is his freakish ability to get girls *not* why he started our club in the first place?"

I turned toward Lenny beside me. "Is that true?"

Lenny shrugged loosely. "From what I've heard, everyone wanted to date Sebby at school, so he saw a chance to commodify himself. Then he found others like him."

"Jesus," I muttered.

Sebastian was too busy chuckling over his oversized drink to hear our little sidebar. "No *women*. I'm engaged to my work."

"Your dating app is really taking over Europe now?" Constance asked. She was mid receiving a tarot reading from Everett, sparkly cards splayed across the table. Guess a full moon was the optimum time.

"Did you know that every college at the University of Oxford owns a pet tortoise," Sebastian said instead, "and each May, they make them race?"

Aiden muttered a low *whoa*, and Everett dropped his focused connecting-with-spirits demeanor to gasp. Even Max lifted his pencil from his sketchbook in awe.

Internally, I rolled my eyes.

Asher, however, deepened his frown. "You're able to take a long-weekend vacation here when your company's just started making millions?"

No one reacted to *millions*. Asher loathed to speak about his brother and least of all his accomplishments, so Sebastian must've been more than open about the size of his bank account.

"The club just means that much to me, little brother." Sebastian lifted his whiskey with a popped pinkie, a heat lamp flame reflecting along the crystal. "Besides, you know what they say: a president should barely work to get all the pay."

Laughter surged around me as I cringed.

Aiden especially found his words hilarious, wiping a tear from his eye. Although he'd probably react the same if Sebastian said *among us sussy imposter*. "We'll have to revolt against our club pres if he tries to snatch up the money we scored tonight. That five thousand's getting split between us whether Asher wants it to or not."

"Your new president's giving out bonuses on top of your base rate?" Sebastian asked. "What a kind gesture." He turned to Constance, who clutched her chest at the sudden eye contact with the king. "Constance, how much has the club made this year so far?"

Everyone kept their lips pressed shut while I stole a quick look at Asher.

His face was downcast, like the last thing he wanted was for his older brother to discover the truth of why we competed in the first place. That there was no more money.

He looked so tired.

"A lot." It busted right out of me.

Everyone's gaze zoomed my way.

I could sense Asher's eyes drilling into me too, but I couldn't bear to meet them. We were supposed to be dead and done, yet here I was, defending him. Had my lemonade been spiked too, or was I really this brainless?

Welp. Couldn't back out now. I straightened on my carved marble stool, which was extravagant at the expense of shattering my tailbone. "Asher's made a lot of money for us. He's making the club bigger and better than ever before."

Sebastian kept his drink hovered below his lips as he studied me like a specimen in a lab. With the sharp glimmer in his eye, it was obvious he wanted me to receive that. Even in his sweatpants, not a designer shoe or bag to be seen, he made me feel lesser than. I suddenly understood how he could entice borrowers into showing up when he first established a hot-boy club.

"I'm glad to hear," Sebastian mumbled once he was through with the inspection, leaning back on his own ass-shattering stool. "Look at you, Ash. You're surpassing me."

Asher waved a strangely civilized, dismissive hand, but his forehead had at least lost some wrinkles. Finally, a sign that Asher Price was relaxing. "Nothing compared to First Datecation. How much is your company up to now? Billions?"

Sebastian's pupils were supposed to transform into money signs as he cackled capitalistically into the night. If anything, the grin he'd worn all night only faltered a hair. "Well, with the stock market, it's always changing."

"It changes that much?"

He ignored the question to clap Camilo's shoulder beside him. "How's the borrower form looking lately? Care to show me?"

I'd never seen Camilo more willing to follow an order. With a quick reach over his stool, he pulled a laptop from his backpack, and Sebastian leaned closer as he bragged about how he'd made tons of improvements that streamlined the borrowing process entirely.

Everyone got wrapped up in separate conversations. With Asher remaining silent to my left, and Lenny roping himself into Everett's divining session to my right, I opted to take a break from the palpable discomfort in the air and search for a bathroom inside.

I wandered back through the kitchen and foyer, then into more confusing halls, and stumbled across one. The high-tech toilet gleamed as much as Asher's rings, and the ceiling soared to the sky. Rich Bitch Street residents were a whole other breed.

With a weary sigh, I used the restroom, then nearly jumped when I caught my reflection in the mirror above the sink. Since Isabella had tossed our costumes at us right before rushing onstage, I hadn't taken a good look at myself. Now that I had the chance, I couldn't stop staring. My shoulders were wide in this suit. The collar shaped my neck perfectly.

I looked like a boy. I *felt* like a boy. I had proved that I was by becoming friends with the best of them.

Did I really need the club anymore? I thought back to Camilo's original plan to dine and dash. Now that I'd made it in, did I need to stay?

I swallowed away the thought once more. I couldn't make

this decision now. I left behind the bathroom and my reflection, taking a left turn through the kitchen instead of a right.

Before me was the exact room I'd been wondering about for so long.

The dining room didn't have three chairs. There were eight. The long oval table had a lace table runner spread over top. There were no crumbs on the ornate carpet. Not a single chair pushed out of place, either. There was no way Asher ate here alone.

Not like I cared.

A door shut nearby. Then a voice.

"How much debt are we talking?"

Asher. My heart rate spiked. The last thing I needed was for Asher Price to think I was snooping through his belongings like a fanboy.

"Just do me a favor and don't tell Mom, all right, Ash?" Sebastian was with him. His words were slurred. "I'm fine. If anything, this vacation has me forgetting all about Oxford."

"You can't run away from this."

"Please, that's not what I'm doing."

"You are." Asher's voice cracked, hitting a high note I'd never heard from him, and my whole body tensed at the sound alone. "You can't fly back to your old high school out of nowhere hoping for a pick-me-up and pretend First Datecation isn't totally screwed."

Was something wrong with Sebastian's company?

Oh God. Was it tanking?

Either way, I heard enough to understand I needed to leave. Now. I spun around and tiptoed through more countless halls, not knowing exactly where I was going but that I would have to pop out around the patio someday. Glancing over my shoulder, I checked to make sure Asher wasn't lurking close behind, ready to catch me in the act, then faced forward again.

The Price brothers stood at the center of the kitchen. They stared.

My legs locked, and my breath stopped. I'd made a loop?

"Uh." *How?* "Hi."

"Hi," Asher said. Slowly.

I pointed left. Then right. Left again. "Patio?"

He gestured over the kitchen island, somewhere past my shoulder.

"Right." I started walking backward. "Big house you got. Many halls."

I turned around and rushed for the patio as fast as I could. Once I made it out alive and reached the sliding doors, the biggest sigh of my life escaped my lungs. The other members were busy talking and laughing as I'd left them, and Pascha had started to play his acoustic guitar. Instead of joining the table again, I hovered by the door.

The uneasiness crawling in my stomach was too distracting, too overwhelming, and my brain kept arguing to turn around and march back inside. Despite everything Asher and I had gone through, I wanted to know if he and his brother were okay.

Thankfully, Pascha hardly got through one song before Asher reappeared. He didn't return to his seat either. He just stood near me.

"Where'd you two go?" Aiden called our way over the music, gesturing his lemonade can toward us with a muscular grip. "You missed Isabella and Max doing a sick BTS dance."

Asher didn't answer. His eyes glazed over as he watched Pascha strum his guitar. There was no sadness on his face. No anger. He simply looked like a boy who had prayed at the Sebastian Shrine for a lifetime and never heard anything back.

"Bathroom," I answered for myself.

The door slid open again.

Sebastian stepped out with a fresh drink and corporate head shot smile. As if his entire business wasn't tanking, his relationship with his brother wasn't falling apart, and his sweatpants definitely didn't have a hole in the back.

"So," he announced. "What have I missed?"

CHAPTER 33

My name-change court date was tomorrow morning, so it was a little too late to be browsing names on my laptop instead of going to bed.

I'd committed to Noah so many years ago that it felt like the name I'd been meant to have all along. It was one of the most popular boy names on ranking lists, and that's exactly what I wanted. Something indisputably *boy*. There was no reason to window shop. But according to these lists, the name Asher was getting more popular each year, too. And wouldn't that be hilarious?

I smirked and forced myself to shut my laptop. One Asher was plenty.

The thought of his name alone made my chest sink. I wanted to know if Asher was still handling his mess of an older brother and what he now thought about continuing to run Sebastian's legacy. Months ago, I would've never expected to feel trapped after finally becoming a member, yet so empty knowing that parting from the club meant leaving my new friends behind.

But here we were.

As I climbed under my covers and flicked on a bedside lamp, I started doomscrolling on my phone. Even that couldn't distract me from all the stress and impatience I had about tomorrow.

Twelve more hours until I was Noah Byrd. *Really* Noah Byrd.

Something hard hit my window and made a *ting* noise.

I startled, lifting my head right off my pillow. The time on my lock screen read 11:00.

Birds didn't slam into windows in the middle of the night. A bat?

Three solid knocks.

Adrenaline spiked through me. Bats did not knock. My curtains were pulled back, but the sky was too dark, and the flickering streetlamps were too dim. I couldn't see a thing. My lamp, though, shone across every wall of my room. Whatever was out there could easily see me.

My heart pounded as I rushed over to my closet and dug around for anything heavy or sharp. Stuffed in the corner was my miniature baseball bat from when I briefly played Little League in elementary school.

Gripping the bat with both hands, I approached the window like the floor could shatter beneath my feet any second.

Living on the bottom floor of a century-old townhouse that had been converted into a cramped apartment complex meant there were definitely ghosts watching me sleep, and also there were no protective barriers installed on the windows. Today was the day I was thankful for that. A gust of cold air blew into my bedroom and fluttered my shirt as I pushed up the window with a free hand, keeping my bat on standby.

A stuffed *Tyrannosaurus rex* on the wide windowsill stared back at me.

"Jesus—!" I swung my miniature baseball bat at the green chunk of fluff. The dinosaur soared across the snowy front lawn. A loud clunk followed.

"Ow! Why?!"

I squinted into the darkness. "Who's out there?"

The sound of footsteps crunching through the snow approached my window. With the help of my bedroom light, I could vaguely make out a figure coming into view. Tote bag draped over the shoulder. Wool peacoat hitting above his knees.

Asher Price, holding a stuffed toy against his chest. The same one we had won together at the winter festival.

No way this was happening. I'd fallen asleep while doomscrolling.

Asher's gaze narrowed at the baseball bat in my hand. "Did you just whack the dino at my head?" His voice was raspy. Loud. And very much real.

This wasn't my imagination. Asher was truly here, looking as frustratingly impeccable as always in the cold, with his rosy-red cheeks and dark hair dotted with snowflakes. And I was in one of Dad's workout shirts he'd won at last fall's Ann Arbor corn-eating contest, which shouted *KEEP CALM AND EAT CORN!* across the chest.

I crossed my arms to cover up the words. "Want to tell me why you put the *T. rex* on my ledge?"

"Did you at least listen to the voice-box message before you ruthlessly attacked him?"

"Message?" I asked. "What message?"

Asher glanced somewhere down the road, then ruffled the back of his hair to get rid of some melting snowflakes. He pointed at a newly added pink heart patch sewn onto the dinosaur's fuzzy stomach, which had *Listen to me* embroidered on it in cursive. "You squeezed the patch on his stomach. Right?"

His voice was suspiciously quiet. I still wasn't sure what Asher was doing at my bedroom window in the middle of the night, but whatever he was trying to do, he was clearly humiliated over how miserably he was executing the plan. I couldn't help but sympathize. "Yeah, kidding. Totally. I listened."

Asher's chest visibly rose and fell like he needed to calm himself. Like he was preparing himself for something earth-shattering. "Do you have an answer?"

What the hell kind of message had been inside that *T. rex*? "Um. I'm not opposed or unopposed. Mostly neutral, I guess. I don't want to take a side."

"What?"

"What?"

"I asked if you'd want to spend time together tomorrow. With me."

I blinked at him. "As friends?"

Asher opened his mouth, but nothing left.

His hesitation already had my thoughts spiraling. Him showing up here, now, with a stuffed animal didn't exactly scream friendship. "Asher, what are you doing? Is this because of your brother?"

"No. He flew back to New Haven this morning. He's fine."

Asher's words didn't match the way his face twisted. Both of us knew this was a lie, anyway. He had looked up to his older brother for so long—as well as the high-tech dating app business he'd developed that was no longer thriving—and I'd walked in while Asher's worldview of his brother crumbled. I took his dismissal as not wanting to talk about it, or at least not yet.

"I want to—" Asher dropped his gaze, then reached toward the windowsill and picked up a clump of snow. The silver butterfly wings protruding off his Anteros ring gleamed in my bedroom lights. Of course, no gloves. I held myself back from grabbing a pair from my closet and slapping him upside the head with them. "I want to figure this out."

"Figure what out?"

"Us."

My pounding heart spread into my legs, my arms, my head. "By us, you mean what?"

"I want to pass your rounds."

"Rounds?"

"Romance the . . . Byrd, for one." An awkward grin spread along his face, and I couldn't deny how cute he was. "You passed the Romance the President round with me at the winter festival, right? Now I want to pass yours. To try to prove myself to you again. And to apologize."

"Oh," I whispered.

He must've taken my *oh* as a negative because his mouth warbled. He took a short step back and focused hard on his Prada sneakers, which shockingly were surviving the snow. "But if you don't want me to, I won't."

The Borrow a Boyfriend Club president really was horrible at romance stuff.

Still, I wanted to be happy about this, whatever this was. I wanted to finally be thrilled about the idea of being with Asher, especially now that dating was no longer as intimidating as I once assumed. I was ready to be myself with someone. For real.

Instead, a mixture of confusion and annoyance overcame me. We'd spent more than a month enduring dance practices while somehow avoiding each other. What was different now?

"You're altering the no-dating club rule, then," I said.

Asher sniffed and wiped the back of his hand along his reddened nose—probably to stop his snot from freezing—and then stuffed his hand back into his coat pocket. "Does after school work for you tomorrow?"

He hadn't answered the question. The only reason why he would stay silent was if the rules weren't budging.

"I'm actually sort of busy tomorrow," I said. "I'm skipping school. I have a court date for my name change at one. I don't know how long it'll take."

The words came out so naturally that they almost startled me. I hardly spoke about these things with Mom and Dad, let alone anyone else. But with Asher, it was always as easy as telling time. I worried if talking about these things would make Asher act weird or back off.

Asher didn't back off, though. As the backdrop of snowflakes fell behind him, landing on his perfect shoulders and perfect hair and perfect nose, he lit up just as much as I did when my court date had been originally accepted. "That's amazing."

His response stunned me.

"Um," I managed. "Thanks."

"Once you're free, then, we can meet up. I'll send you my location later. It's a secret spot I know. No one will see us."

My stomach dropped. Because he wasn't going to adjust the rules for me. He wanted us to stay hidden.

I was so sick of hiding. For so long, I had ducked and dodged the world from underneath sweatshirt hoods, and I never wanted to go back to that life again.

The last thing I ever expected was for Asher Price to come to my window and confess that he wanted to act upon his feelings for me. Even more, I never imagined I would turn him away when he did.

"I'm not going to be your secret, Asher," I forced myself to say. "If you really want to *figure this out*, then we're not hiding."

Asher found the snowy ground again and nodded a couple of times. I couldn't make out his expression with his longer, messy hair draped over his face, but my imagination filled in enough blanks to break me. "Right. Yeah. I get it."

That was it? I wanted to scream at Asher to take his words back, to grab my face and kiss me right then. Not stand there like a coward in defeat. Weren't we worth more than this?

Wasn't *I* worth more than this?

"Why are you holding on to this dating rule so tightly?" I finally asked.

He huffed, and a puff wisped in the air. "Because if I don't make it a rule, guys like Camilo will destroy our marketability and appeal by dating their girlfriends for real."

My brow shot up. "So you do know about him and Constance? That your rule is being broken? If other members date, it's fine. But it's not for us?"

"That's not what this is."

"Then what *is* this?" I gripped the windowsill and leaned closer. "What, are you trying to guard your own grumpy heart from the very thing you sell at your club?"

There was a pause. A long one.

Then, finally, he muttered, "Maybe."

The way he spoke so pained and soft, I assumed I'd imagined it at first. But as he stared down the street to avoid my gaze, I knew he'd admitted something he never wanted to.

Asher wasn't open to love.

"Good luck tomorrow," Asher eventually added. "With the court date." Having said everything he wanted to, he set the stuffed dinosaur back on my windowsill.

I picked up the animal and gave the stomach a squeeze. A deep, demonic-sounding voice came out like it'd been drenched in water. Or hit with a baseball bat.

I hated that Asher was giving me yet another reason to reconsider him being a rude know-it-all. I hated how he was walking away in the freezing cold and leaving me with more questions instead of answers. And I hated how happy I was that he had come here in the first place.

The dinosaur spoke again, grumbling and glitching out. By the time I lifted my head, Asher was gone.

CHAPTER 34

The court hearings were running late.

I swung my feet in time to the ticking clock on the wall as I sat on a hallway bench. My trial was supposed to start a half hour ago.

Mom and Dad sat across from me, both glued to their phones. Neither seemed to notice how long we'd been waiting. Did they even remember the original time? Or how any of this was supposed to work?

I did. That's all that mattered.

Dress nicely. Bring your legal documents. Get there early. No phones. No talking. Those were the guidelines I'd read on the internet prior to coming. I kept repeating them in my head to control my fears, to convince myself that I'd done everything right so far, even if Mom and Dad hadn't done anything except walk me here.

Everything would go perfectly. I'd become Noah Byrd without any problems. I'd prepared my legal documents and medical forms. I'd rehearsed in the mirror three times that I'd never been convicted of a felony or lost a lawsuit. I currently didn't owe back taxes, nor had I ever declared bankruptcy, your majesty.

No—shit. Honor. It was *your honor*.

I checked the faraway clock on the wall again. One-thirty.

School would be out soon, but my phone hadn't buzzed with any messages from Asher. I despised how disappointed his silence made me. It was irrational considering *I* had rejected *him* last night. But a piece of me wished that he'd say he changed his mind. He didn't want to hide anymore.

It was wishful thinking, but I pulled my phone out of my back pocket to make sure I hadn't missed any messages. The screen wouldn't light up.

I clicked every button. Nothing. Shook it. Still nothing.

I had been so busy preparing for my court appearance and dealing with a wild Asher that I'd completely forgotten to charge my phone. I wasn't thinking. Today was the biggest day of my life. Overnight, I had morphed into a new creature composed solely of fear and panic who was about to go before a judge and prove who I was.

I glanced out the window above Mom's and Dad's heads. Melting snowflakes streamed across the glass.

There was no reason to be daydreaming about Asher right now. All that mattered was becoming Noah Byrd. Really Noah Byrd. Legally Noah Byrd.

The clacking of high heels started down the hallway.

A suited woman approached. "It's time, Mr. Byrd."

* * *

The hearing took even longer than the eons we'd waited in the hallway.

I stood alone at a podium during the whole session. My legs ached toward the end. Even though I provided my whole life story to the judge through pounds of documents and paperwork, she asked everything about me except what I'd eaten for breakfast.

While answering a question about taxes, a phantom vibration tickled my back pocket. I wondered if it was Asher until I remembered once again that my phone was dead.

"Mr. Byrd."

I snapped out of my thoughts and continued to recite that indeed, I was sixteen, and *indeed*, I did not file taxes.

In the end, there were no problems. My name change was approved.

I was officially Noah Byrd.

"There you go, kid!" Dad's voice boomed unnaturally loudly as we walked down the courthouse steps. He was wearing earmuffs as orange and fuzzy as a Furby, which clashed impressively with the rest of him. Though anything probably would've clashed, since he was wearing a bulky camo parka with cargo shorts. "The paper's official."

"Remind me that we need to rewrite our wills," Mom said. To Dad, I hoped.

I stared at the name-change confirmation in my grasp, my whole face aching from grinning so hard. "I *did* it."

Noah Byrd. Noah Byrd. Noah Byrd.

Now Mom and Dad would finally know that my name was true. That I was enough. And so would the rest of the whole freaking *world*.

My eyes stayed glued to the paperwork as we walked through downtown on the way back home. The combined smells of Korean barbeque and seafood and greasy burgers flooded my nose, but I couldn't even think about eating.

I was too busy holding myself back from cheering and jumping up and down and screaming my head off in public, just like how everyone else had described their own official name-change days online.

This *was* real.

Mom said something beside me I didn't catch, and then Dad was stopping into a McDonald's to buy a medium fry. Probably because Fridays were his cheat days, and he didn't want to waste one.

When he came back out, and we started back on our journey home, he offered me a fry. "How about a fry to celebrate, N?"

I stopped dead in my tracks.

Really?

Really?

Just like that, my smile was gone. Rage churned inside me, but I wasn't even sure who I was mad at anymore. I was supposed to be mad at myself for not being enough for them. And I didn't want to blame them. I *didn't*.

But I was. I was furious. After months of effort. After a whole name change. Nothing was different. I still, *still*, wasn't enough for them.

Would I ever be?

"How come you never call me Noah?" I said.

My voice was loud enough to make Dad and Mom stop right in the middle of the sidewalk. They turned to face me. A few pedestrians swerved around them.

Dad's fry wilted in his hand. He blinked at me. Mom. Then me again. "What was that?"

"You call me N. Just like you have all my life. Is it because that's the name you can still get away with calling me from back before?"

"Honey—," Mom started.

I cut her off. "Is it because it's too hard for you to call me Noah? Does it not make sense to you? Do I not look or act or sound boy enough to be called that name?"

Dad approached and grabbed my puffer-coat sleeve. He pulled me closer toward the road so I stopped being a human traffic cone in the middle of the sidewalk. A mixture of chocolate and sugar drifted our way from the crepe place across the sidewalk, and it reminded me of the fancy hot cocoa I'd bought Asher at the winter festival.

Stop thinking about Asher, you lovesick loser.

"Whoa, whoa, whoa," Dad said. "How long have you been thinking this way?"

I opened and closed my mouth a few times. I'd been thinking these thoughts for so long that I didn't know anymore.

"We told you to talk to us about this stuff," Dad said.

"I have. I've told you. But then you never changed." I tugged my arm out of Dad's grasp. "You were fine with me organizing this court date by myself. You're fine with me working at Bitterlake so I could raise enough money for my surgery and cool new clothes and to get my name changed. You were fine with me requesting to transfer to a new school."

"Of course we were."

"And I'm thankful for that. I am. But I didn't want to do

this alone. Except I *had* to do this alone. Because neither of you get it."

"What don't we get?"

"Nothing. You don't get anything I'm going through. But the internet is right there. Researching is so easy. And you haven't done it once. All I keep thinking is that it's because you don't care enough to try. Because you don't accept me. You just tolerate me because I'm your kid."

I was saying more than I'd even ever consciously realized, and so much so that the words even shocked me into silence.

Mom grabbed my shoulders, her chunky charm bracelets knocking against my coat. "Honey, this isn't how we feel at all. You've always been so on top of things. So responsible. We thought you were okay. Of course we accept you."

"Then why do you call me N?"

"Because that's what we've always called you." Mom's voice was hitting a sweet spot between her *Oh, God, I don't know how to handle this* and *Oh, God, I feel so attacked right now* voices. I didn't exactly understand how this had become more about her than me. "And what did you mean by *enough*? Of course you're enough. We just didn't realize you felt like this."

"Okay, now you do. What happens next?"

"Well, of course we'll—"

Dad rested a hand on Mom's shoulder, and she stopped. "We didn't mean to hurt you, kid. But that doesn't erase the fact that we did. We should've been figuring this out with you."

Mom finally took the hint. The panic showing in her creased brow and the crow's-feet around her eyes faded. "You're right, you're right. We're sorry. Things will be different from here on out. We promise, Noah."

Mom and Dad were talking, and talking, and telling me I was enough, and that things would be different now. But the frustration inside me didn't go away.

Something still was missing.

That didn't make sense. I'd gone through the changes. I'd finally earned a permanent spot in the Borrow a Boyfriend Club. I'd legally changed my name. Now my parents were telling me that I was enough, and all I felt was thankful that they had listened. There was nothing left to prove to them. To anyone.

Except . . . myself.

CHAPTER 35

Constance and Isabella were sandwiched between two aisles packed with cowboy hats, water goggles, and sets of kitchen knives. At least, from where I stood, I could only make out Isabella's high ponytail with her being taller than ninety percent of the scrambling crowds.

When they texted me to come to Kiwi's Thrift Sale way too early on a Saturday morning, and on my day off from Bitterlake at that, I nearly performed an exorcism on my phone upon seeing those cursed words. Kiwi's was a hidden downtown gem that opened once a week at eight in the morning and closed at noon sharp, and the locals treated the event like church.

"There you are!" Isabella whipped a bubble-wrapped knife out of a kitchen set as she noticed my presence. In the next aisle over, a rope soared over her head.

I followed the rope with my eyes, then scanned the remaining crime scene. "Yep, I showed up."

Though I was surprised I showed up in one piece. On the way, I'd run into two lampposts, crossed on a red walking signal while traffic was coming, and dodged getting hit by a bus. I was exhausted, and the store's musky wool aroma was already giving me a headache.

Isabella met me at the end of the aisle. "Congratulations on becoming a certified, official, locked-in member!"

Even if I was unsure how I felt about being a part of the club now, I suppose I had overcome huge odds. "Thanks."

"So, listen to my vision." Isabella pointed the knife at other concerningly conflicting objects in the aisle. "Since we won the show, our request rate has never been higher, right? Our beautiful CFO, Constance, thought up a genius idea to do professional member head shots to add to our request form."

A snort shot right out of me. "You really think Asher will be on board with that?"

"If we see profits increase, of course he will."

Because this was still a business.

"Right," I muttered.

"Each member has a theme," Isabella went on. "We got the basement's costume racks at our disposal too, so maximum variation for maximum audience. There's something for everyone." She snatched up a cowboy hat with a pink sequin star and matching fuzz trim, and slapped it on my head. "Oh, we're going all-American cowboy for you."

"I'm included in this?"

"You're a member now, aren't you?"

Before I could respond to that, Camilo turned in to our aisle and stopped me.

We locked in a stare.

He looked up at my cowboy hat. "It's giving Giddyap Type."

"Camilo decided to join us." Isabella winked at me, then glanced at Constance farther down the row. "For some totally random reason."

His face tensed so much that his glasses slid down the bridge of his nose. He shoved them back up with a single finger. I never thought I'd see the day when he was embarrassed instead of embarrassing others. "I needed a new protractor."

"And?" Isabella said.

"And I got one." He waved around the flimsy protractor, then followed Constance. She kissed him on the cheek, and he blushed.

Isabella sighed as she watched. Her arms were magically full of even more props than she had ten seconds ago. "They're a mess, sneaking around like this. Sucks about the club rules, huh?"

A pang struck my chest. "Why don't they just quit? Aren't they missing out on being together?"

"I suppose so. But then they'd be missing out on the club. For all of us, it's more than just an after-school activity or side hustle."

I thought about what Aiden had told me, that the basement was Asher's home. Lenny's, too. He'd even claimed it to be his own at times. Clearly, he wasn't alone in these thoughts.

Not only that. Every member was borrowed because of a talent they had. One they could use to entertain others and simply have fun. Max could paint. Pascha played guitar. Everett gave astrology and tarot readings. Aiden was an all-star athlete. And Lenny genuinely loved selling the idea of love, just how Sebastian wanted the club to operate. Meanwhile, I hadn't wanted to sign up for the club because of the borrowers at all, and my talents were limited.

Sebastian once told Camilo that the club wasn't around to prove himself to his parents. Only to *serve love*. More or less, that sentiment made me gag, especially after learning Sebastian had only been interested in getting girls and making money off that slogan. I felt wrong for being a member when I had joined the club to prove myself instead. Now I didn't even feel a desperate need to prove myself anymore on top of having no desire to *serve love*. My motivations were weak.

Still, leaving the club meant losing the basement and everyone inside it.

"What if I were to quit?" I muttered. Isabella instantly stopped fiddling with a broken baby doll head on a shelf. The sudden confession on my part must have seemed ridiculous to her, since she had witnessed me endure one million rounds to reach this point.

"Do you not like us anymore?" Isabella showed a perfect set of white teeth. Not her infamously wide, tight-lipped PR smile, either. A real one.

I couldn't help but smile back, even if the topic wasn't fun. "Of course I do. Just, when I first transferred here, I didn't sign up for the club because I loved romance. I signed up for a reason I shouldn't have. I wanted to prove something. Not because I wanted to fake-date people."

I felt a pull in my chest to tell her even more.

So, I did. "I wanted to prove I was a boy. But I got my name legally changed yesterday, and I don't know. That act lifted a weight off my shoulders. I honestly don't feel the need to be a member anymore." I held up protective hands. "Not that

I don't enjoy the club now! I just think everyone else cares about *borrowing* way more than I do."

Worry crept into my chest as I waited to see how she'd react.

"That makes sense, I suppose," she said. "Well, congrats on the government-official change! I've always seen you as Noah, though, and he . . . deserves the best cowboy hat in here!"

That was it. So easy.

"Yeah." I blinked. "Thanks."

Isabella returned to her hunt, flicking through more hats at the end of a rack. Behind her, Constance grabbed a sweater with a creepy Santa Claus head protruding from the center and held it up to Camilo's chest. He covered his mouth with one of his to-do–list hands as he laughed.

"You know," Isabella spoke up again, pulling back my focus, "the other members would be super pumped to hear about your name change. I think they'd want to congratulate you, too. But only if you'd want me to share."

The weirdest part was, I didn't even have to think about it.

"Sure," I said, my heart full. "You can tell them."

*   *   *

"What in the huh?" Isabella muttered. She was staring down a *Michigan Day-to-Day* newspaper stand in front of Kiwi's Thrift Sale.

Constance and I halted on the sidewalk, but Camilo was too busy messing with his new protractor to notice. Constance tugged him back by the hem of his polo shirt, and he grunted. Short and stocky newspaper stands were always set up around the city streets of Ann Arbor but faded into the background so well that I typically forgot they existed.

Balancing her three reusable bags brimming with props, Isabella struggled to pick up a copy. Right before the bags slapped onto the sidewalk, I snatched them.

"Our school is in a headline." She flashed the front page my way. "Asher's name is in it."

Constance gripped onto my shoulder with the force of a hydraulic press. "Please, no, I can't do another round of damage control."

I leaned closer to read the headline. *Heron River High School Fails to Implement Safety Measures* and *students fight to be heard* instantly slammed into my eyes. A whole half-page recounted the robbery incident last October that constantly weighed on Asher's conscience. Same for his prior unsuccessful efforts to convince the school to improve security with lights or cameras. This must've been what he was waiting to hear back on before changing the base rate.

Finally. *Finally*, someone had listened.

Even if Asher and I weren't on the best terms, I couldn't control how proud I was.

"You'll be all right, Constance," I said. "If anything, I think this'll put an end to damage control once and for all." Our president being a town hero was promising news.

Just as Constance showed me a confused look, the door to Kiwi's Thrift Sale swung open with a jingle.

"*No magic noise tubes allowed,*" someone shouted on the way out.

I looked up. I knew that voice.

Nasal and high, the one Everly Walsh used to complain about contradicting with her carefully crafted hard-core skateboarder persona. She still must've not given up on that image because she stood behind us with a beat-up skateboard tucked under her arm now, plaid shirt and obscure band name tee included.

Jas trailed behind her out the door, a polka-dot noise tube swinging in her grasp. "But it'll be so metal if you attach the tubes to the side of your board—it'll moan while you skate." She flipped the tube upside down. A deep, rattling noise followed.

As they headed farther down the sidewalk, oblivious to my presence, I took in their familiar arguing. Jas had always been the opposite of Everly, flaunting pink pom-pom clips in her bleached-blond curls and bright glitter makeup that popped against her darker brown skin.

I had no clue when I'd accidentally run into them next. Months. Maybe years.

"Hey," I shouted at their backs.

Everly swiveled right around and froze. She tugged the camera strap around Jas's neck to grab her attention. Jas squinted before spotting me, too.

My heart rate zoomed up to a million. *Why* had I gotten their attention?

Constance nudged my arm. "Friends of yours?"

"Yeah." Everly closed the distance between us. She waved a free hand at Constance while readjusting the skateboard under her arm. "We're Noah's friends from Pinewood."

I couldn't decide what was more shocking: that they used

my name or considered me a friend after I ignored them for over a year.

"Nice," Isabella said, pointing a thumb my way. "Noah's in our club."

Everly's brow popped. "Really?"

Jas faced me. "We spotted you at the winter festival downtown, but"—she raised her film camera to snap a photo, and the flash went off in my eyes—"you were gone in a flash!"

I blinked away the spots in my vision, chuckling awkwardly. "Right. Sorry about that."

"I get it. I mean. You have other—" Jas scanned the three people beside me, then me again, and chewed on her bottom lip. "S'all good."

Everly picked at a frayed infinity sticker on her skateboard instead of paying attention to the others as well. My obvious new friends. Who were not them.

There was no easy way to explain myself. How my old classmates had me assuming even my closest friends would eventually join the crowd, or that they secretly never saw me for who I was. And how finding out those fears were true would've tipped me right over the edge, so I ran before I gave them a chance.

Maybe I didn't have to explain myself yet. We could start slow.

I wanted to start *somewhere* with my friends again. That much I knew.

"We should check out Shakespeare in the Park once school's out," I willed myself to say, but my still voice came out too shaky.

Everly and Jas just stared at me. The longer they remained

silent, the more doubt coiled in my stomach. Had they only called me a friend to be polite?

But then a grin slowly broke across Everly's face. "I'm down. We'll let Rosen know when he gets back from his piano competition."

Jas rose a hand. "I wanna go, too!"

"We should all go," Constance said.

Relief burst through me. Maybe I'd caught them off guard. In a way, I was also surprised by my offer. But no matter what Everly and Jas thought of me in the end—what anyone thought—the basement would be there.

No, everyone at Heron River High School would be.

I smiled back. "Cool, I'll message everyone."

As Jas switched back to pitching her moaning skateboard invention, which Isabella found much more inspiring than it really was, my phone buzzed in my back pocket multiple times. I assumed the call was spam until the contact *Asher Prick* caught my attention.

He was calling me. Like we were in some ancient nineties movie.

Camilo also eyed my screen suspiciously. He clearly hadn't forgotten about witnessing Asher and I smack lips in my apartment. "You going to take that?"

I swallowed hard as I placed the phone to my ear. "Hello?"

"Hey."

The sound of Asher's recognizable baritone alone shot a warmth through my whole body. "You're calling me."

"I thought you deserved more than a text."

My heart pounded so violently in my temples that I nearly passed out on the sidewalk.

Isabella dropped the magic noise tube, which at some point Jas must've handed to her. A whining groan resounded. Everyone laughed.

"Are you with someone right now?" Asher asked.

"Yeah, that was Isabella."

He didn't speak again for a moment. "Sorry to interrupt you two—"

"No, what's up?"

Another beat of silence settled on the line. "If you're not busy later, do you want to meet up?"

"Has anything changed?"

And then Asher said what I'd been wishing for so long, I asked him to repeat himself.

"Not yet, but I want it to."

CHAPTER 36

As much as I wanted to hurry through the downtown streets on my way to the pinned location Asher had dropped, I refused to be an Asher Price fanboy. I kept a steady, doubtful, jaded pace. He was still a mile away, closer toward my old high school. The opposite side of town.

What kind of hide-and-seek game was this?

When my phone led me to the Pinewood Park entrance, my feet came to an abrupt stop. I hadn't been to this park since I was a kid, but I remembered the place clearly. The one time Mom and Dad had taken me hiking, I climbed down a hill and got lost for two hours. The park was bigger than downtown Ann Arbor.

As I walked the trails bordering Heron River, falling snowflakes slapped against my face, and each step I took felt colder than the last. I jumped over logs and rocks, keeping my eyes glued to my phone to make sure I didn't pass Asher. Another twenty minutes passed until my phone showed his location was nearby.

The trail was hardly visible now, mostly dead leaves and patches of snow crunching beneath my feet. There were no more park signs telling me which way to turn either, and pine trees towered over my head. This wasn't Pinewood Park anymore. I was deep in the woods.

My phone pinged to tell me I was right beside him. I glanced to my right. Nothing. My left. Three wooden docks leading onto Heron River.

Asher sat at the edge of the dock on the very right. He watched the river, frozen over and covered in a light dusting of snow. His back was to me, and his gray wool peacoat fanned out behind him. For some reason, he was holding an umbrella over his head.

He was here. Waiting for me.

I jogged onto the wooden dock. The moment he heard the sound of creaking planks beneath my feet, Asher glanced over his shoulder. His usual dark hair left half down and half up in a bun was frizzy from the wind, and his legs were pulled into his chest.

Once I reached him, visible short breaths heaved out of me. So much for not trying to walk here too fast.

"You missed me, huh?" Asher smirked.

I rolled my eyes as obviously as possible. "I didn't want you to, you know, be soaking from the snow. Like a stranded, wet puppy."

"The only wet puppy is you." Asher rose to his feet and held the umbrella over our heads, leaving hardly any space between us. Until he'd said it, I hadn't noticed the dampness of my clothes.

He was close. Too close. Rather than peer at his face, I drilled a pointed stare at the buttons of his peacoat. "You know that's snow falling, right? Not rain?"

"Still gets the hair wet. Rule number five: members must always look good."

He did look good today.

"I saw, by the way," I said. "The newspaper article."

"Oh." He rubbed the back of his head as if to blow off the accomplishment, but the goofy little grin tugging at his lips told another story. "Vice Principal Elrod already reached out to me. Said there should be lights and more cameras up in the next week."

My whole face lit up. I itched to ask what this meant for the club finances now—if he had enough confidence to charge borrowers now that he'd repaid the school—but stopped myself. Celebrating came first. "That's amazing! Seriously."

Asher's face softened in a way that only came off as shy. Asher. Shy. "How was the court date yesterday?"

"Good. I'm Noah."

"I know." He grinned. "Congrats. That's huge."

"Thanks. I guess it is." I lowered my gaze even farther toward the wooden dock that led into Heron River, the other two docks beside ours, and finally at all the pine trees towering over our heads. "What is this place?"

"The docks. Lenny and I used to come here all the time during freshman year. They're pretty much abandoned. Rotted, too."

"So, you've brought me onto some hazardous abandoned dock in the woods, essentially."

"Essentially."

"And you brought me here to kill me, or?"

"A couple of reasons." He fell quiet a moment. "Were you busy?"

"Not really. I was just with Isabella and Constance." I conveniently left out Camilo.

Now seemed like the right time to explain that I'd been reconsidering being a club member. But I wasn't exactly foaming at the mouth to reveal that I wanted to quit after all the time he'd invested in the process.

"You've never told me why you let me pass your round," I decided to say. "At the winter festival. Why you thought I was a good enough boyfriend for the club."

He bent down to search my face. "Where is this coming from?"

I shrugged, hoping my cheeks weren't flushing from the close contact. "I just—I'm Typical, remember? There's no way I should've scored high enough on that date to—"

"You were you," he interrupted. "You didn't try to suck up to me. I liked that."

My brain glitched out. I thought back to how Lenny's mom's dating video had instructed me to be kind and patient before that date, and how Lenny had told me to be bold instead, and how I'd literally told myself to be anyone other than myself.

"I could've been faking who I was the whole time," I said, somewhat guilty now. "Trying to win you over like everyone else."

"You weren't."

"But—"

"The rose? Yes. The hot chocolate? Yes. But you slapped that hat on my head behind the carousel and yelled right in my face, even though I held the fate of your membership in my hands. You cared about my well-being over me quite literally being Popular Type. You treated me like anyone else."

I didn't know how to argue with that. "There really wasn't a score?"

"You can't put a scoring system on being good enough for the Borrow a Boyfriend Club. It's a feeling."

I stood there, digesting this information. This whole time, I'd assumed there was some secret to being accepted. That there was a secret list of ingredients that made up the perfect boy, and that Asher had been analyzing my every move for months. Deducing if I was a good boyfriend, a good conversationalist, a good everything.

I was wrong.

It was always so simple. The whole time. Just vibes.

A shaky breath left my lips. "You've probably caught on, but I wanted to be a part of the club to prove I'm, well, a boy, to everyone at school. So, I don't think I should be a member when I never cared about its mission."

A slight frown on Asher's face wouldn't leave. I couldn't tell if that was from irritation or disappointment or both. After a moment of taking me in, he stepped closer to readjust my knit hat, which must've tilted after walking all the way here and was probably soaked from the snow. "Noah, you have nothing to prove."

A burning pressure built behind my eyes. He was right. Mom and Dad had said this, too.

The last person who still hadn't was me. If I could believe the words, then no one else's would matter.

"Yeah. Thanks. I know that now." I found the planks beneath us again, too embarrassed by how often I found myself opening up to him. "Sorry. You invited me here, and I'm doing all the talking."

"No, I'm glad. Because I think you just answered the question I had for you."

My head snapped right back up. "What question?"

Asher took a deep breath. "Before I get to that, I want to say that I'm really sorry."

"For?"

"My constant back-and-forth. Ignoring you while I was sorting things out for us. You didn't deserve that. What I said on the phone was true. I do want to change things. Because you were right about"—he pressed his lips together—"my grumpy heart, as you put it."

I didn't fully understand what *things* meant, or anything else for that matter, but too much hope was surging through me to care. "But the rules—"

Asher interrupted me with a heavy sigh, stuffing a hand in his coat pockets and toeing the rotting planks. "Seb's the one who decided to run the club like a business. He always thought of us as products, not people. That's why he brought on Constance and Isabella and wanted members to be as marketable to the school as possible. Even if that meant sacrificing their happiness for everyone else's. Hence, the handbook. Stay single. Look good. Essentially be"—he hesitated—"perfect. Ridiculous to even think. Turning a normal after-school club into a secret business? Why can't we just play some billiards and hang out?"

"I guess. Yeah." I even laughed a little.

"And I've been thinking about what you said. About the rules." He paused. "I think I should stop trying to run this club the way Seb would want."

My heart pounded. Okay . . . What did this mean for us?

"What does this mean for the club?" I asked instead.

Asher studied the frozen river. "I want to focus more on what I want. And that's to focus more on everyone in"—he awkwardly ruffled the back of his hair—"the club."

He cared about us. His family in the basement.

"After that, I'm not fully sure, but we could put a space in between *boy* and *friend* for some. Or cut the *boy* from *boyfriend* completely." Asher's words quickened as the ideas came to him. "Who doesn't need friends, right? Or we cut down on the number of dates we go on, or even spend time in the basement relaxing more with our own borrowers, playing pool and stuff with them there." By the time he finished, he was nearly out of breath, then his jaw clenched.

My hand drifted toward him, but I pulled back just as quickly. I couldn't. Not when the lines between us were still blurry. "What is it?"

"It's just hard to say aloud. Seb would kill me."

I shuffled my feet a bit on the wooden planks, trying to think of what to say. Asher had spent his whole life chasing Sebastian's legacy and wanting to just be seen by his mom. Wanting to be enough.

In the end, Asher and I had wanted the club for a similar

reason—to prove something. Now Asher was letting go, just like I was, and I was genuinely proud of him. But a hint of guilt struck me, too. Before the club existed, Asher had always been alone. Meanwhile, I'd always had family who tried their best. Of course, he had a grumpy heart that he'd been trying to protect the closer we grew. How could he trust me when no one else ever stayed in his life or showed him sincere affection?

Maybe he hadn't gone about us the right way, and I'd need time to forgive that, but I couldn't blame him for being terrified, either.

"If it helps," I said, "I also want you to run the club the way you want. I'm sure everyone else in the basement does too. We're family, right?"

"Right. We are." A hint of a smile rose to Asher's face. "Then I will."

"Will what?"

"I'll change the rules."

I nearly melted right then and there.

We stood a chance. We actually stood a chance.

"There's another reason why I brought you here," Asher said before I could even think to form a response. He let out another short exhale, and I could sense the nerves radiating off him. "If you'll let me, then I still want to try to pass your round."

"In the middle of nowhere?" I asked slowly.

"I thought I could show you how well I can dance now. Because of you. I've been practicing a lot. In my bedroom."

"We had to meet in secret to dance?"

A familiar crease formed in Asher's forehead, the crease that popped up whenever he was embarrassed about his messy footwork during practice, and wiped away any nervousness he showed a moment ago. "Only because I'm new to this whole dancing thing, I promise. I'd really rather not have anyone see how bad I am. After this, let's go to Bitterlake." He stopped like he'd misspoken and bit his lip. "*If* I'm allowed to try to pass your round, that is."

I glanced at the underside of the umbrella above our heads, trying my hardest not to make it too obvious that butterflies were throwing a rave in the depths of my stomach. "Might be hard for us to dance with an umbrella."

Asher lowered and set the umbrella on the ground. Snowflakes landed on the top of his head, and more dusted the shoulders of his peacoat. He took my gloved hand into his bare one and led me off the dock, toward the snow and the pine trees, deeper into the woods. Once we got into a proper position, he placed another hand on my hip without me having to tell him. Even through my puffer jacket, his touch shot a nervous shiver through me.

"Follow my lead," Asher said.

I couldn't think, could hardly remember to breathe. I just nodded.

Asher took the lead as promised, swaying to the left. He started humming the melody of the club theme song while we moved. We were improvising. *Asher* was improvising. The temperature was dropping every second, and my Converse were so soaked that even my double layer of socks were damp. I didn't care, just like those rom-com movie characters I'd researched. They taught me that it was impossible to feel cold when your whole body was burning.

Once Asher finished humming, he pulled me closer into

his chest. His hair was dusted with snowflakes, his breaths wisping from his mouth after the routine. "One last question."

I nodded.

"Is it too soon to ask if I passed your round?"

I studied the way his deep gray eyes perfectly matched his peacoat and the overcast late-winter sky above us. The way his cheeks turned pink in the cold. The way there wasn't even a hint of condescension on his face. "Why are you doing this?"

"Isn't it obvious?" His gaze flickered toward my lips. "I like you, Noah. A lot. And I'll go through as many rounds as it takes to gain your trust."

I couldn't hold myself back any longer. I grabbed Asher's face in both my hands and kissed him. Asher was too stunned to react at first, but he caught up, pulling me in close by the waist. His lips were snowy against mine, freezing cold and soft, but everywhere else was warm.

We didn't pull away until we lost track of time, until our faces were redder than they already had been from the cold. We pressed our foreheads together and laughed, the only thing we could do, knowing the knives dangling above our heads were finally falling, but we were dodging every single one.

CHAPTER 37

Asher Prick: Come to today's meeting at 3:00 p.m.

My brow furrowed as I secretly checked my messages beneath my chemistry lab desk. The text had come from him about an hour ago. School ended at two, and the Borrow a Boyfriend Club meetings went until four. Three didn't make sense.

Noah Byrd: not 2?

My phone buzzed in my hand a moment later.

Asher Prick: Try not to be late.

I fought the urge to roll my eyes. Silly me to think Asher would stop living up to his name once we started dating. Still, the time to update it had come.

As I changed *Prick* to *Price* in my phone, I bit back a smile. If I'd been told a few months ago that I'd stop calling him that *willingly*, I would've assumed donkeys could also lay golden eggs.

When the final bell rang, I headed to the library to try to finish my world history homework, but I couldn't concentrate on the Han dynasty for the life of me. Even though Asher had scrapped the no-dating rule days ago, I hadn't given him a definitive answer on if I would remain a member. Mostly because I didn't know myself.

I didn't want to lose my friends. But I didn't have the same passion for *serving love* to strangers as they did. Sticking around while having never cared about their motto felt selfish.

Asher had claimed the club wouldn't revolve around business anymore. Out of the options he'd considered, what was their goal now?

Ten minutes before three, I drifted into the theater and then onstage. I passed a few leads from the school musical calling my name from the lower bowl, and I waved. Once I disappeared backstage, I headed to the basement.

The cluttered space packed with overflowing costume racks came into view. Mustiness clung to the air as always. I wiggled my way through the costumes until I stumbled onto fuzzy maroon carpet.

Balloons were scattered across the floor. Streamers dangled from the rhinestone maroon curtains covering up the concrete walls. On the rolling whiteboard, every member and Type was written down in a long column. Except Asher's no longer said Popular Type. A few new words were written beside his name instead. *Changemaker? Trailblazer? White Knight?*

I grinned. The options were written in a mixture of Lenny's and Asher's handwriting, as if there'd been a whole conversation. About time he was ditching Sebastian's Type.

All the love seats and couches were abandoned. So was the billiards table. The jukebox glowed, but no music played.

No one was here.

"CONGRATULATIONS!"

I screamed at the top of my lungs as a herd of people lunged out from behind the curtains on my right. Isabella and Aiden blew party horns.

Camilo stepped out of another curtain later than everyone else, looking exceptionally bored. "Congrats."

"Congratulations."

I swiveled on my heel. Asher stood over to my left, holding a tray of cupcakes. The tops spelled out a full sentence in very warbly, very melty, blue frosting letters.

YOUR NAME IS NOAH?

I tilted my head. Was this a trick question? "Yes?"

Asher glanced down at the cupcakes. "That's supposed to be an exclamation mark. Not—" He wiped the squiggly exclamation-point cupcake with a finger to fix it.

I blinked around at everyone. "What are the cupcakes for?"

Aiden wrapped his beefy bicep around my shoulder, and the combination of his trained football muscles and heavy leather varsity jacket weighed me down like an anchor. "We're trying to celebrate you, man. Congrats on the name."

"Asher's the one who baked all those pretty cupcakes," Lenny said. "What do you think?"

I was speechless.

This was my surprise party.

Everett walked up and pressed a single fingertip to my temple. "He believes the cupcakes are a thoughtful gesture, but the decorating is subpar."

Asher slammed the cupcakes on the billiards table. "No one told me that you have to wait for the cupcakes to cool off before you do the frosting shit."

"They're perfect," I said.

Asher's attention snapped back to me. The iciness invading his furrowed brow and frown melted away in a flash. "You sure?"

"Of course. Shouldn't you be discussing the weekly to-dos, though? There are huge events coming up this month. Like prom?"

Lenny squeezed me into a hug so tight that I nearly threw up. "You're what's most important right now."

Liam laughed. "You out of anyone here should know Asher's stopped with the dictator persona. Aren't you why he dropped the stay-single rule?"

My face flushed with heat.

"You're killing him," Asher grumbled, and snatched me away from Lenny, who pouted back. He took my hand into his own. "He helped, but he's not the only reason. We deserve to enjoy ourselves more. Everyone here. Lots of changes are about to go down."

I squeezed his hand back. "Already showing off your influence?"

Isabella and Aiden smirked toward each other. They disappeared into the *Do Not Enter* room and shortly returned holding either side of the SERVE LOVE banner that hung over the Sebastian Shrine. Except now, two new letters had been painted before *serve*.

A grin cracked along my face. "Deserve love."

"Isn't our president clever?" Isabella said, winking at Asher.

Asher turned red. "It's cringe, I know—"

"Absolutely not," I said. "I think it fits our new president." I glanced at the whiteboard, where Asher's new Type options were listed. "Which Type you gonna choose, president?"

"Not sure." He gestured toward everyone in the room. "Thoughts?"

"I think you're Noah's Type," Lenny said, his voice muffled by the massive bite of cupcake in his mouth, half left in his hand.

I covered my face with a palm. This was embarrassment overload for a single day.

"I vote White Knight," Camilo said.

"'Cause he's heroic?" Lenny asked.

"No, 'cause he's white."

Asher pinched the bridge of his nose. "If you're not going to help, shut up."

"Wait, wait, wait," Lenny practically yelled, dramatically tossing his arms out to both sides to stop all conversation. "We never gave Noah the formal acceptance!"

Camilo rose onto his tiptoes to swipe Lenny upside the head, and the rest of Lenny's cupcake hit the carpet. "That's a Sebastian tradition. Read the room."

Asher let go of my hand to stand by Camilo and Lenny and slapped them both on the back. "You know, I think we should keep that one."

Lenny cheered while Camilo sighed and wandered toward Constance to rest his forehead on her shoulder. She patted his back sympathetically.

Asher spun his finger in the air, signaling the others to break off into factions. Another surprise?

As they did, Isabella yanked on my shirt sleeve. "You *are* staying in the club, right?"

I bit the inside of my cheek. I *had* admitted to Isabella that I was considering leaving. Not only that, but that I did all this to prove I was as much a boy as the others.

But these guys weren't perfect. Being perfect was never how Asher determined acceptance, anyway.

Now the mission statement had changed. The rules had changed. We were all shaping this club like the odd, mishmash family that we were.

Was there really anything wrong with staying?

Someone cleared their throat by the couches, pulling my attention. The members had formed a line in front of the club's double-*B* heart flag on the wall.

Asher stood before them with an outstretched hand. His other gripped the handbook, which was open to a back page.

"Congratulations," he recited directly from the handbook in a voice so robotic I bit back a laugh. "On behalf of my members, I am happy to inform you that you have passed all three rounds of our membership process. We would be happy for you to join us. Do you accept our invitation?" He gestured at the whiteboard where our names and Types were listed. Mine was written last.

Not N. Not Byrdie. Not Byrd. Noah.

I grinned at the board, then at him and the rest of my friends.

"If I say yes," I said, stepping forward to shake his hand, "will you stop talking like that?"

With a smirk that came off as borderline prickish, Asher chucked the handbook full of rules over his shoulder. He wrapped me in a warm hug and whispered in my ear.

"Welcome to the Borrow a Boyfriend Club, Noah."

ACKNOWLEDGMENTS

The first person to ever tell me I should become an author was my high school AP English Language and Composition teacher, Mr. LaPlante. He was an ex-Marine and looked like one. We were working in the computer lab and had to go up to his intimidating desk, one by one, to have him read our college essays. I wrote mine about how I failed precalculus twice. When he finished reading my essay, all he did was look up and say, "Page, you should be a writer."

Then, across the computer lab, Michael McSomething threw up.

Mr. LaPlante felt like a sign. *Do it*. Michael also felt like a sign. *Don't do it*. I guess Mr. LaPlante won.

First and foremost, thank you, reader, for picking up this story. If you heard about this book from your librarian, bookseller, or teacher, please tell them thank you on my behalf! Right now, it's tough for them to fight for authors like us, so I appreciate their work more than they could know.

This silly book found a perfect home at Penguin Random House thanks to the Delacorte team. Bria Ragin, I'm so thankful that someone as intelligent and hardworking as you read this in a whirlwind of a day, saw literally anything in it, and became my editor. Because of your dedication, you challenged me to make something I never could have created alone. And with our shared love of highlighting joy, we made *The Borrow a Boyfriend Club* even funnier! Thank you to Wendy Loggia, Beverly Horowitz, and Barbara Marcus for allowing me to infiltrate Random House, as well as Lydia Gregovic for the vital feedback along the way. I'm so appreciative of my in-house designers, Angela Carlino and Kenneth Crossland, for nailing the visual vibes of this story. Not to mention my dream cover illustrator, Steffi Walthall, for drawing a dinosaur plush that made me laugh so hard I shed tears. Colleen Fellingham, Marla Garfield, and Tamar Schwartz—thank you for copyediting and managing-editing, and sorry you had to read "among us sussy imposter." Kim Small, my publicist, apologies again for having to thoroughly discuss the f-word in our first-ever correspondence. And to all the book bloggers, reviewers, booksellers, and marketers for getting this out into the world.

To my United Kingdom team, thank you for being some of the cheeriest people I've ever met. Tig Wallace, my former editor, I'm eternally grateful that you acquired this and allowed me to experience Hachette UK's jaw-dropping professionalism. I miss you! But this way I got to meet Lena McCauley, my current editor, who is equally a joy. So it's a good thing you left. Just bants, mate. And Georgina Mitchell?! I love you, girl! You've overseen this book as assistant editor since day one and have been the glue through all of this. Make Tig and Lena take you to Spoons. Hannah Bradridge, thank you for being an incredible publicist. Nils Jones and Bec Gillies: don't tell anyone, but you've almost made me sob happy tears due to how much marketing effort you've put into this book. And, of course, Bex Glendining, for illustrating a brilliant UK-edition cover and trading card-ifying the club members.

None of this would've been possible without Natalie Lakosil, the most showstopping champion of an agent ever. Gold trophies to Grace Milusich for objectively being the best agency marketing assistant, Antoinette Van Sluytman for being the best agency assistant, Heather Baror-Shapiro for being the best foreign rights agent, and everyone else at Irene Goodman Literary Agency and Baror International. And to my film agent, Lucy Stille, for convincing me to give Noah a new name. I still don't know what I was thinking.

My mentors, Sophie Gonzales, Amelia Coombs, and Carly Heath, deserve cupcake platters bigger than Asher's ego. Thank you, Sophie and Amelia, for taking this book under your millennial wings during Pitch Wars and making this love interest even more of an insufferable Fitzwilliam Darcy. That's what mentorship is for, right? Also, Carly, for being the first person to take a chance on my writing.

To my early readers who blurbed this book, it's an honor to have your names on the cover so that I look very important despite the truth.

Christian Banas, I must've made a deal with the devil and forgotten, since there's no other way I could've landed you as my audiobook narrator. Now when I play *Genshin Impact*, I'll hear my own character? What? Thanks, CL Montblanc, for the hilarious succession of texts that led to this, as well as to Desiree Johnson, Brady Emerson, Emily Parliman, and everyone at Listening Library.

Thank you to Emily Charlotte and M. K. Lobb for being my ultimate omega readers since no one else can keep up the fake smile and tell me I'm a genius for as long as you two. To Sarah Poultney, for helping me survive the week this book went to auction. To Kathleen and Johann, for helping me figure out who I am. Sort of. Ish. To the Performing Arts Technology Department at the University of Michigan School of Music for teaching us students that nothing is impossible. To everyone who helped Noah's journey along the way—you're the best! Special shout-outs to Sonora Reyes and Carrie Gao for helping from the very beginning.

And most importantly, to Reiner Braun. Just kidding. Kind of. Most importantly, to anyone who finds themselves in Noah's shoes, it's okay if you're still figuring things out or aren't ready to show who you are. I promise the right time will find you. Just like him, and me too!

See you in the next story. Maybe at an all-boys boarding school?

ABOUT THE AUTHOR

Page Powars was raised by his favorite gay-coded anime and video game characters. They taught him how to soften his gaze at a homie, sacrifice his lifespan for a bro, and, most importantly, metaphorically kill or kiss his definitely-just-a-pal. Now he writes books with this wealth of knowledge. Page also helps with music soundtracks and unfortunately plays *Genshin Impact*. Originally from Michigan, he currently lives in Los Angeles. *The Borrow a Boyfriend Club* is his debut novel.

pagepowars.com

[Instagram] [Twitter] [TikTok]